MW00974959

CLUB DAZE

& The Subtle Realm

N. J. SIMAT

WWW.CLUBDAZE.NET

Copyright 2021 © N. J. Simat
All rights reserved. 1-10851208011
Contact: Nancy@canaryagency.com for use

Published and Edited by: The Canary Agency
Atlanta, Georgia.
www.TheCanaryAgency.com
Cover Design by Betty Martinez
Author Photo by Kelly Lewis

ISBN: 978-1-7379030-1-7, 978-1-7379030-5-5
E-ISBN: 978-1-7379030-0-0
LCCN: 2021919546

FIRST EDITION
Printed in the United States of America

Dedicated to:
My Father, Larry Bryant
August 29, 1957 - September 9, 2013
&
My Grandfather, Vincent Eschbach
May 18, 1931 - March 14, 2019

Thank you for encouraging me to dream.

"Gonna change my way of thinking,
Make myself a different set of rules.
Going to put my good foot forward
Stop being influenced by fools."
—Bob Dylan

Acknowledgments

We will begin in gratitude

First and Foremost, I want to thank the readers. Without you, there's not much of a point to writing a novel. I am honored that you chose this one, and I believe in someways it chose you too.

1) Gary Simat. My husband who loves me through my weaknesses and is my biggest supporter. Thank you for making a space in the world for me to create in. I know it takes an incredible amount of time away from everything else, and I appreciate your patience.

2.) My mom, who gave me life, and minds me to not take life so seriously.

3.) Joseph McCurdy. My older brother who has served our country his entire adult life, for the last *several* decades, as a Master Sergeant in the Airforce. You make me so proud to be related to someone who *pretends to have* —I mean, has their shit together.

3.) To my Beta Readers: Leah Downie, Farris Lewis, Teal Lingenfelser, Cameron Alkhasraji, Lauryn & Chris Macfarland and Erica Chastain. Thank you for your honesty and encouragement.

4.) My AR's: Megan Flores, Brianna Gonva, Gaby Goumas, Steph Cannoles, Richie Wallace, and Anastasia Muratovic.

5.) SweatHouz. This was my sanctuary. I came up with so many ideas through my meditations in your wonderful establishment.

6.) Ivy Mcneil and Courtney Lytle. Thank you for your legal advice concerning my intellectual property. (See I was listening.)

8.) My Nightclub Muses: Melina Wade, Jaynie Branum, Tongue & Groove, Mitul Patel, Courtney Foster, Benny, and the Gidewons, for a lifetime of laughs and industry material.

9.) To my literary teachers: Zoe Fishman & Jody Lynn Nye, Thank you for imparting your wisdom.

10.) My Cheerleaders: Shermine Khakiani, Kristen Schnak, Chrissy Aneq, Alexia Joyner, Katie Hill, E. J. Adams, Omar & Mari Rodrigues, and Blake Miaoulis Thank you for all the love through the years and encouraging me on my crazy ideas.

11.) Brad Hancock, "HOLD—at some point that's on you."

12.) Kim, Emily, & Eric Bryant thank you for your support.

13.) Dave Alkhasraji. Thank you for saving our lives that one night in Barcelona, so I could be here to write this novel.

14.) Illy Coffee. It would not have been possible without you—really.

15.) Nadim Ukani. I actually forgot why I was putting you in here but I am sure you did something nice.

16.) Janelle Ortiz-Simat. Thank you for your encouragement when I needed it most!

17.) The Coopers, Billy McDaniel, Brandon and Brittany Browne. Thank you for being there when I had no one and nothing. I'll never forget the kindness you showed me.

18.) To Hoather my Spirit Guide, and every other Spirit & Angel, that assisted me along the way.

19.) Emory's Creative Writing Program, Atlanta's Writers Club, Dekalb Writing Workshops, and Dragon Con's Writers Track thank you for giving this baby-author her paper wings.

20.) To the city of Atlanta, the Alanna Baes, and all of my fellow Atlantans. We survived...that in itself is encouraging. (I'm looking at you ATLSCOOP)

21.) To my dogs Nikko and Kane, (*and Kuma & Yoshi*) gah—I love you so much. Thank you for all the material.

22.) To my palm reader Nhu.

*To anyone I didn't mention and is reading this thinking, "Well damn." I owe you a drink...

CLUB DAZE

and The Subtle Realm

1

CLUB DAZE

...Has it gotten bigger?

I could never tell. The ridiculous circumference bore so much importance in our industry, that finding it objectively in my crowded mind was hopeless. My phone flashed, interrupting my internal debate, alerting me that the night was calling. I silenced the alarm. It was almost nine p.m. and my girls should be arriving any minute. I looked back longingly at our lockers, and particularly to the one that held the key to my apartment captive. For a moment, I imagined crawling into it and shutting everyone out for the night. My phone flashed again, this time igniting a subtle groan from my soul. I was officially late for my shift but my lower back throbbed in protest. This industry was taking its toll, as do all industries sooner or later, but this one was greedier it seemed. It stole things from me that I didn't even realize were up for grabs. Lately, my smiles felt foreign on my face, like something I could reach up and peel off, and press back on as needed.

On my way out of the dressing room, I stopped in front of a gilded, full-length mirror that guarded the exit. A weekly ritual I performed before every weekend to take inventory of my assets. False lashes slightly refused the inner corners of my eyes, something that would have bothered me a few years ago, but now seemed too much of a hassle to correct. Instead I refocused my attention on my perfected scarlet lips, and a glistening décolletage with masterfully contoured cleavage. With one final surveying gaze, from my head all the way down to my pink patent stilettos, I concluded my assessment, pausing only to reconsider my corseted waist. I sighed.

Yeah, it's definitely bigger.

I breathed in the last sweet moments of privacy before exiting our dressing room, and walked out onto the open stairwell that led me further and further from the security of our employee lounge. Under the ambient light, both of my hands fumbled to snap on a name tag, ignoring the handrail's offer to assist. Someone powered on the stage lighting from below. Cool-toned beams of light glazed over my nameplate revealing remnants of white powder stuck in the crevices of the carved letters; "TASHA," listed just under, "CLUB DAZE." As I neared the bottom of the stairs, my leg stubble tugged at my fishnets. It was always cold down there, before the bodies filled up that big empty space. *This beautiful empty space.*

I stood at the bottom of the stairs for a moment captured by the glamour of our building. It was the most impressive in Atlanta, especially since it was renovated just last year. The ceiling was an exaggerated wooden lattice in black that softly reflected any scenes from below. The floors were lacquered oak and glasslike in appearance; they complimented the structured leather-wrapped couches and grandiose center bar. The couches, reserved for our *very important persons,* were arranged in pairs and faced one another. They created perfect rectangular sections and bordered exactly half of the nightclub. To save the club from looking sterile or too pristine, there were rustic golden accents scattered about in the form of frames, sconces, and chandeliers. When all of these elements were combined: the adaptive up lighting, hypnotic sounds, and dancing bodies, Club Daze was intoxicatingly sexy.

I drew in a deep breath. The air was pregnant with the smell of new leather and citrus cleaning products—notably absent of any cigarette fumes that penetrated the older nightclubs. A weird thing to be proud of probably, but I had always smelled of cigarettes growing up and I appreciated not having to smell like them now. The impression of someone staring pulled my body around in a semicircle, but I didn't see anyone looking in my direction. Then I felt a cold, small hand grasp my bare shoulder.

"Hey sexy," Jesmitha flashed her bright white teeth and cat-like canines.

"Oh, hi Jes," I still could never decide when—or if—I was happy to see her after what happened last year. "Rick will be at table two tonight. You can have him." I said.

I saw confusion—or maybe suspicion, stream down her small face, "No, why would you do that? That's easy money for you...and Justin will be here at one. I've gotta be completely open for them."

"Yeah, I should probably start saving anyway," I said, mostly to myself.

"What are you talking about," she asked, nearly laughing, "and why are you passing up Rick?" Jesmitha's face stilled, "Did something happen?"

"No, nothing happened. I just can't deal with him or groping hands tonight, and my back is killing me."

"Tasha, you're probably just having one of *your days*—" Jes's voice was snuffed out under the sounds of our DJ starting his set.

'Your days,' why did a bad day have to be labeled explicitly mine? My mom called the days that my anxiety would get the best of me, "High-Five Days," although I can't quite remember why. She'd remind me it was just my brain needing healthy stimulation so that I could burn off the restless mental energy. "Just breathe," mom would say, and then find me something new to learn. I wished I could call her— hear her voice again—even if it was just one more time.

It seemed louder than usual tonight, too loud actually. I made a mental note to tell Bryan to check sound. I glanced down at my watch —9:55 p.m., and then looked up to witness my first table enter the nightclub, Five women, all ranging from their late thirties to mid fifties. They followed tightly behind the host and made sure not to leave any gaps whatsoever, as if they might actually get lost moving through a wide open dance floor. Fortunately they made it safely to my section despite a few shaky ankles connected to fresh pedicures. Their designer shoes that looked like they had never seen dark of night. If I had to guess, they'd probably been gifted—or won—a VIP table at Club Daze from a bid at a charity-auction event. Regardless, you can always tell when people arrive that weren't truly a part of our nightlife society. Sometimes it's style and sometimes it's body language, but this was painfully obvious for all of the above. Another dead giveaway was that show up early, but truth be told, it's manufactured this way for both parties' benefit. It kept us busy, kept them safe, and filled the room with warm bodies until the real players arrived. I confirmed my snap-judgement from our internal registrar. They were, in fact, a promotional table, but not from a charity. They were corporate employees from a popular liquor brand, and possibly not even true patrons. I grabbed a bottle menu—and of course a Club

Daze smile—before heading over to greet them.

"Hi ladies," I slapped on the smile, "I'm Tasha, I'll take care of you tonight. It looks like you have a complimentary bottle of vodka on the way, is there anything else I can get you?"

They all looked at each other, but none of them answered. The big hair, clutching her Louis Vuitton and wearing the knock-off Valentinos, refused to look at me throughout the entire exchange. It was if she believed that eye-contact translated directly into sales. Ironically kindness, being as rare as it is in our business, *could* substitute for sales—to some extent.

"Oh-kay, well, here's a menu, and if you need anything I'll be around." I handed the nearest one the oversized and backlit book in vain.

I need a new job. I was nearly thirty and there was barely room for all of us at Daze as it is, but where would I go? All of my connections only benefited a woman in their early twenties, or someone willing to be compromised for attention—attention that may, or may not, lead to an actual dollar. I didn't exactly have many day-walker skills left, just a dusty Bachelor's degree in Science. In today's economy people were probably applying to McDonald's with their Master's degrees. Somewhere in my brain an internal channel widened and allowed anxiety to flood into every part of my being. *I'm stuck here until they're all through with me—until Bryan's fed up with me.*

"I can't do this tonight," I said to myself, at least, not without some chemical support. I glanced back at my table. It was just past ten, I had at least forty-five minutes before any real money showed up. I rushed back upstairs, not slowing in my pace until I reached the employee lounge. We had an elevator but it was out of the way. It was also usually backed up with table-guests trying to access the second floor bathroom; the stairs kept my legs tight anyway. I plopped down behind the security desk, that sat right inside the entry, to catch my breath. All of our security guys must have been on the floor. Through their security cameras, I could see all of my tables, the center bar, the first floor bathroom hallway, the main entry, and all of the exits. The liquor-ladies were exactly as I had left them. I would make sure to bring out their bottle as soon as I got back to the floor. They seemed happy enough, although, I couldn't help but feel thankful for the twenty-two percent auto-gratuity on the bills now. Ironically it was something I had initially fought Bryan on. I searched for Jesmitha in the security cameras and I found her, not surprisingly, flirting with

Bryan who was behind the main bar. I knew them both so intimately I could practically script their entire conversation. I watched Jesmitha lean over the bar and check her reflection in its black mirrored surface.

Jes extended her neck to meet Bryan's eyes with her own. 'Want me to send a round of shots to Tasha's promo-table on you?' Jes pointed to my section.

'Cute, but I find it refreshing when the non-club dwellers show up here. They're un-entitled and easy to please,' he sliced a lime with precision into equal parts. 'they also make my staff—and some of our regulars—feel better about themselves,' Bryan looked up pointedly at Jes.

Jesmitha put on her best smile as she shifted her weight from one sparkly pump to the other.

Bryan had a way of making people's secrets surface to the outer layers of their bodies. He could read anyone at anytime. It was something I both loved and hated about him. But Jesmitha? She just admired his muscular frame, smoke-grey eyes, carelessly tousled hair, and most of all, his position of authority.

'Where's Tasha?' Bryan looked up at my table, whose inhabitants were none the wiser of my absence.

'She's around,' Jes threw her hands up, flicking her wrists back, 'she's been having one of her nights, she tried to give me Rick of all people.' She looked around the nightclub.

Bryan's face formed concern but he said nothing.

After a brief silence between them, Jes looked up at the stairwell, 'I'll go check the lounge,' she pushed off from the bar and walked away.

I laughed at my rendition of their interaction, and tried my best not to go into a dark place watching Jes—or *anyone*—flirt with Bryan. It took a lot of compartmentalization, especially given our recent history, but in this industry I'd be driven mad if I let every little flirtation ruffle my feathers. Besides, he was my ex now—and more importantly, he was still our boss and the owner of Club Daze.

I met Bryan about four years ago, the same year my mom died, when I started working for him at the Top Key. A piano bar that existed as an extension above an exclusive neighborhood steakhouse. It was frequented mostly by the local celebrities and businessmen accompanied by their *dates*. The piano bar was a members only club, and you had to play a three-key-code on the baby piano out front in order to be permitted entry. You also had to pay two thousand dollars annually for the membership—for which they'd graciously remind you of the code if you forgot the little melody. The code was mostly ceremonial, unless of course, you were someone's guest trying to enter or re-enter, then it really depended on who was working the door.

I pushed my chair back from the security desk and stood up, leaving a generous and shimmering imprint of both thighs and buttocks from my body bronzer on the worn-in leather chair. I headed towards the changing rooms to grab my little leather backpack from my locker, assuring myself all the way that I still had a few Adderall mixed in with the mobile flea market that was my purse lately.

In the dressing room, in the center of the vanity counter, sat a large crystal jar filled to the brim with loose community Advil. If you didn't know any better you might have assumed that they were candies, chocolate M&M's perhaps. They might as well have been at the rate we consumed them. I fished out two of the sugar coated NSAIDS, walked over to open my locker, and twisted the knob: 33-88-99.

The hook-strap was stretching at the seams under the weight of the bag. I pulled it off the hooks and flipped over the top flap, then peeked in the tiniest pocket along the back wall of the bag. *There you are.* Huddled together in the deepest corner sat the little orange tablets, like two baby birds that had fallen out of their nest. I placed only one of them on my tongue, lint and all, and reached for any of the abandoned water bottles sitting on the vanity counter. Then I added the other two pain relievers to the mix. The warm water hugged my throat as the pills floated down. *Now that I'd be able to work through tonight, I could finally, 'Just breathe.'*

LIL' ORANGE PILLS

"Natashaaa? Tasha? 'Sha—you in here?" I heard Jesmitha's call all the way from the entry of the employee lounge.

"I'm in the dressing room," I answered quietly, as if she were standing right next to me.

Jes appeared in the doorway, "Tha' hell are you doing in here? It's getting busy and your tables haven't seen you all night! I brought the liquor-ladies at table eight a bottle of goose and mixers, but I didn't use sparklers or any—

"Jes I'm not—I can't—I can't go out there." I said.

"Oh-kay…Tasha I love you, but this whole woe-is-me thing is getting annoying, can you suck it up and we can play therapist later."

"What? No, I mean I took the wrong pill," I said, each word coming out quieter.

"Huh?" Jesmitha squinted as if she couldn't see me, as if I wasn't sitting on the floor at the base of the lockers right in front of her.

"I thought I was taking an Adderall, but it was not that at all," I explained.

Jessica's eyes lit up like a six-year-old having just arrived at her first amusement park. "Are you telling me…that you ate…one of those orange pressed pills from the festival a couple of weeks ago? A whole one?" she asked, trying to hold back her laughter.

I nodded, keeping my gaze towards the floor. I was annoyed that she found the whole thing was amusing.

Jesmitha released her laughter.

My floor-stare shifted into a face-glare, aimed at Jes and her ridiculously tiny plastic nose. She put her hands on her knees to support her weakened-boisterous state, and then apologized with one hand in the air. I wondered how much of a laugh-load that delicate nose could even bare before it collapsed under the pressure. Finally Jes regained a bit of composure, but only to let the remaining laughter trickle out a few seconds later.

"I wish you would stop laughing."

"I'm sorry." She cleared her throat. "Babe, it will be fine, I'll get the other girls to cover our side tables, and I can handle Justin and Ricky by myself. Just make sure you call an Uber home…or, go to a rave." She grinned from ear to ear.

I raised my hands in the air to her like I was five years old. Jes grabbed my wrists and pulled back on her heels, with all one-hundred-and-ten pounds of her being, and helped me unfold from my crumpled position.

"I'll close out my table before I go home," I said once we were both standing—never eye-to-eye, "sorry I'm a complete idiot. Please don't tell Bryan about this." I gathered all of my things out of my locker.

"I'll just tell him your back was hurting. You are so lucky boss man loves you, lucky, lucky, 'Sha," Jes said, as she re-applied her lipstick in front of the full-length mirror at the exit. Jes leaned over fully to re-adjust her new breasts into her corset. Her small hands barely contained the two masses. "I'll call you when I get off to check on you," she added, right before she walked out.

A few minutes later I made my way back down the stairs to go home, this time accepting the handrail's assistance. I stopped mid-way to scan the room for my table, but the lights were already shining brighter from the pill, making it difficult to see. To my surprise, my table was empty and completely turned over for the next guests. I should thank whomever did that for me...

Now, what was I doing? Oh, look, Bryan is still here and behind the bar. He must be training someone new. He looks so good in a black v-neck. I miss his smell. I guess that means Jes will be here all alone with him tonight. There was something I was forgetting to do though—that I needed to focus on. Yes! I need to close out my table, and I then I could slide out the back—but that's right...my table was already closed out. Well, okay then, things are looking up for me. Wait. How will I get home though? I shouldn't drive like this. Uber? Yes, Uber. Okay, see I can do this, I can do anything! I bet I can get any job I want...if I really tried—If I applied. Ha, that rhymes. I could be a poet. I could be anything I want to be! I'm not going to worry anymore. I've got this...and even if I don't, this place is not so bad? All the pretty lights. It's so, so... beautiful and look at all of the people, they're glowing—dancing—happy. It's not such a bad place to die. To die? Wait. What?

My stomach dropped. My entire body hummed and sweat beaded along my hairline. I had maybe five minutes before the ecstasy took over the reins completely. Thankfully an exit was only a few steps away, so very close.

"Hello, beautiful," a low, confident, and tequila-infused voice rustled my inner-ear fuzz. His breath, so close to my skin, made my whole body goosebump. At the same time a firm hand pressed into the small of my back. *Rick.*

"Hey Ricky, you're here, uhm, early," I said trying to focus on his face through the shimmering lights.

"Am I?" He smiled.

I leaned down a bit for his hug, and he kissed me lightly on my cheek. Both felt wonderful. Rick looked more handsome tonight than usual. It's not that he was particularly unattractive, but I've never really been attract-ed. He had severe Italian features and easily could have been photoshopped into the cover of GoodFellas without anyone questioning it. He was barely 5'7 in height, but his personality was seven feet tall, and his clothes appeared as though they were made just for him.

"Are you leaving already?" Ricky asked, noticing my coat and the little black bookbag.

"No! I gave all my tables away to take care of you and your friends tonight," I blurted out with the fuzzy euphoria pressing heavily on my brain.

Rick was already a little drunk, but if he registered my new affectionate disposition odd, he was too smart to question it—lest he scare it away.

"I guess that calls for shots!" Rick announced to his entourage, a group of about ten to fifteen hungry people that were standing a few feet behind him. They seemed to always be waiting for his mark, and they followed him wherever he went. The men were sometimes attractive, but the women? The women were all hand-selected from Aphrodite herself.

"Yes sir, forty-two for the crew," I dumped my personal belongings on the confused check-in girls, and unclipped a strobing flashlight from my waist. I pulsed the light in the air to guide my guests to their table for the night. All of my chances of escaping an inevitable disaster, slipped out through the door, just as Rick walked through it.

"Can I get a vodka soda with lime?" yelled a slender man with dewy skin from across the swarming table. He looked like he came straight from a Guess photoshoot. He was so beautifully androgynous, it was impossible to even speculate on his sexual preferences.

"Sure," I leaned over the table to grab a glass to make his drink with.

"Here's a clean one," Rick said smiling, while handing me a clean glass from the stack on the table.

Confused, I looked down, and my face flushed to what felt like an even deeper shade of red. I had someone's dirty vodka cranberry in my hand and was about to pour a new drink into it.

Rick leaned in close and gently cuffed my upper arm, brushing my breasts with the back of his hand, "Need a little something to sober up?"

"I can't," I said, almost certain that he was referring to blow. "I'm at work." At that we both laughed, as I had clearly abandoned any sober righteousness for the night. "Right, okay," I said, acquiescing to his suggestion, "that's probably a good idea."

He grabbed my hand in his, and pressed a small plastic bag of powder into my palm, his grasp lingering longer than necessary. I mouthed the words, "Thank you," and excused myself to make a mad dash to the upstairs lounge.

Once I was inside the bathroom stall, I locked the door and sat down on the top of the commode. At this point in my shift, taking the weight off of my feet and lower back was better than any man-made ecstasy could ever provide. I carefully stuck a nude coffin-shaped nail into the teeny bag. My five-inch heels were precariously balanced on the toilet seat rim—only one slip n' slide away from disaster. I quickly shoveled a few heaps into each nostril. Then I closed my eyes and rested my head on the back of the wall.

In that moment I considered never returning. After what seemed like only a few minutes, my blood rushed like white water rapids. I was wide awake and ready to move. I was still a little muddled, but now I could at least focus. Eager to get back to my table, I hightailed it downstairs and pushed through the humid, congested, dance floor. I almost pulled Jes straight out of her heels when she tried to flag me down.

"Tasha, why tha' hell are you still here!" Jes said, with her big brown eyes reaching impossible widths.

I couldn't tell if she was yelling at me, or just above the music. "I know, it's crazy right? You can't win 'em all." I shouted back at her.

"What?" She shook her head.

"Ohhh right...so I ran into Rick on the way out, but it's okay, because he helped me with the glass and it's fine now," I sniffed and wiped off anything that might remain on the underside of my nose.

She stared at me for what seemed like a solid thirty-seconds, with her face crinkled up like she smelled something sour,"What?"

"I'm good Jes! I did some blow in the bathroom—to just...sober up." I realized that I was dancing while we were talking, and that maybe, just maybe, I should have tested the potency before I snorted the Godfather's share.

"All-right, well I can't *make you* leave," she said, looking around as if she was hoping for backup to arrive. "I guess, uhm, just let me know if you need me, and do not leave here without me Tasha," she had each hand on my shoulders, "and no more drugs!"

I nodded, then floated back to my table. Throughout the night I must have made at least twenty more drinks, took shot after shot with my clients, and participated in four bottle parades, all without a single stumble—that I can remember. I did have to make a couple more stops upstairs with the help of Rick's entourage, but other than that, I felt proud of myself. This night could have gone terribly wrong, but at two-thirty a.m., I had officially made it through the night. Although tomorrow, and possibly even through next weekend, I would be a complete mental and emotional nightmare.

The withdrawals would hit me hard, as they always do. I'd likely need to call out of work due to a case of crippling anxiety, if not lower back pain. But, tonight was a success. I even enjoyed myself while flirting with Rick, which was an especially rare occasion.

I was mid-conversation with the ringleader himself when the ceiling lights flashed once, signaling closing time. Rick immediately reached into his pockets and handed me a Xanax. I looked down at the little white bar in my hand like it was a live mouse, then quickly closed my fingers around the contraband to conceal it. I strained to control the knee-jerk reaction to scan the room to see if anyone—mainly Bryan—had seen the deposit.

"Thanks." I said, too shy to question it. I'd never actually taken a Xanax. I was only familiar with them from my friends…which was why I had never taken them before.

"It'll help you come down, you know—sleep tonight—function tomorrow," Rick said, slurring slightly. His index finger pointing to his temple punctuating his last word. The diamonds on his watch sparkled fervently under the blue and pink ambient light.

The bright lights flashed again but this time they remained on, inciting the routine groan from the surviving crowd. Although our closing-flashes were never welcomed, I always considered the illumination to be merciful—a gift even. It gave our clients a chance to evaluate some of their choices that night, thus the quality of their immediate future. The culmination of their night's decisions, smiling and swaying right in front of them, and escape from him, her, or they —if need be. Then again, I guess if you were the person that people usually left when the lights came on…then groan away.

Rick signed the tab and left his usual forty percent gratuity. "I'll text you the address to the after party if you're up for it," he said.

I gave him a kiss on the cheek and wished him a goodnight. He signaled to the remaining pack that they were on the move and they left through a private exit. Then, as if compelled by some strange force to dispose of the evidence, lest Bryan catch me with a random closing-time-Xanax, I promptly swallowed the entire pill in my hand.

After the club had expelled most its visitors, I began to feel—strange. Warm, then hot. Hot enough to start sweating profusely—but also cold, shivering and weak. I was *very weak*. So weak that just holding my jaw shut was too difficult for my body. I tried to retreat upstairs, mouth agape, and wait for Jes and Bryan to help me, but my legs disappeared from beneath me on the first couple of steps.

I fell straight backwards, grasping at air on the way down. I hit the floor with an audible smack. The back of my head broke my fall. When I tried to get up, I was too distracted by how difficult it was to take in a breath. Pain fastened my neck to my back like a stiff board. Waves of nausea pounded my stomach and spread out into my throat. The tidal waves were followed by gut-wrenching tsunamis of embarrassment. An embarrassment only relieved by bouts of terror. My mind couldn't decide which horror to process first. It defaulted to crying. The salty tears blurred my vision. Hyperventilations stole oxygen from my brain. Everything seemed to play out so slowly, like my life was submerged in Jell-O.

When the lights went out, I could feel hands all over my body. I heard muffled sounds that might have been my name. I thought I saw my mom's face hovering over me. Finally everything went still. Only a single repeating thought remained, like a blinking cursor on a blank page: *Just Surrender*.

2

A MESSAGE

Fluorescent yellow dashes hovered above the dark rivers of road before her. Approaching rapidly to her right, Tasha saw headlights bounce off a gray apartment with maybe two bedrooms at most. She recognized this home and turned her whole body to face the car's back window as it passed behind her. She furrowed her brow in concentration and tried to keep the building in sight long enough to place it in her memory, but it shrunk down the road too soon. She slumped back in her seat disappointed, and looked up just in time to see a child standing right in the middle of the street! She slammed her foot down to the floorboard to stop the car, but there were no pedals—there was no steering wheel—she wasn't driving! She opened her mouth to scream, but no sound emitted from the gaping hole.

A Driver, who she noticed suddenly sitting in front of her, swerved around the child and avoided her harm. The child dissipated into a cloud of shimmering gold light as they passed by her.

"What is a child doing out at night?" Tasha said, looking through the fingers on her hands that were holding her head.

The Driver peered at Tasha through the rearview mirror. "Young souls are everywhere Ms. Price, especially in dark places. It's our responsibility to look out for them —at all times."

Tasha stared at his abbreviated reflection. His eyes were captivating, but only because they seemed to know her, or maybe she knew him, yet, she was reasonably sure that they had never met before.

"Are we almost there?" she asked.

"If *there* is where you want to go," the Driver said.

"Then, yes, I suppose we *are here* now," she pointed to the gray building that was approaching slowly on her right.

The car stopped in front of a three-story apartment complex. The building was covered in horizontal wooden panels with navy blue accents presenting as shutters and doors. Tasha knew this place: Dogwood Park. She got out and stood in front of the apartments that she and her mom moved into shortly after her dad departed. Tasha had high hopes for this community because it had a decent pool. She would need all the help she could get to make new friends since they moved to a new city right in the middle of the school year.

Her and her mom celebrated her fourteenth birthday there, just weeks after moving in. She didn't expect much for her birthday, after a recent move, and being down a dad, but she did hope for more than just a candle-less cupcake and a dream journal. It would have also helped if her mom hadn't broken down into tears the middle of her *Happy* Birthday song. Tasha turned around to get her luggage from the car and gasped. Before her was a dark and empty parking lot.

"Where did the Driver go?" she shouted.

Tasha's cheeks warmed with embarrassment, she had forgotten to pay the driver for the ride.

"Natasha come give me a hug already!" a familiar woman's voice called from behind her.

Tasha turned to see her mom standing halfway inside the front door. The sky had flipped into a neon sunrise, and her mom's image was painted pink by the sun's rays. She was 5'8, almost as tall as Tasha. On the floor, beside her mom, Tasha was relieved to see her luggage with all of her belongings: a microscope, a white stuffed dog toy, and her glasses. She picked up the pace to meet her mother's outstretched arms. Her mom's hugs worked some kind of magic on Tasha, it was like her stress was butter and her mom's arms were heated wires. The scent of white roses, her mom's favorite flower, entered her nose and energized her entire body with the sense of well being.

"I've missed your hugs, Mom," Tasha said, "and you look so beautiful."

"Thank you dear," her mom said, twirling. "Are you tired, would you like to come in and rest?"

"No, not tired, but I need to talk to you. I've needed you a lot lately...where have you been?" Tasha held her mom's hands in her own.

Her mom looked at her, her bright eyes turning dark and heavy, "I know, I miss you too, honey."

Light tears began to trickled down Tasha's face, "We can't keep avoiding each other like this. I haven't seen you since..." her voice trailed off to a whisper, "the hospital."

Time froze. Tasha remembered at once that her mom was gravely ill.

No, not ill—dead.

Her mom was dead!

Am I dreaming? Tasha trembled at her words, as the scene blinked in front of her.

Her mother re-appeared on a velvet black backdrop, but her image was altered. She was no longer fully solid. Her body continued to shift, moving apart slowly into abstract shapes. It reminded Tasha of watching cloud people, how they slowly drifted into something no longer recognizable. It was if Tasha's awareness of the dream, and the emotion that came with it, had swept her mother away until all that was left of her was shadow and sound.

The motherly figure whispered, "I love you, my sweet girl. You must *try to remember* this when you wake, both worlds are created for you, and every tree tells the same story —your roots are still here on earth!"

Before Tasha could clarify her mother's words, she was jerked away to a dark and empty space. Tasha felt as if her essence was being poured back into her body. Toe by toe and finger by finger, she became aware of her flesh and bones again, and the empty space around her became a lighter shade of black.

3

WAKING WORLD

The awareness continued to spread outwards until a small seed of consciousness rested behind my eyelids that remained tightly shut. I opened them slowly—one, then the other—allowing the outside world to intrude. In my sight were two pairs of eyes, Jesmitha's and Bryan's. They were seated just to the right of me in a large chair that was made for only one person.

Had they been holding hands?

My heart sank as hazy images took their turn filing into the forefront of my memory. It was like the memories were waiting for the main office to open, to document their complaints. Maybe I could just close my eyes again and play dead.

"Oh my god Tasha," Jes exhaled.

Too late.

"We were worried," Bryan said, placing his hand on my ankle, an ankle inside a in a thick white sock—a stark contrast from the fishnets I had on last.

"People have been asking about you," Jesmitha said, "we've told them that you're fine —that you were just working too much and are taking some time off."

Bryan shot Jesmitha a disapproving look.

What's with all the 'we' talk? I rubbed my eyes.

The tubes pulled at my arms and it hurt. I opened my mouth to speak but my words only drew in a breath.

"Rest. I'll go get your nurse," Jes said, before leaving the room.

Once Jesmitha was out the door, Bryan moved closer. "Just focus on healing right now. Your job is safe—I don't want you worrying about that," Bryan said, he waited to see if I would respond, before adding, "there will be some stipulations, but we can talk about all of that later."

I nodded.

I was embarrassed and uncomfortable. I was also too tired to explain the whole story; a story that inferred only a momentary lapse of reason, versus some type of problem like it seemed he was suggesting I had. *Oh God, is that really where we're at?* Apparently, there were two falls I would need to recover from, the physical one and the proverbial fall from grace. *How did I go from head manager to lead charity case within twenty-four hours? Had it been only twenty-four hours? How long had I been here?*

Jesmitha re-appeared with a nurse who couldn't have been much older than her, and definitely not older than me. She wore a set of cornflower blue scrubs that swallowed her petite frame but complemented her blonde hair that rested at the top of her shoulders.

"Hi Na-tasha," the nurse said, reading my name from my hospital bracelet to make sure it matched my chart. She looked at my hand and frowned, "I'm just going to replace your IV catheter real quick." She gently removed the tape securing a catheter in the back of my hand, placed a cotton pad on top while she pulled it out, then reinserted the needle in a more comfortable spot in the corner of my arm.

I watched all of this unfazed, I was never squeamish around needles. After all, I graduated in hopes of becoming a ER doctor in the first place. The nurse checked a few screens on the computer directly beside a nearly empty bag hanging above my bed. She replaced the bag with a full one—the color of highlighter ink. Then she placed a muted burgundy, kidney-bean-shaped, container on my bed.

"I will try to get your next meds here as quickly as possible, but you might still feel a little nausea in the interim, if so, just aim for this," she said.

What a hideous object, surely there's a more pleasant shape and color combination to look at when you're in a risky heaving situation. The nurse noticed my disgust, although, I doubt she knew the reasons behind my aversion.

The nurse said, "Sitting up will help with the nausea as well. Your doctor will be in shortly," then tapped something into a tablet before exiting the room.

I looked at Jes and Bryan. I needed to apologize for scaring everyone and for being so careless, but nothing came out when I went to speak

N. J. Simat

—again.

It dawned on me, *what if I can't talk? What if I have brain damage from the fall?*

My heart quickened. Tears began to gather in my eyes and a raspy whimpering followed. Slowly I realized that the whines were actually coming from me. My cries transitioned into hysterical laughter. Bryan and Jesmitha, having bared witness to this entire exchange, sat in suspended animation from a state of confusion. I'm not sure which vexed Bryan and Jesmitha more: the tears or the laughing.

"Are you okay?" Jes asked.

Bryan echoed, "What do you need?"

"A drink," I said, rubbing my throat.

To which, Jesmitha laughed aloud, and Bryan frowned at both of us before he said, "I assume you mean water, I'll be right back."

Once Bryan was out of view, Jes leaned in, "He's been on edge ever since...you know—the fall...but, everything is going to be okay, because you're going to be fine now." Jes grabbed my hand. I felt the cold hard metal from all of her rings press into my skin. "Oh, and before you freak out, I've been taking care of Yumi[1], so she's good. She's very concerned about her Mommy, but completely safe. We tried to bring her into the hospital to see you but they wouldn't let us," Jes stuck her bottom lip out.

"Yumi," I said, drawing out her name, invoking all of the warm mental and emotional impressions I'd attached to it over the years.

My mouth tasted like ink, my eyelids were heavy, and I craved sleep, but a thin layer of fear kept me awake. I didn't know the extent of my injuries, or if I even had any. I took a deep breath and tried to think about something lively and exciting to stay alert. My mind flipped through violent movie scenes to sex, to concerts and festivals, back to sex, and finally settled on the fluorescent lights above my head. They were a lot less interesting than any of the aforementioned, but they were bright and carried no hidden anxieties within them. They also took less energy to focus on.

"Oh my God!" Jesmitha cried.

Jarred out of my sleepy trance, I jumped, and then laughed, upon realizing that I must have looked dead staring up at those lights with such stillness.

---

[1] Pronounced; Yew-Me

18

"I'm okay Jes. Sorry, I'm just exhausted." I closed my eyes.

"I'm going to let you rest," she said without a single inflection in her voice. "I need to go check on Yumi anyway, my apartment isn't exactly the most dog-friendly, I'll come back tomorrow morning though…I think Bryan is staying the night if they'll let him."

She tried her best to hug me goodbye, but horizontal to vertical embraces always made for awkward experiences—unpleasant for everyone.

I was happy to hear that Bryan would be staying, but I also felt a bit guilty. I tried to rationalize that he'd probably extend this treatment to any of his employees. After all, he was the reason why we had great benefits in the first place, and why I was in this nice room I supposed. Yet I knew that he was also hyper-aware that I had no family to speak of. I had no one else at all other than him, Jes, and Yumi.

Bryan and I were alike in that way, and it's what initially drew us together. We fell in love rhythmically: conversation by conversation, work-lunch by work-lunch, and after shift drinks. Unfortunately, soon after our friendship turned into something more, the conflicts of interests manifested much quicker than either of us had anticipated. Surprisingly, the whole dating-your-boss thing, wasn't our main issue. We were great at keeping things professional in front of the staff, in fact, most of them were none the wiser the first few months we were dating. But the red flag that had *always* been there, waving earnestly at us both, was me having to flirt with our high-profile clients five feet away from him.

Our breakup, about two years into the relationship, was probably the most civilized and mature conversation that I'd ever had. Even though I initiated it, I think we both understood that it was either part as friends or eventually end as enemies. We respected each other too much to see that happen, nor did we want to abandon our synergy. We worked incredibly well together.

I remember the night that Bryan told me he had bought Club Daze with his inheritance money, and he asked me to lead the VIP cocktail team. There was no hesitation or question in my mind what my answer would be. I followed him out of Top Key's doors, right then and there. I can still see the look on the owner's face, as Bryan played and sung, *'Bryan' Had a Little Lamb*, on the mini piano out front; right before we left hand-in-hand. We may have had a few, "last-day-cocktails," in celebration of Club Daze on our last shift together at Top Key. I was content to finally be rid of that pretentious place, and I never looked back. Yet even if I would have liked Top Key, I was so blindly in love with Bryan, I would have followed him anywhere.

Maybe we've just been lying to ourselves these past two years, but we've remained somewhat stable in friendship. That is, if you ignore the few drunken and passionate hookups that spurred jealous outbursts, as well as, weeks of avoidance.

Bryan popped back into my room in faded blue jeans, a red pullover, and his ever-pristine white sneakers. He had a pillow tucked under an arm that also held a single coffee. The sight of that lonely little coffee, swiped away all of my fond reminiscence. It was a curious point of contention in our relationship: he *never* brought me a coffee when he got one, and he also never ordered me a drink while we were out. It was like he had an etiquette blind-spot in that specific area. It made me feel like he thought I was supposed to only serve him. Possibly a by-product of working for your lover, but it annoyed me to no end. I'd usually react by bringing everyone else drinks too, excluding him, hoping that he would catch on, but he never did.

I searched his face for any signs of sleep deprivation as a clue to my length of stay, or maybe even to his invested interest in my well being, but there was none, save for a five o'clock shadow. But that wasn't much of a clue on Bryan's face, because he was part-Syrian, so you could still see his pitch black hair under his tanned skin even right after he shaved.

"Hey," I said, sticking my toe in the water to see how cold it would be if I were to jump all the way in.

"Has the doctor been in yet?" he said, still standing halfway in the door.

I shook my head no.

"So a woman wakes up from blacking out, and a possible concussion, and the doctor can't be bothered to stop in," Bryan said, "I'll be right back." He threw his pillow across my bed, onto the empty visitor chair, and left again.

Shortly after leaving, Bryan returned with *someone's* doctor. I wasn't surprised in the least, I knew him well enough to know that he never returns empty-handed. In fact, I can't recall a single event in which he said he was going to do something, and it wasn't done *exactly* as he said it would be.

"Uh, Hi...Ms. Price, your primary doctor is tending to an emergency, but he's aware that you are awake. I've read your history —briefly." The Doctor glanced at Bryan, "We will most likely be able to discharge you tomorrow after you speak with the Psych Department."

"The Psych Department?" I asked, sitting upright in my bed.

"Isn't tomorrow a little soon?" Bryan asked.

The doctor looked at Bryan, and back at me. "It would be better if we spoke in private Ms. Price," he said, as he nodded his head up and down assuringly.

"It's fine, just tell me—us," I said.

The young doctor pressed his lips together before he asked, "Technically, you could leave today, we're just waiting on labs and paperwork. As long as all of your vitals are stable and your tests are unremarkable, there's no reason to keep you here. However, due to the nature of your incident, we require that the psych department sign a release declaring that you are not a danger to yourself."

"I'm sorry, what exactly do you think happened?" Bryan said.

The doctor looked at the charts, then at me, and paused. He said, "are you sure you don't want to speak in private—

"Yes!" Bryan and I said in unison.

The doctor stiffened, "Ms Price, you overdosed on quite a concoction of drugs. We found Amphetamine, Methamphetamine, Cocaine, Opioids, Benzodiazepine, and of course high blood levels of alcohol, in your system," he added, "you also presented with a mild concussion from a presumed fall that exacerbated an already fragile situation, as you were suffering from hypoxia as a result from the overdose."

I was so shocked, that I didn't notice Bryan's face was now an impressive shade of red, and outpacing his hoodie in vibrance at alarming rates.

Perhaps I should have had this conversation in private. "I'm sorry but did you say Opiates, isn't that painkillers? And what is Benzod-a-whatever?" I asked.

"Yes, some Opioids are painkillers," he lowered his voice before saying, "but they are also heroin. Benzodiazepines are anti-anxiety meds such as Valium or Xanax." Then doctor said, "It's a lot," raising his eyebrows.

"'It's a lot?' I'm sorry sir is that a technical term?" I snapped.

I said a quick prayer for a sink hole to open up and swallow me whole. I felt like a teenager getting reprimanded by her dad. Although, it's not like I could—or would—ever really know what that felt like.

"I didn't take heroin, I would never do that," I said, "and the weed was from a gummy bear, a couple days before." I added as if it would make *all of this* better.

"I didn't mention THC." The Doctor quipped.

My face reddened and my whole body warmed.

"...Look, all I can tell you is that the Opioids were in your system, but then again, there is always the possibility that you were unaware that you consumed it," he said calmly, "we see it more often than not, people being admitted to the emergency room, and even dying from various additives, especially in the case of fentanyl in Georgia. The drug gets unknowingly mixed in with their plans for the night, and if that was the case, you're incredibly fortunate. Most people don't get a second chance like this Ms. Price, I hope you can appreciate that."

"Yes...thank you," I whispered, withdrawing my attitude.

I refrained from saying *that will be all sir* to the man in the lab coat in front of me. A man that actually had his life together, and a man who looked no older than me.

He pressed his lips together once more. He nodded, and walked out of the room—leaving me alone with a pacing Bryan.

"Heroin," Bryan said, with one hand closed over another in a fist at his mouth like he was cold. "You know I can't just let this go Tasha, right? *You do* know that?"

His eyes peered deep into mine. They were searching for the confirmation he needed in order to continue his one-way conversation.

"I need to make it clear that if you expect to continue working at Club Daze, or anywhere near me, you will have to get therapy for this —no exceptions. I won't have that in my life." He sat down and then stood right back up. "Were you trying to kill yourself! Why else would you do something *this* dumb? Haven't you seen it take enough of our friends?"

"Bryan—

"What? Look at me, and promise me, that there is no way that it could have gotten in your system—that it's impossible." Bryan looked down upon me for a bit, for some type of acknowledgment, or reassuring correspondence, to anything he just said.

I thought it better to invoke my right to remain silent. Defending myself now would only be in vain. He had already made up his mind about what happened that night. After a while of obvious brooding, I watched him seemingly agree to something internally, nodding his head up and down, and answering his own questions as it appeared.

He looked down at his phone and began to type for a short while.

He said, "I'm going to head home since the doctor seems to think that you'll be fine. Jes will pick you up in the morning."

I shut my eyes and focused on my breath. I didn't want him here anymore, but I didn't want him to leave either. The last thing I heard were his heavy footsteps carry him out of the room, without so much as a get well soon.

LONELY RABBITS

"Good Moorningg," Jes sang, as she entered my room.

Warm hazelnut, cooked eggs, and toasted bread, grappled in the air as she walked over to me and placed a pair of crinkled paper bags and two coffees on the bedside tray.

It was obvious that Jes had the whole day off, because of the intentional lack of effort she put in her appearance. This was a signature *Daze-Girl* habit. On the days we didn't have to get all dolled up, we'd save every single measure of energy that otherwise went into perfecting our image. This meant no makeup, hair in a messy bun, slip-on shoes, and an outfit that made us appear a tad homeless.

However, Jesmitha's beauty was never disturbed and her trademark sandalwood and vanilla fragrance was always present. Her skin was an ever-steady flawless wonder of deep henna, and her body alluded to its perfection through the thin fabric that hung off her small frame and perky breasts. She wore an oversized t-shirt that was intentionally faded black. It had some American rock-n'roll band on it, that I'm sure she'd never listened to. Underneath it were very short and stonewashed, denim shorts. Tied around her waist was a grey heather sweatshirt promoting some prestige college, of which her mom was an alumni, and that she probably was—or had been—expected to attend as well.

She sat down in the visitor chair.

"Good Morning," I said, comforted at the sound of my own voice.

Jesmitha plopped down beside me on the hospital bed and said, "I brought you breakfast—not sure if you're hungry—but I know you want this coffee though."

I wasn't hungry, but I actually wanted food for once. Eating breakfast felt like a very normal thing to do, and what I craved was normalcy more than anything else. Anything normal to put distance in between me and this horrible incident.

"Thanks," I accepted the warm coffee, "but can I have some water first—the pitcher is empty."

My mouth was dry and rough. I could feel indentions on my tongue from where my teeth had sat solitarily pressed against it for far too long.

"Oh!" she said jumping up like she'd seen a spider, "sorry—I'll be right back."

When Jes left the room, I realized that I was alone for the first time since waking up yesterday. For a breath it was nice, but the little tick of peace dissipated under the onslaught of troubling thoughts and mental images of *the fall*—as Jes so delicately put it. I felt a wave of nausea that could have actually just been anxiety. I sat up a little and tried to distract myself with some television. Unfortunately, despite my fumbling with the remote, the one that hung in the corner of my room remained a flat black rectangle. Either the batteries were dead, or this was some type of karmic punishment, because the TV's only channel was a distorted image of me in a hospital gown. My reflection on its matte surface—not helpful.

On top of a dresser beneath the television, I noticed for the first time a modest condolence corner in my honor. There was a lightly-stuffed, grey rabbit, sitting about two feet tall. He was slightly slumped over, and from what I could discern, neither cheery nor sad in his disposition. Behind the bunny, was a swirling blue and green glass vase that held a bouquet of sunflowers sprayed outwards and their stems were resting in cloudy water. There were no cards though. I imagined that most people in my predicament might have woken up to perhaps more than one stuffed animal; maybe a plethora of flora, but most assuredly, at *least* one card. Despite their intention, the hare and flowers made me sad, and I wished they weren't there at all.

I laid back down. Something moved me to run my hands against my bare stomach, from the base of my ribcage down to the top of my hips. I felt a subtle moment of relief with the realization that alongside the loss of my dignity, I'd also managed to lose some water weight. *Silver linings.*

"What are you smiling about?" Jes asked, matching my own dumb grin with one of her own as she re-entered my room.

"I'm just happy you're here," I said.

Jes handed me an oversized styrofoam cup with a bright red straw and said, "Well, I'm not going anywhere. I'm just glad you're going to be okay girl."

"I am, it's really not what it seems."

"Don't worry, we can talk about it later. Don't feel like you have to explain yourself to me, I'm not judging you," Jesmitha said, "let's talk about something else, anything else…well anything else but Daze. I've got the whole day off."

"I'm really more embarrassed than anything else. My head hurts and my body is sore—but like after-the-gym sore. I really just want to take a shower and cuddle up with Yumi. Oh, and I had the strangest dream."

"I love dream stuff," Jesmitha said as she edged closer to me.

All of her enthusiasm encouraged me to sit up a little more, but before I could fully explain my dream, a serious woman marched into my room. She had short and natural red hair that ran strictly alongside her jawline. She wore a long black pencil skirt, with opaque black stockings, and a pale blue blouse that tied into a knot along her neckline.

"Hello, Ms. Price. I'm Doctor Rivers, but you can call me Kathy. I'll be doing your psych evaluation, but there's no need to be nervous, it's really just standard procedure."

"Like right now?" I asked.

"Yes, if you're ready," She looked at Jesmitha, and then back at me.

Jes hugged my neck, grabbed half of the food that she'd brought in, and scurried out. At the same time Dr. Rivers took a seat in the leather recliner beside me, the one that Bryan had been in. I missed seeing him in it. After asking me a few preliminary questions, that I can only assume were to rule out any extreme psychosis: like believing I could fly, or wanting to harm the president, she changed her tone. She also read the questions out more slowly, and her pauses for my answers became more attentive.

"How often do you drink alcohol?" She crossed her legs.

"Maybe six or seven drinks a week," I said.

"How often do you use drugs?"

"I don't…typically," I said, realizing the absurdity of the answer after the sounds left my lips. "Well, I use Adderall sometimes when I have to work all night, or as an appetite suppressant, and I'll have a mild gummy bear for anxiety that I usually only take the night after a work weekend, and *very*, rarely—"

"But you're not prescribed adderall correct?" she asked.

"Correct," I said slowly, as my chin jutted forward, and I peered over my nose, to see what she scribbled down beside the question, immediately regretting my honesty.

"Do you believe that you abuse alcohol?"

"No...it abuses me though," I smiled unashamed. She didn't laugh, smirk, or even look up to acknowledge my joke. I sighed in disappointment.

"Do you believe that you have a problem with drug use?"

"No," *Unless you consider this a problem. The problem we're existing in at this very moment.*

"Do you ever have thoughts of suicide?"

Sometimes, but doesn't everyone? "No."

After a few more questions she finished writing up her notes and closed the notebook. She seemed satisfied, or at least content, with what she could do within the confines of the system. As it turns out *standard procedure* was tragically accurate.

She stood up and handed me a few brochures, "Here are a few numbers to call. They're all local and they can help with any questions you might have. They are real professionals. People that you can talk to and sort out any personal, or professional, struggles. The two on the back are specifically for addiction. Based on your answers, we cannot keep you here, but I strongly recommend that you contact at least one of those office's before you leave today," her eyes looked tired.

I accepted all of the antidepressant-blue pamphlets that she handed me with feigned interest, solely out of empathy for her, and thanked her sincerely before she left my room. Jesmitha must have been waiting directly outside, because she returned no less than two minutes after Doctor Rivers was out of sight. She approached my bedside slowly, maintaining eye contact, like she was unsure if I was comfortable with her presence.

"Well this has been fun," I said, in a weak, yet effective, attempt to lighten the mood.

"Alcohol abuses me?" She said shaking her head and giggling. She approached my bedside more confidently, "So, tell me about your dream."

"I told you most of it already, except for that I visited my old apartment complex and I spoke with my Mom there. I think she told me something important—but now that I say it aloud, maybe it was just a normal dream. It felt so real."

"That's it?" She asked, quickly followed with, "Sorry. I just thought there would be more to it, you know, since you said it was crazy." She smiled.

"Yeah, I guess it's not that strange after all, or maybe it's too difficult to put into words what made it feel different. I felt like I was really speaking to my mom you know? It was like she was here again. It's so hard to explain."

"Maybe you were 'Sha," Jesmitha said, "my family believes in all of that stuff."

"You're free to go Ms. Price," a voice interjected from the door, startling Jes and I. It was the same young doctor from yesterday, "your panels look good, we just need you to sign your discharge papers, and a nurse will be around with the wheelchair to roll you out," the Doctor said, barely entering the room, and leaving as fast as he had appeared.

"Yay!" Jesmitha threw both hands in the air dancing. "Slumber party at your house tonight. Man, Yumi is going to be relieved! She's so tired of me. You can literally see it on her face when I walk in, but then again, I've never been good with dogs—I can barely keep plants alive." Jes noticed me tense up and said, "Don't worry, Bryan's got her right now. I'll text him. I'm sure he can drop her off for a little welcome-home party."

In someways, I got lucky having Jes as a friend. She was my first hire the week I started as the VIP Cocktail manager at Daze. We've gotten along really well ever since. There's only been one major hiccup in our relationship—yes, only one uninhibited blast of a belch in our history as friends. It's a night that we do not speak of. Other than that, our personalities have gelled well.

We followed the opposites-attract model, and we couldn't be more opposite, not only in personality, but in appearance. Jesmitha was petite and was feisty. Some might even refer to her as a bitch, but I liked to call her, "tiny but mighty." Let's just say, she didn't take any prisoners. In spite of all of that, she was a loving person at her core; once you reached underneath her vapid—and somewhat plastic—exterior. On the other hand, I was long in every direction and always calm on the surface. I was warm to strangers, but somehow increasingly cold to those who got close to me. Physically, we only shared one single feature, and that was our extremely long and dark hair.

"Bryan said he can drop off Yumi tonight," Jes said. Just as the blonde nurse who replaced the catheter arrived in my room with a wheelchair.

The nurse freed me from all of the machines and tubes. She wheeled me outside of the room and to the exit. The turns were familiar to everyone but me. Once outside, I was surprised to see how late it was. All of the cars, that were lined up for their respective pick ups and drop offs, already had their headlights shining. There was barely any blue left in the sky. I guess I hadn't looked at the clock, not even once, while nestled in my fluorescent lit room. I also had the window's shades drawn throughout my entire stay.

I stood up from the wheelchair with ease, another ride of standard procedure I'm sure. I climbed into Jes' antique and white, Jeep Wrangler and finally plugged my phone into a charger. On our drive home not one word was spoken. Instead, we listened to David Grey and let him bare the burden of filling up the quiet space between us for the duration of the trip. A few times along the way I caught light from the oncoming headlights reflected in the fluid building up in the base of Jes's eyes. I pretended not to notice, because I didn't know if they were happy or sad tears, and didn't want to risk another lecture. The one from Bryan was enough.

We were less than five minutes from my apartment when the album ran its course and the stereo system had defaulted back to the radio; and so came the radio talk-show host in between the abrasive and needy commercials.

"…great having you on the show today PhD Lim, so you know…we have to ask you about your eccentric boss Dr. Stepanov. Some say that he's a Russian spy, or that he's actually an alien from outer space," the hyperactive DJ said too close to his mic, "what do you say to these rumors?"

"Like I have said many times before, he's a simple man—well more or less. He's a man that appreciates his privacy, and has always been hyper-focused on his life's work," a slightly mature female voice responded, with each word perfectly enunciated and round. Her voice was soothing.

"Spoken like a loyal employee, but we all know he's gotta have some big secrets in those glass houses." The DJ laughed obnoxiously, "is there any mention of *him* in your new book, or any personal—

"Actually the book is not new, it's a relaunch. I guess you'll just have to pick up a copy to find out if he's mentioned or not, but I will say that we're all very pleased with how it's been received this time around."

The DJ shouted into his microphone rendering it's use completely redundant, "To all of our listeners out there, you can order Min Lim's book today, *This World is Made for You*, use promo code

OURWORLDS15 to save—

I reached up and slapped Jes's radio off, opting for the awkward silence instead, but the title of the book echoed in my ears, and resonated with me. Something about it seemed familiar, like I had heard it somewhere before. I made a mental note to search the title when I got home. *Home.*

I couldn't wait to squeeze Yumi, not having her beside me for the last few days was heavily weighing on me. She was the one thing I could always count on in my life to make me feel better, without any negative side effects.

We turned into my apartment complex. At the entryway stood a solid black square of stone, with the words *Vivid Stream Apartments* embossed in gold on it. We snaked through the streets until we reached my building. My place was on the second floor, unit #222. It faced the parking lot. As we pulled up closer to my apartment, I could see Yumi's eyes shining through the large living room window. They were reflecting the light back from the jeep, and shifted from metallic gold-to-green. Her eye-lights vibrated wildly—her butt wagging so much that it shook her entire face along with it.

I hurried past Jes up the stairs and sprinted to my apartment. I was so excited to see Yumi, that I almost dropped the keys—my hands clumsily trying to unlock the door. Once unlocked, I barely got it open before my entire world embraced me. Yumi tried her very best to give me a human hug within her restrictive four-legged blueprint.

Jes walked in shortly after. She looked around the empty apartment, "I guess Bryan just dropped her off, he must have had work stuff to do tonight."

"On a Tuesday? Yeah, probably not," I said, looking up at her from the floor, with all of Yumi's eighty pounds sitting on my lap. She sat on me just as she did when she was no bigger than a loaf of bread.

"Yeah, probably not," she echoed, "let's watch something scary." Her eyes went wild in a clear attempt to change the subject.

Jesmitha pulled out a personal crash-kit that she kept stored under the bathroom sink at my house, and then made her bed on the sofa. Luckily she was passed out within ten minutes of being horizontal. As soon as Jes fell asleep, Yumi and I retreated to our room. Both of us were thankful that we didn't have to sit through another one of her awful horror films. Yumi *hated* the screaming, and I hated the cheap love scenes.

Finally I snuggled into the plush familiarity of my own bed, and

Yumi curled up beside me. Nothing felt more like home. She must have been really worried while I was gone, because anytime I would stir awake, I was met immediately with her copper eyes staring at me; it was like she had been watching me sleep all night.

4

THE QUANTUM TREE

The steam from our coffee and scrambled egg-whites collectively flickered and swirled into the air. Jes and I had breakfast around the coffee table in front of the television, as we looked for potential halloween costumes for this year's festivities.

"Let's do zombies—oooh or better yet, an outbreak theme?" Jes raised her eyebrows.

"You can't be serious," I said.

"Yeah, probably not the best idea…what about aliens?"

"I dunno," I flipped through a halloween store's catalogue. It was uninspiring, or maybe I was just in a bad mood.

"I probably need to head out soon. I have Latin night tonight." Jes shook two imaginary maracas in each hand.

"I know! Badges, Babes, and Boos—any profession with a badge is fair game." I closed the magazine.

Jes slapped her hands down on the coffee table."Did you just think of that off the top of your head?"

"Yep." I tilted my coffee mug all the way back.

"It's great. I love it, and we already have a couple firefighter outfits for the girls, if they want to use them," Jes said.

"I think I'll go as a park ranger and find someone to dress as a bear," I got up from the floor and brought our dirty dishes to the sink.

"Bryan would do it." Jes followed me to the kitchen with her empty mug.

"Yeah…maybe. Well, we have one night down—only three more to go." I rolled my eyes.

"We're kinda behind this year...but we can figure the rest out tonight and have them all posted by Friday."

"It'll be fine, no-one in this city plans more than two weeks out anyway."

Jes left to go home and relax before her shift. I had never worked Wednesday's but Jes swore that they were the best nights to work. She loved everything about latin night. She loved the music, her co-workers, and the vibe. She had also mentioned how much it entertained her that a few of her loyal mid-week clientele, have failed to realized that she was actually Indian. But, she did speak Spanish, and her true accent only peaked through when she spoke with her mom. Jes also had a fair amount of cosmetic work done. So I couldn't think less of anyone for being confused about her ethnicity—especially on Latin night.

A passing cloud stole the light from my living room and reminded me that the day was still moving forward even if I was not. I hadn't moved an inch from this kitchen barstool since Jes left. I sat scrolling through social media, and then ended up reading through all of the comments on Club Daze's IG account. I scanned for any reference to my incident. Surprisingly, there wasn't much posted about it. I found a few comments here and there, some of them were actually wishing me well, but nothing derogatory like I had braced myself for. I guess there weren't as many people left in the building as I remembered—or it's possible Bryan could've already erased the comments before I got the chance to read them—probable even. I wondered if I should call him or wait for Bryan to call me. It bothered me that he just dropped Yumi off last night without so much as a word.

"12:45 p.m.," posted on the top corner of my phone taunted me. I should at least take Yumi for a walk, even if I didn't accomplish anything else today. I can't exactly remember when or why, my entire life shifted into one nagging obligation. I used to look forward to these walks with her. Yumi would flirt with all of the dogs along the way, with her elegant strut that was seemingly intentional. It didn't matter which season either, I would embrace every class of stroll for its own atmospheric pleasures.

"Roooph," Yumi barked from the couch, as if she could sense the very second my thoughts geared up for action.

"At least you're still excited to go."

The thought of her wiggling, wagging body allowed a smile to creep across my face. I amused myself by testing her super-sonic hearing.

As low as audibly possible I whispered, "Want to go for a walk?"

Yumi's face exuded expansive joy and she panted with the anticipation of something wonderful to come. She jumped from the couch and ran to me, nudging me off my chair. I stood up, laughing at her pushiness, and grabbed our park-bag. After I latched on her Crayon-purple leash, we walked outside into the blinding-white sunlight.

The birds along our path were clearly none-the-wiser of my burdens, or anyone else's for that matter. Their songs of jubilee were disembodied incantations coming from up above. Their delicate bodies were camouflaged within the remaining autumn leaves. The choir followed us all the way until we reached the dog park.

The park was a retired highschool baseball field from a team that they had re-located up north a few years ago. The batting fence still remained, and the bottom bleachers were kept for seating, but that was it. The Diamond had been completely covered in grass and the dugouts were demolished. Scattered about the field were bright blue and yellow enrichment structures: in the form of tunnels, stairs, fire hydrants, and sway bridges.

Usually the dog park was always busy regardless the time of day, but for whatever reason there was only a quiet-stillness present. There weren't any other people, nor dogs, roaming about.

After Yumi seemed to be content with her usual park errands: a few sprints back and forth, refusing to engage with any of the enrichment equipment despite my pleading, and investigating the perimeter thoroughly, I re-attached her leash and laid down a blanket from our park-bag. Once she was settled, I handed her a bone and sat on a bleacher seat with a blanket of my own. Her leash was wrapped around my wrist, just in case an unmannered dog entered abruptly.

I embraced the quiet that surrounded us and stared off into the thick layer of trees at the opposite end of the dog park. Unlike most of the other neighboring trees, these were evergreens, so they were still thick and opaque. Despite Fall beckoning them to shed their leaves, they refused to expose their resident's homes.

During this time of the year, when it was cold and the holidays were just around the corner, they looked like rows of Christmas trees to me —which always reminded me of my mother. Her favorite thing about Christmas was buying and decorating the tree. The year of her physical death, I was praying that she would get just one more Christmas with us, but she passed mid-October. In reality, I had lost her years before then.

The book from last night, the thought emerged out of the mental fog that lingered from my incident.

On my phone I typed, *This world is made for you, PhD Lim,* and the book appeared at the top of the search results immediately. I clicked on the thumbnail of her cover art. The image was a golden seed with a tree growing out of it on a white backdrop. The trunk was made from a colorful DNA helix, and the seed had seven roots emerging from it. Yet, the tree, its trunk, and rooted seed, were completely incased within a second seed's shell. The encasing seed was a translucent pearl shade.

A philosophy book, not exactly my typical Monday night, bubble-bath read; but if there was ever a time in my life that I should branch out, it would be now. The book had been very well received, as was obvious from all of the colored in stars listed below the thumbnail. The fifth star was colored in half-way as to not short the author's praise just for the sake of whole and complete stars. Some reviewers claimed it, "life-altering," or, "eye-opening."

The synopsis read, *"The work is about enriching our lives through the expansion of our minds. PhD Lim and her team, enlighten us on how to readily extract gifts from the physical world by means of exploring the marriage between Science and Philosophy."*

Intrigued, I invested the $13.99 on the download. On the very first page—the very first line—read an all too familiar phrase: *"This world was created for you, every tree tells the same story."*

Yumi's leash snapped taut, startling me. I looked up, expecting to see another person or animal, but there was just Yumi at the end of the cord: She stood growling, with her hackles raised and teeth bared, at something in the distant tree line. If someone *was* lurking about, they would have to wait their turn for my attention. I was still struck with awe that the very words my mother uttered to me in my dream were now digitized on the screen in front of me.

"Yumi, what is it baby? It's okay,"

I rubbed Yumi's back to console her, but it was no use. She continued in her demonstration without pause.

"All right, let's go, you don't have to tell me twice."

We decided it best to make our journey home, thankfully, in opposition from the evergreens. Once we were safely inside our apartment, I felt my shoulders relax. Yumi ran past me and pounced on the couch. The same couch that I initially fought to keep her off during the first few months after I brought her home: the girl sheds just as she breathes. Ever since she won that battle, and advanced her territory, she seemed to enjoy jumping on it as hard as she could as if to remind me of her victory. Unfortunately for me, her stark white fur stands out alarmingly against the deep grey fabric. I have a hefty lint-roller expense as it were.

I suppose I could just have bought a different sofa, in a more Yumi-esque color, but I purchased this one specifically to match my kitchen counters—both of which, can be seen directly from the front door. At least my guests couldn't see Yumi's contribution upon entry, no that surprise was for later once they've stood up from the sofa and looked down at their clothes.

My apartment is otherwise surgically clean, which I guess comes from not having bi-pedal children, or much of a life outside of work. Every room was decorated with a minimalist approach: flowers in a white vases, a couple thick black frames, lots of books, and a candle here and there, but that was mostly it. It was peaceful, uncrowded, and effortless.

I locked the door behind me, a habit I wasn't always so diligent at, and checked my phone. I set it to *do not disturb* during our walk.

I had a missed call, and two unread text messages:

1 missed call from Bryan <3, October 13 at 2:33pm, and 1 message from Bryan <3, October 13 at 2:56pm, "Call me."

I resolved that I would call Bryan after reading for a few minutes to settle my nerves. I wasn't sure how the conversation was going to go, or if I still had a job to discuss.

1 message from Jesmitha DAZEGIRL, October 13, at 2:36pm, "Hey babe do you need anything?"

I replied to Jes, "No, I'm good, more weird dream stuff, but I'll tell you about it later."

I walked over to my wine cabinet, and pulled out a red blend that I grabbed during my last grocery run simply because I liked the label. It was black and had a metallic gold tree etched into the paper—it seemed fitting for tonight. I poured myself a glass, poured Yumi a bowl of water, and sunk into my soft sectional.

I lit a rose scented candle and began reading the first chapter of the book. It largely focused on the idea that the physical world we experience is *created intentionally* for all souls to evolve in. PhD Lim cited plants as just one example of evidence for intelligent design under a chapter titled: *The Quantum Tree.*

In the beginning of the chapter, an illustration of photosynthesis presented in a microscope-box that jutted out to the left side of a tree. The figure consisted of sunlight, as rays of photons, shining down into a green leaf's Chlorophyll. Inside the leaf were circular waves of energy—like a ripple-ring on the surface of water.

Beneath the image, a few words described the miraculous mechanics that make photosynthesis possible. The crux of the miracle was a process called superposition: a single particle's ability to exist in multiple places at the same time. With superposition, a particle can become three-hundred and sixty degree waves of energy. The process was familiar, some type of Quantum Biology that I couldn't fully understand, but only recognize from my undergrad.

The main text read, "*The sun supplies energy to the trees and empowers them to manifest into their essential role of carbon up-taking machines; thus, supplying us with oxygen and making life possible on earth. This seemingly primitive process employs quantum mechanics to ensure maximum efficacy. As a result, photosynthesis is more efficient and accurate than any masterful human technology that has ever been created on earth. Yet, these natural quantum marvels, that rival the most powerful computers existence, are expressed from a simple seed; a seed that is only born from matured trees. How could this be, you might ask? Could it be the product of a pure genesis—a true intelligent creation? This predicament is not unlike the chicken and the egg scenario. Only as far as I know, we could sustain life without chickens—but I digress. My point is: A respectable answer can be found for any of life's curiosities, once they're placed under a powerful enough microscope. We will eventually understand every 'how,' of intellectual design; but, in that heightened moment of discovery, we run the risk of tragically losing sight of the bigger picture—'the why.' Why was it all done? Why was the world constructed in such a way that our food grows on trees? Why are our bodies secured to this spinning green and blue marble by an invisible force known as gravity? Why is this astro-rock tucked in under a lush green blanket; a landscape that collectively cleanses the carbon from our breath, in order to provide our lungs with a sweet breeze of life-sustaining air? Why? Because this beautiful piece of art, called Earth, was purposefully commissioned for the evolution of all souls—and we can back it up with science.*

I continued on, although I couldn't understand everything that I was reading. It felt a bit like groping in the dark, but I kept at it because I knew there was something there on those pages—between the lines—speaking to me. I took a gulp of my wine and let the pleasant bitterness coat my mouth, relaxing my mental palette. Yumi's curled up body appeared in the bottom of my wine glass. She laid on the hardwood floor, asleep, a few feet in front of me—just *outside* of the very expensive dog-bed that I had just bought her. I scanned through the second chapter. It appeared to redefine the entire world in terms of energy: waves, frequencies, and vibrations.

It read, *"We experience life on this Physical Plane through a system of code—a sacred geometry of intervals. The waves of information are received through all of the body's senses, and interpreted in the brain to the best of its current abilities. Then the signals are transmitted into a vast ocean of illusion, or rather, a network of subjective reality."*

I searched for something to stand out, or resonate, as a message that my Mom would send to me. Everything I was reading was interesting, but nothing felt like *the* message. I was getting impatient. I scrolled to the middle of chapter three. There she discussed alternate states of consciousness, as well as something about the different planes of reality.

PhD Lim writes, *"While we can't fully access the Astral Plane in this life, we can make contact through an awareness-transfer. Just a few moments of exposure to this plane can cause a paradigm shift for us on the Physical Earth, because of the Universal Knowledge that exists there."*

Again, the text was intriguing but I wasn't finding what I was looking for, whatever *that* was. I had almost finished my bottle of wine, which made an already rich subject material impossibly viscous. I laid my phone down. The book wasn't helping me remember my mom's full message. It crossed my mind that she was just reaching out from the grave to help my anxiety by creating a 'High-Five' day for me—the thought brought a smile with it.

I stood up—a little too fast. Once the dizziness ceased, I rifled through my mess drawer at the kitchen counter for a pen and a notepad. I knew Mom was trying to tell me something important. I could almost feel her pushing me forward to find it. I just wasn't getting it.

On the paper I wrote down everything that happened the night that I spoke with her in my dreams. There had to be a way to reach her again. Maybe—maybe, if I Just took half of everything from the night I saw her, I could visit her without hurting myself. I was pretty sure I still had the little bag from Rick tucked away in my corset's interior pocket.

I looked at Yumi, she was still fast asleep, paddling her paws in a dream land of her own. I searched my bedroom for all of my new plan's components. After I had everything in my possession, I carefully divided them all into half-portions as best as I could. The only thing I didn't have on-hand was the Xanax. The heroin must have been a mistake—possibly a false positive of some sort? The night was blurry in my mind, but I don't think Rick would have given me anything like that—*but his entourage?* I pushed the possibility out of my mind. I looked over at the empty wine bottle. Perhaps this wine was too strong, or maybe I suffered some brain damage from my fall, but I desperately needed to get to the bottom of all this so I could move on with my life.

I grabbed my phone and tapped on my last text thread. "Hey Jes, do you have half a Xanax I can have?" I hit send and held my breath.

Jes responded immediately, "What? 'Sha, why are you asking me for that?"

I typed, "I know it sounds bad, but trust me, I need it for something important."

"I don't know…"

"So you do have one."

An ellipsis danced on the screen for a moment. It disappeared. Then reappeared for a second, before she responded, "I do."

"Jes, you know me." I sent.

My phone started flashing with Jesmitha's name at the top. I answered and explained to her what I was trying to do. I tried my best to sound certain and sane, even though I wasn't sure of any of it. Luckily, I'm an incredibly persuasive person, admit-ably sometimes to my own detriment.   Jesmitha remembered my dream, and the obnoxious radio DJ, so it was easy to explain the book coincidence. I was able to capitalize on her, "wow," moment and sway her just enough to hand over half of the pill.

"I can drop it off in an hour. I'm getting ready for a date. I met this new boy at work." Jesmitha said.

"That's great."

"Are you trying to do this thing tonight—while you're home alone?" Jes asked.

"I was thinking about it," I said.

"Thats probably a bad idea 'Sha, but I can stop by after my date. Do you still have the house-key under your mat?"

"Yes, I do."

"Okay…if you promise me that you're just taking half of the MDMA as well, and not taking anything else, then I think you'll be fine. It's going to be a low-key night for me anyway, so I shouldn't be too late. He's an EMT—hubby material," she said.

I could practically hear her beaming through the phone. "Really, hubby material? And you met him at Daze—that's rare."

I heard Jes giggle emphatically on the other end of the line.

"Jes, tell me he wasn't *my* EMT—that he's not a guy whose carried my lifeless body?"

"I gotta go! I need to get ready, but see you t'night girl!" Jes hung up.

When Jes stopped by, she honked her horn outside my apartment. I ran downstairs to meet her. A butterscotch sun was disappearing below the tree line.

"I'm late, or I would come in for a bit," Jes shouted over her engine. She tossed a small blue wristlet at me through the Jeep's window and added, "and he's definitely going to be on time—if not early. He's responsible." She smiled.

"It's fine, thank you for bringing this." I held the wristlet up.

Once back inside, I laid everything out on the coffee table, like pieces of evidence to a crime. I also poured three double-shots of tequila; one for each puzzle-piece before me. I wanted to recreate everything as closely as possible to that fateful night; so I planned to ingest them in the same order and time apart. I picked up the first piece—a jagged orange half—and threw it back with a warm tequila shot. My entire body shivered in disagreement. Right on cue, my phone started flashing again, this time with Bryan's name displayed across the screen. I silenced it immediately. Hopefully he would think I was already asleep. I scrolled through the ebook to search once more for my mother's hidden message, while I waited on the alert to consume what little was left in Rick's bag.

A passage read,"*The Astral Plane, sometimes referred to as the Subtle Realm, can be reached multiple ways: meditation, Astral projection, Lucid Dreaming, near death experiences, and some other (more controversial) methods…*"

I scanned through the text until it was time to snort the next piece of the puzzle, which was followed by another tequila shot. I set the next timer for thirty minutes, and scrolled through Instagram until it went off. I saw a few costume ideas that I liked and saved them for later; as well as, an ad to freeze my eggs that I marked as offensive. I also saw a post from Jes's dinner-date. Her picture was of a large glass of red wine, with a thick menu placed conspicuously in the background. The menu was easily recognizable as one of Atlanta's nicest sushi restaurants. I noticed she left EMT-guy out of the frame and untagged. When I zoomed into the photo I could almost make out the side of another glass that looked like it contained water, and the tip of a clean man's fingernail. A few pictures beneath hers, I saw a rare post from Bryan's personal account. He proactively ran the Club Daze account but hardly ever posted anything under his personal handle. The image was a promotional flyer for the upcoming Halloween weekend at Daze. I felt a twinge of guilt knowing that this post was probably made to compensate for the promotional reach that my account would have had if I wasn't...unwell.

Halloween. Oh yet another joy, stolen by father-time. The holiday was once my favorite before the nightlife industry forced me to associate it, indistinguishably, with mankind at it's worst. At Daze we even had a seasonal closing game: body paint, makeup or vomit? It referred to the smudges on our clothes that our patrons imparted on us, as we walked through the compact and moist crowds. That game was a new low for me. I double-tapped my screen in habitual support. Then shared the post on my story to appease my guilt.

No! No-No. I forgot I was ignoring Bryan! My hand covered my mouth. *Real fucking smooth.*

The phone buzzed and dropped into my lap, as I jumped ten feet in the air. He must be calling me. I took a deep breath and rehearsed what I would say to him to convey a sense of sobriety: *Heyy Bryan, I'm just journaling about my goals and aspirations, can I call you back?*

Only...the phone's vibration pattern felt different from an incoming call. The phone wasn't ringing at all. It was only the timer buzzing—it was time to take the last set. My body thawed and I consumed a tequila-chased Xanax.

I waited for sleep. Yet, a final part of the experiment still remained on the coffee table—something that could have only been found in my room. I slid it off the glass surface and into my hands. It was the last happy photo I had taken with my mom. The moment was captured nearly a year after my college graduation, and about three years after Mom's diagnoses: early onset dementia. In the picture, we were holding up plane tickets and a yellow folder. Our smiles were so big that they were unflattering; the facial muscles were powered by pure joy, and pushed our skin into awkward folds and divots.

Mom had surprised me with a trip to California. She wanted me to visit a campus that I was interested in. One I hadn't pursued because I didn't want to leave her. Mom worked on the folder for months, because her traitorous mind slowed any of her projects to a crawl. The folder we held in the photo was composed of three very tidy sections of pre-filled paperwork: applications, scholarships, and housing options.

My mother was incredibly thoughtful and uniquely skilled at helping people excel to their fullest potential. She removed the unexpected barriers to success—the small hurdles that people didn't necessarily consider—but the very ones that caused stagnation. Our photographic images blurred, partly from my chemical-cocktail, but mostly from the tears. I laid back on the couch, clutching the photo to my heart. A heaviness pushed me into the eternal depths of the couch cushions. It was if my blood had become lead—and my muscles stone.

BRYAN'S NIGHTMARE

"Tasha, --ke up. wake -p! I'm calling 911. --at have you done, -atasha wake up!"

My eyelids felt like velcro as they slid open. Bryans face, his furious face, was the first thing that welcomed me back to the land of the living. His hands were shaking my shoulders. I saw relief blink through his anger but only for a moment. He was mostly just a blur of hot rage.

"What time?" I mumbled.

"It's after one a.m.—what did you take?" he asked.

I looked through the space under his arm and above his lap, at my coffee table. It presented: three shot glasses from the Vegas trip we took together for the Nightclub and Bar Conference, an empty bottle of Clase Azul Tequila, an empty bottle of wine, and a suspicious white smudge directly beside a straw—a straw way too small for any drinking glass.

I concluded that the answer, "nothing," might infuriate him even further so, "everything," it was.

"Let's go," he said, "now, get up." He pulled me to sitting.

"Go where? I'm so tired, no Bryan I'm fine I just want to..." I realized I had failed.

I hadn't reached my mom. I hadn't reached anything but a dark nothingness. The thought of never reaching her again brought tears alongside it. In a surprising act of sympathy Bryan pulled me close to him. His natural smell was comforting in a familiar way, and his cologne was inviting. He smelled like the ocean. I buried my face in the little space under his defined jawline. I softly cried as he held me in both arms.

I wanted him back. I wanted him more than I could ever remember wanting him. As my tears dried, the space between my thighs became wet. My lips found his skin. I kissed his warm neck softly, and then twice more moving closer towards his mouth. I straddled his lap, and leaned in to kiss his lips, but he turned his face away from mine.

"Tasha, stop," he said, "let's go to the hospital, your body is on fire and your eyes are damn near black."

I didn't budge. I sat frozen, with his icy, steel blade of rejection wedged into my heart.

"You can ride with me, or I can call the police and you can ride with them, your choice," he said.

High, heartbroken, and rejected, I was in no condition to fight—especially not with Bryan. I sighed, then stood up slowly and wrapped the blanket around me—like a wobbly human burrito of disaster—before following him outside to his black truck. He buckled me in, and returned to my apartment and let Yumi out to pee. I waited, shivering under my blanket.

We drove in silence all the way to the emergency room. I passed out a couple times along the way, jerking awake each time and forgetting where I was for a second; only to feel ashamed all over again. We arrived at the hospital. I swiped some sunglasses from his truck, and kept the throw blanket wrapped around me. I prayed a silent prayer that none of the staff: Cornflower Blue Scrubs, Doctor Doom, nor Sad Kathy, would recognize me—*especially* after Bryan lied to the receptionists at check in. He told them that I was drugged at a party, but he left out the fact that it was a party of one, and that it was *me* who drugged *myself.*

A dainty male nurse, named Derick, took me into a room—almost immediately after we arrived. It must have been a slow morning in the

Emergency Room.

"Whew 101.8," he said, pulling his lips into his mouth.

I feigned surprised at the not-news. I was well aware of how badly MDMA pills affected your body's ability to control internal temperatures. It largely explained why people ended up in the hospital after taking them—well that, and the severe dehydration. The young nurse read my blood pressure, drew blood, took me through a series of questions. Then he collected my urine.

When Derick returned to the room, he handed me a cold and heavy, styrofoam cup. "Drink up baby, don't stop, or put it down, until it's empty," he watched me for a moment, and added, "go on, the faster the better. I'll be right back." Then he turned on his heels, and whipped out the door.

The thirty-two ounce cup was filled to the brim with what looked like a milkshake made of coal. I brought it to my lips and the proximity chilled my face. I closed my eyes and tipped it back. I anticipated something awful that never came. The bizarre drink was minty, not the worst thing I had ever choked down in the name of peer pressure. Still, be that as it may, about three-fourths of the way through the black sludge, my stomach cramped and turned on me. Before I could stand up and move to a private place to vomit, every ounce of it erupted from my throat and mouth. Dark and lumpy puke covered the floor between Bryan and I. He stared at me in horror.

The nurse ran in, probably alerted by my heaving sounds, and began to clean me up. He handed me a gown to change into. Then that sweet little nurse walked me hand-in-hand to the closest restroom. Once I was puke-free, I settled back in my newly made chair-bed hybrid. Bryan walked back into the room. The corners of his eyes were bright red, and his under-eye area was darker than usual.

"You don't have to stay Bryan, I feel fine. I promise," I said.

Derick was walking in behind him, but he was completely eclipsed by Bryan at first. The nurse carried something in his hand, "let's try this again baby," he said, handing me a new, and completely full, charcoal shake.

Bryan stared at the shake, then quickly turned around, and walked out of the room without a word.

5

LEAVE OF ABSENSE

Not a single image danced in the darkness. After all of that, I didn't have a single dream about anything—or if I did, I certainly did not remember it. It was all for nothing. The only thing that I actually accomplished, was convincing Bryan that I was emotionally unstable, and possibly a drug addict. I woke up in my bed alone with a few missing pieces of recent history to account for; such as, getting home from the hospital, finding my bed, and changing into this bathrobe—I looked down and cringed. I wasn't upset with Bryan seeing me naked, he was more than acquainted with all of my parts. What disturbed me was the mental reel of Bryan struggling to rag-doll my unconscious ass into this robe. I rolled over and covered my head with the pillow. How unsexy that must have been, and I was so very bloated from my stupid experiment. I sat up in bed. I avoided looking at the mirror that sat directly across from me, in order to spare me anymore embarrassment.

Where was Yumi?

There were no concerned faces to greet me, not even stuffed ones. I would've settled for that lonely rabbit and his dead eyes—no judgement there. My head was pounding. My throat was a desert. *Water, must find water.* After a few more moments of rest, and an internal pep talk, I slithered out of bed in search of any life giving source: water, coffee, tea—Bloody Mary. When I turned out of my bedroom I ran smack into another human being. I was relieved to see that it was Bryan. He was carrying breakfast in a paper bag, and he had only a single coffee in his hand.

"You're up already," he said.

44

"Mmm hmm." I rubbed my eyes. I was caught off guard at having to hold back an onset of tears with everything I had. *Why am I so emotional? I will not cry again—I will not! I am a mentally stable person. After all, what I did last night had a purpose. It was a controlled experiment, and intentional—sort of—mostly. I'm almost positive that I'm not a head case. I'm especially certain that I'm not an addict.*

All of those self-proclaimed truths might have been enough to stop my tears—if they were sad tears—but unfortunately for Bryan, they were happy tears. I swelled with relief. Bryan was still here, still supporting me, after everything I had put him through.

"You're a mess." Bryan laid a heavy hand on the top of my head.

"I know." I stole a hug.

In that quiet moment, I had a sense of clarity. The kind of lucidity that hindsight delivered. I regretted not fighting harder for our relationship. I regretted asserting my sacred independence by flirting with other men in front of him; and most of all, I regretted declaring to Jes that he was fair game, one drunken night. A declaration that no doubt contributed to their halloween-hookup last year. 'The hookup heard round the world,' and the act that single-handedly put a full stop to our on-again-off-again love saga. Bryan was dressed as a doctor, and Jesmitha—a sexy-nurse.

My theme for Daze that night was: *Most likely to be Brought home to Momma—Professions with Prestige.* So their costume pairing was mostly by chance. Yet, it nonetheless, added to their momentary pseudo-connection—their simpatico-romance—on the night they came to know each other biblically. It was also the same year that I had just started dating one of our top clients. A client that Bryan truly hated, which of course didn't help either of us make good decisions that night. We were all *so* drunk. It was an over all shit-show of a night, but then again, every halloween is. Jesmitha had been too terrified to tell me, so she just avoided me completely for weeks. When I confronted her, she mostly just cried. Not a word has been spoken about that night since. Bryan however, told me on Thanksgiving Day at his friend's uncles house—while we were eating pie. It completely ruined the pie.

"Where is your mind at?" Bryan said, finally releasing my hug.

I searched for the right words. I wanted to explain everything, and sum it all up into one sentence. A sentence that he could easily understand. One statement that would assuage his fears; but all I could think about was him and Jes now. It was almost a year later, and still the thought of them together made me sick to my stomach. I have always told myself that their sex must have been clumsy and awful, and that it couldn't have been more than just a blur of moving limbs. If it had been any good, then they would have kept doing it. *But what if they were?* Jes didn't tell me the first time. The situation kind of just… went away. Maybe I had been in denial this entire year. The bile in my stomach swirled, and saliva filled my mouth to capacity. I felt a projection rush through my body. I snatched the bag out of Bryan's hands, and let my anxiety-riddled puke fill in between it's carby-contents. His face showed disgust and disappointment for the whole scene, not only for the vomit-glazed donuts.

"I'm sorry." I looked up at him and quickly put the bag behind my back. "I'm so sorry. Let me throw this away—just give me a minute." I stepped to the guest bathroom.

I shut the door and turned on the faucet. I placed the bag carefully in the waste bin, and rinsed out my mouth. The person looking back at me from the mirror startled me. My face was puffy and my eyes were bloodshot. My hair was greasy and frizzy; it looked like I had been tossing and turning all night. So this is what rock bottom looks like. Staring at my reflection brought a whole new level to Bryan's devotion. I really couldn't for the life of me begin to rationalize why he was still here. I wasn't his responsibility any more. I rinsed my face and pulled my hair back with a faithful hair tie around my wrist, that was better—not great—but better. I walked back over to Bryan who was waiting patiently outside the door, leaning on the doorway to my bedroom. I was unsure of what to say, so I stood awkwardly in silence and waited for any merciful direction.

He said, "lets go some place to talk."

"Like this?" I gestured at my appearance.

"Yeah, I guess not," he said.

"We can just talk here," I said.

"That's probably not a great idea, I'm going to head out so you can shower up…then maybe you can meet me at the Leaf N' Bean in the park?"

"Why, are you afraid to be in my apartment while I shower? I'm not a freak Bryan."

"I am not af-raid," his eyes narrowed, "I'm just trying to keep a professional relationship with you--while you're healing."

"Wow, okay. I'm not your patient. You have yet to ask me what really happened—you just assumed the worst!" The way Bryan was talking to me was infuriating—like I was a child. Suddenly, his kindness felt patronizing.

"You should lower your voice. I'm trying to help. I wanted to tell you this gently, but clearly you are going to take everything I say wrong anyway. So here it is, I'm giving you time off to get some professional help—to clean up your act. If you can do that, then you can come back to work. Jesmitha will temporarily handle your clients until you come back."

"Un-fucking-real Bryan, 'giving me time off,' you really think the best way to 'help,' me is to fire me? Just so you can date Jesmitha openly without feeling guilty? It's the perfect time to move me out of the way isn't it?"

Yumi ran past us and into my bedroom. I'm sure she was heading to the closet, one of her favorite places to hide when she's upset.

"What? No, where is this coming from? I'm not trying to date Jesmitha, and this isn't about her...it is *about you* though, and I never said you were fired. I'm just giving you the time you need to sort out your shit. I get that you're hungover, and being a little crazy right now, but one day you'll thank me," he studied my face before tilting his head to the side and squinted, "I think."

Bryan's phone rang. He answered immediately, "Hey I'm here now, I'll call you back later." Hanging up as quickly as he answered.

He controlled every situation with such authority, but not to satisfy his ego, it was a leadership persona he effortlessly identified with, and one he tempered with humility. I admired how he was seldom ever wrong—*he was probably right about this too. Maybe I did need some time off to focus on my life.*

Bryan gently picked my chin up from the floor, "I'm giving you two weeks leave of absence. I know you'll figure something out. Find someone you can talk to, or maybe even a program you can join. Whatever it takes—I need you to be mentally and physically healthy if you're going to lead my team at Daze. If you haven't put forth a serious effort after two weeks, then we will need to have a different discussion, but I don't see it coming to that—I know you." He pulled me in for another warm hug.

"So you aren't still hooking up with Jesmitha?" I said into his shirt.

He sighed, "That's what you're really worried about?" He set me back to look me in the eyes, "Tasha, you were standing in an emergency room last night with black vomit all down your clothes. You look like you had just stepped out of a scene from the Exorcist, and your main concern, *right now,* is a name in your ex's little black book?"

I nodded unashamedly.

Bryan looked tired, "No, and to be completely honest with you, I don't really remember the night that it happened exactly, it was a rough night," he closed his eyes and rubbed his forehead. "Please start on this today, because your two weeks begin now."

I knew it. I smiled, showing way too much candid relief, but I didn't care. Bryan looked down at his phone and started texting someone. I had a pass to be crazy for two weeks anyhow. While it could have just been my brain trying to re-stabilize my dopamine and serotonin levels, I started to get excited about this time off. It *really could* be just what I've needed. I couldn't picture a life without anxiety, and maybe that was cause enough in and of itself. Who knows, maybe the nightlife industry was finally getting to me, just like I had seen it warp everyone else. Who was I, to think that I'd be the exception. Everything was relative, and when you spend the majority of your time around any group of people, it's hard to keep your original baseline in clear sight. At the very least I could look more into this whole dream thing. I could try a better approach to figuring out what my Mom was really trying to tell me. Or maybe I could search for a new job.

I smiled at Bryan, "So...do you want to go get breakfast and get to work?" Although, I already knew what his answer would be.

PLAYDATES

Bryan politely declined my offer, with a final hug, and kissed me on my forehead as he left. He said he would call me in a week to see how things were going, and suggested that it would be better if Jes met me at the coffee shop. I leaned against the front door. He confused me the way he bounced to both ends of the spectrum: on one hand going the extra mile to help me stay on track in my personal life, on the other, going to even further lengths to, "keep it professional." The thought crossed my mind that his kindness could be out of pity, but I quickly shoved that idea down. I couldn't bare that reality. What I did know, is that I needed to find another way to reach my Mom. Some method that didn't include an all-expenses-*unpaid* trip to the emergency room. Yumi who was probably still hiding in the closet—God bless her—must have slept on the couch with Bryan last night. She had not greeted me this morning either, sometimes I thought she liked him more than me.

"Yumi!" I called.

I heard nails galloping across the bathroom tile, then the hardwoods. The distance between the taps lengthened as she approached me in the living room. After tending to Yumi's needs, and cuddling her for good measure, I convinced the both of us that everything was going to be fine.

I needed to clear my mind and reset my body. I walked into my bathroom and turned on the shower as hot as my skin would bear. I disrobed and stepped into my sanctuary—my holy ceramic temple. Eucalyptus hung from my shower head. The medicinal minty vapor enveloped my naked body, and opened my sinuses. There were few places I adored more than my shower. My little square of heaven, contained within two adjacent planes of glass and two walls of matte taupe tiles. The shower boxed me in and blocked the world out. I stayed in as long as I could before I felt like I might faint from the heat. When I swung the door open, the steam manically escaped as fast as the cold air rushed in, making me uncomfortable in my own skin once again. I grabbed my oversized terrycloth robe and draped it around me before I flopped back on the bed. My swamp of hair soaked the bedding beneath it.

Bryan was right, I needed to find someone to talk to. I wanted a mentor or a life coach, someone enlightened, someone who knows about this stuff—perhaps a guru of some sort. I fanned my arm up and down and groped around my bed for my phone, without moving any other part of my body. I was always losing my phone and keys around my house. They would usually be found under piles of clean laundry neatly placed in different areas around my room. My underwear were left in the basket at the foot of my bed. My shirts and pants were folded and stacked on the top of my white dresser. I'm not quite sure why I stop my projects right before completion, but I've always seemed to begin everything with a surgical-like precision before I lose motivation.

Having no tactile luck, I sat up and scanned my room. My phone was nestled between a growing pile of mail on the nightstand. I barely had the will to get up and grab it, but I eventually exerted the least effort possible to reach it. My body was still a little weak from the past few days. The worst thing about drugs are how they seemed to drain you of the willpower to accomplish anything for weeks, and only deliver fleeting high that you may not even remember.

Once I had my phone, I typed the words, "Dreams + Meditation + Guru," on the browser's search bar and the results quickly filled my screen. Scrolling past the ads, reviews, and products for sale, I started to encounter some more promising links. But I still couldn't find exactly what I was looking for. There was too much information to find anything of value. Finally I noticed a familiar event page that was promoting a free meditation class titled,"The Secrets of Happiness through Meditation," nestled in the web of links. This could be a good start. The class was conveniently scheduled for tomorrow at one in the afternoon. I filled in some preliminary information then tapped the orange rectangle which read, "attend event." Almost simultaneously, my phone illuminated with a message confirming my attendance; right before it turned black and flashed, "Jesmitha Daze Girl."

"Hi friend," I answered.

"Hey doll...Bryan called me," she paused, "so I thought I'd come over tomorrow and we could go grab coffee or whatever," Jes said.

"Yeah, the whole experiment didn't exactly go as planned. I just need to set up some appointments to show Bryan that I'm taking it seriously, and I could use the company—but I don't *need* the company. You know, because I'm fine doing it by myself. So feel free to join, but as long as you're coming over to hang out and not like—watch me. If that makes sense...you know what, never mind." I said, and wiped away a single bead of sweat trickling down my underarm. I was fully annoyed with myself—and Bryan—and Jes, while we were at it. But I was also thankful. I was conflicted as hell.

I could hear Jesmitha smiling through the receiver as she said,"I totally understand, see you tomorrow Sha."

While it felt great to have support, I was fully aware that Bryan had initiated Jes and I's little playdate. That bothered me enough on its own, but what really ate at me was the pervasive thought that Jesmitha could be supporting me to impress Bryan. I tossed my phone somewhere on the bed, and went to go see if I had an eye cream that helped with puffiness and a quarter-life crisis.

6

THE CAFE CONVO

We heard Jesmitha's Jeep engine and stereo blaring outside my apartment, as if my living room walls were made out of pure imagination. Yumi, per usual, recognized the vehicle and its owner immediately. She shot a look at me—one full of anticipation—like this was a clear indication of an outing to come. Her brows pushed and bunched towards the center of her forehead as her head tilted. Her mouth hinged opened, just shy of closing. Yumi's furry muzzle was frozen in query.

"I'm sorry girl, not today Yumi—mommy has to work on saving her job that puts the kibble in your bowl," I said, rubbing her head as I passed her to unlock the door.

She must have understood because her entire body deflated. She moped over to her bed and laid down with her back turned to me. Yumi didn't even greet Jes once she walked through my door.

"What's up with her?" Jes asked.

"Oh, Yumi? She's just mad at me, but she'll live."

I put my laptop in an old leather messenger bag that once belonged to my Mother.

"Okay. I guess we can go ahead and walk over to the cafe if you're ready." I said.

"Yes, and you can fill me in on what the hell happened last night. Bryan called me pretty pissed off—he especially wanted to know *who* you got Xanax from." Jes stuck her neck out and widened her eyes to the point I could see white all around her irises.

"Sorry." I winced and quickly walked out the front door, as Jes

51

followed behind me.

The air outside was thick with the smoke of burning leaves. Although I couldn't imagine it would have been the best day for leave-burning because the wind was aggressive. I immediately put my keys and cellphone in the exterior pocket of the messenger bag, to free my hands and secure my hair out of my face. Our teeth chattered and our bodies shivered. The air currents cycled out any internal warmth I had through my thin sweatshirt, which wasn't much of a feat, because the sweatshirt's neck was cut out across the shoulders, exposing my sports bra. My skin-thin leggings weren't much help either. I fully regretted the absent minded wardrobe choice. But, anyone living in Georgia as long as I had, knew that there were actually about twenty seasons here. We experienced the same four seasons as everyone else but they flipped back and forth—alternating almost every two to three weeks.

I shifted the camel colored satchel in front of me to block the brunt of the wind as we walked, then I pulled Jes in close. Huddled together, we walked straight into the wind head first, giggling at the absurdity of our plight. In our small and private pocket of warmth, I filled her in on the details of Wednesday night; specifically how it was—in my opinion—blown way out of proportion. She teased me about Bryan and his, *second full-time job,* also known as Tasha. We marched through the park like a couple of mountain climbers braving Everest—seeking refuge and refreshment.

We arrived at the Leaf N' Bean cafe right as a Barista flipped a sign over on a purple door—chalkboard, hanging on twine—that now read "open." We were the first ones in line, and stood at the counter looking up at another, larger, chalkboard. I scanned the options like I might possibly order something new, and stray from my usual circulation of the boring drinks I always get. This cafe had been here since before I was born, and I had been coming here almost that long. It was the last standing original coffee shop in Atlanta; the only one that had survived the great green and white commercial wave in the beginning of the twenty-first century.

Leaf N' Bean was always packed, and if you weren't here when it opened, you would be lucky to find a seat. Despite its steady popularity, I had an irrational fear that surfaced every time I decided to visit. I feared that I'd arrive in front of a torn-down sign—in its place only a shadow of dirt, outlining where the letters had been in. In my hypothetical fear-story, there would also be a letter taped to the doors apologizing to their faithful patrons—explaining why they couldn't keep the doors open. Then Leaf N' Bean would be completely gutted and replaced by some pretentious coffee bar, or simply by another Starbucks—the default cafe of the world.

I ordered my unsweetened hot green tea. Jes ordered a dirty-chai latte and a pumpkin bread to spice things up. I took the tea, and we secured both of the highly coveted oversized armchairs in the far corner. They were upholstered in a soft ever-green leather, that had long outlived its expiration. Each of them had their own little bohemian ottoman, if you wanted to put your feet up. The fire place was only an arms-length away and was already crackling. They had finally brought back the cozy, plaid throw blankets. The culmination warmed my flesh and my soul. This was the part of the fall season that I adored.

"Soo, my date went well," Jes gushed.

"You're going to see him again?" I asked, "I guess you should thank me?"

Jes looked down at her phone for a minute, "Sorry, what?"

"You owe me…"

Jesmitha stared at me with discomfort.

"You know, because you wouldn't have met the EMT if it weren't for me?" I said.

"Oh right—thats funny." She didn't sound like she thought it was funny at all. She looked at her phone again for a moment, before popping her head up, "Let's talk about that night actually, what's going on Sha…what do you need from me?"

The steaming green tea arrested mid-way to my mouth. "What do I need from you?" I thought I caught Bryan's name on her phone, "Jes, I don't *need* anything from you." I blew on my tea. "I'm not quite sure what you think I'm dealing with, but I've just been having bad luck," I said.

"But what about the stuff with your mom?" Jes asked.

"It was just a dream." I said, in an effort to convince us both.

"Yeah, but I know you think that she's trying to reach out to you from the grave, and we—I, I was just worried about…well I wanted to make sure that you weren't trying to…go back to her?"

It took me a minute to realize what Jes was implying, "Oh God no, Jes I'm not trying to *kill myself* if that's what you're saying?"

Jes shoved a large piece of pumpkin bread in her mouth and didn't answer me.

I shook my head, then pinched a piece of Jes's bread off and ate it,

"So what's this EMT's name?"

"Brenden," Jes said, "are you going to try the dream thing again?"

"No, not like that again—maybe not at all. Maybe it was all just wishful thinking. I've never really dealt with mom's...accident, or whatever you want to call it, and I think it's starting to affect me. I just don't know why it would—after four years? Why now?" I took a sip of my tea, it was finally cool enough to drink, "I really believed that she was trying to send me a message..." I looked out the window to our left, and I saw a homeless person on a park bench, who was arguing with someone who wasn't there.

"I might be crazy, but I'm not suicidal—or an addict, I would hope that you know that."

"I know you're not an addict, Tasha. Addicts don't turn down Adderall prescriptions, just so they won't get reliant on it—even if it was a major inconvenience to their *entire* staff," Jes beamed.

I shrugged.

The Barista called from behind the counter, "Jes...Jes-smeetha?"

Jesmitha rolled her eyes at the mispronunciation of her name. She frequently visited Leaf N' Bean, but never corrected them. Jes got up to retrieve her latte from the coffee bar.

When she returned, she said, "We—*I* think that you should talk to someone because we could have lost you last week—even if it wasn't intentional—but I don't think many overdoses are." She breathed in the spice vapors flowing from her cup. In a lower voice she said, "I didn't want to scare you, but the night you went to the emergency room, Brenden was concerned that you might not make it, and Bryan...I've never seen Bryan look like that. It was like he didn't know what to do for the first time in his—

"Okay, well I'm still here though—so there's really no need to talk about what could have been right?"

Jes took her first sip of Chai Tea.

"I'm going to use the restroom," I said, but I really just needed space.

When I returned, Jes had her phone opened to a profile of a woman named Malinda Brown.

"This is my mom's therapist," she said, pointing to a headshot of a woman that looked like she was in her mid-forties, "well it's her old therapist, but you'll love her."

"She looks like a lovely woman, and if your mom likes her than I'm sure I would too, but I've already made an appointment so..." I smiled.

"Oh with who?" She asked

I opened my laptop and pulled up the confirmation email. I clicked on the class's website, which was something I hadn't actually done until that very moment. Their webpage was a little more sales-pitchy than I had expected, but I concealed my own surprise. I turned my screen so she could see my one o'clock. Jes was visibly unimpressed.

"That looks very promising. While you're at it, why not go to a side-show hypnotist, or how about a psychic who lives in a tent off I-75?" Jes said.

"Great idea!"

I googled, "hypnotist near me." I clicked on the very first link that surfaced under the ads; I immediately booked first appointment available from their online scheduling form. It was for *October 17, at one p.m.*. I turned my screen to Jes, excited for her reaction. She couldn't help but to laugh.

"Very funny Sha, but I'm serious," she whined, "you're like my best friend, and I want to make sure that you're okay." She buried her face in an oversized mug. Into the cup she said, sheepishly, "...and Bryan is scary and I am supposed to get something legitimate in motion."

I nose laughed, then let my head fall to my right shoulder for a moment to consider her proposal. "Okay Jes, I'll see your shrink, but while you set that up I think I'm going to set up a meeting with an actual psychic too. I was joking at first, but maybe someone could really help me with my mom to find some closure."

"Like *a hast rekha*, I think thats fair," Jes said, as she started typing away on her phone.

"Yeah, sure..." I searched my laptop for a psychic.

After a few minutes, it was clear that finding one would be harder than I thought. I found nothing appealing. Every one of them seemed to fall into two categories; either they were too commercial and Ms. Cleo-like, or they were booked up for months. I looked up at Jes texting a stream of kissy faces and hearts to *someone*. I strained to see the contact's name.

"Did you find your psychic?" Jes startled me, and set her phone face down on the table between us.

"No," I said.

"Good, because I have one for you," she gleamed, "my mom uses a lil lady over by Buford Hwy. She is always on point and she's very sweet. The Palm Reader can see you tomorrow—and Malinda can see you Monday morning." Jes looked pleased with herself.

"Does it have to be Monday *morning*?"

"What's wrong with Monday morning, it's not like you'll be recovering from work, and it's just an intake Sha—like a short interview to set up the future meetings; it won't take long and she comes to you. Does that work for you princess?"

"Does she bring coffee?" I glanced up to the corner of my laptop at the clock, "I've got to go if I want to make it on time for the class, do you want to go with me?"

"Uhm...no I don't think so. I'm probably going to stay and...read," she said, with her face now glued to her phone. She was giggling at something I wasn't apart of, that may have involved more obnoxious emoticons.

"Since when do you read?" I let the words run away from me.

"Wow that's rude."

Now I had her attention, "Sorry I didn't mean it that way—

"Just because you went to college, doesn't mean you're the only one that reads." Jes said.

"I know that. Again—sorry."

Jes took a deep breath, "It's okay, but I do have to be at work extra early tonight—and for the next two weeks—so it's probably best that I relax when I can."

"Gotcha. See ya later Jes."

I gathered my things, while a heavy silence hung between us, and walked out the door.

THE PRICE OF HAPPINESS

I braced myself for another chill as I stepped outside the cafe, but the afternoon wiped away all of the clouds and the sunshine warmed my goosebumps flat. The sky had completely flipped from its previous fog-white to a cartoon shade of blue, and the tone was consistent in every direction. The sun was plopped right on the cerulean canvas like a ten-year-old had painted it there. If it weren't sixty degrees outside, you'd never guess it was autumn in Atlanta. We must have been entering our eighteenth season. The day welcomed a self-reflective stroll. The meditation class was only three blocks away. Yet the idea of being submerged in a group of random people, only permitted itself without paranoia when I had overgrown bouncers at my beck and call; so I stopped by my apartment to drop off my laptop and take my car—

for my own peace of mind.

After finding a spot in the crowded parking garage, I still had about fifteen minutes to spare before the class started. The class was held at a yoga studio that was hidden on the back side of a shopping plaza, on the bustling West Peachtree Street. The only access to the studio was through the parking deck, as it had no street-level entry. I recognized this place from a two-week promotional pass I took advantage of a few years ago, but I ultimately decided not to spring for the membership and I can't remember why.

"Hello!" an excited voice blurted behind me as I walked towards the entrance, "Are you here for the meditation class?"

I turned around to see that the voice belonged to a slender Indian man. He wore dark slacks and a blue button-down that made me think he came straight from work—possibly during his lunch break.

"I think so," I said, quickly slapping on a smile from work.

"Velcome, my name is Sonny," he extended his hand, "how did you hear about this class?"

His accent was thick and pleasant to listen to. It reminded me a bit of Jesmitha's mom's but unique in way that I couldn't put my finger on.

"Tasha." I shook his hand, "A friend recommended it to me," I said, breaking eye-contact.

I was a bad liar, so I rarely did so. Yet in this case, *I might be in the middle of a mental breakdown and I have no idea what I am doing here*, wouldn't be putting my best foot forward.

Sonny ushered me to the Yoga studio, of course asking me detailed questions about my imaginary friend the entire way. We walked past check-in, and Sonny waved to the tenants behind the desk as they nodded. The class was a standard square room, with bright orange wooden floors, and mirrors for walls. On the floor the instructor had set up seven by seven rows of folded blankets. Adjacent to each pile, laid a blank notecard and a pen. To my surprise, the class was already one-third of the way occupied, even though we still had several minutes before it began. In front of the class sat a woman, serene in her stillness, with her legs crossed on the floor. Her spine was elongated, and her eyes were closed. She wore a gentle smile, and I couldn't help but envy her state of peace. Most of the back rows of blankets were already sat upon, so I chose a pile one row back from the instructor, and one row away from the door on my right. Shortly after I was settled, Sonny plopped down on the only blanket between me and the exit.

"What do you do for work?" he asked.

"I'm a waitress," I said.

"I'm in sales, where do you waitress at?" he asked.

"Uhm, a place in Buckhead."

I didn't like telling strangers where I worked at for two reasons: it's the busiest club in Atlanta, and something odd always happened once people found out that I work there. It's like my flesh began to glow golden yellow as all of my humanly features crinkled into a gilded aluminum. All they seemed to see in me was a golden ticket; one that should grant them access to the front door—on the biggest nights— and should also come with a comped bottle or two. The other reason why I didn't like to reveal my employer, is because I didn't want to be pigeon held under any preconceived notions that a nine-to-fiver might have about my profession.

"How do you like it?" he asked.

But instead of enthusiastically awaiting my answer again, he positioned himself towards the front of the class, and became very still.

I followed his gaze to the instructor, and noticed that she had opened her eyes. She sat quietly smiling at the congregation before her. Like a school of fish, everyone synchronized their positions towards the front to mirror the instructor, myself included.

Once she had everyone's attention, without having to ask for it, she stood up and said, "Welcome to this class on peaceful meditation. Thank you for spending your afternoon with me. How is everyone feeling today?" She spoke so softly that everyone had to pay close attention just to hear her above the air conditioner.

The crowd responded with mostly, "goods," and, "greats."

"Well, that is pleasant and easy for me to hear, but let us try that one more time. This time I would invite you to be honest with me and your neighbors. So I will ask you all again in this safe place—how are you *really* feeling right now in this moment?" She maintained a constant smile as she spoke, and her eyes were happy almonds.

Now with open permission the crowd sincerely responded. There were still a few scattered, "okays and greats," that were spoken louder; but this time there were also some *depressed, angry, and tireds,* muttered. I belonged to the "okay," group.

"Very good, now that we are being truthful with ourselves, and with our neighbors, we can proceed from a place of sincerity, and hopefully we will end our session in an environment of peace." She sat back down on her blanket in the front of the class. The she said, "I would like for everyone to gently close their eyes and inhale as deeply as you can, hold it for a moment, and then sigh it all out through your mouth—we will do this three times."

The entire class followed suit, some audibly expelled their air each time.

After the last exhale, the instructor said, "For the next cycle, lift your hands in the air with open palms for each inhale, then *fiercely* exhale through your noses with your mouths shut, as you bring your outstretched arms downward with closed fists."

The movement resembled a lat-pull exercise at the gym, like pulling a bar down to my chest. Each repetition caused my head to become lighter and lighter, until I felt as if I might pass out. Finally, once my head was a helium balloon, barely tethered to my body, she instructed us to relax our hands on our knees, with our palms open to the sky. The darkness swirled.

"I want you to listen to all of the sounds that surround you," she instructed, "let them become part of your practice today, invite them in, welcome them, you are in complete harmony with your environment."

I listened. I heard the gentle hum of the air conditioner first, then the people around me quietly shifting their positions on their blankets. I could also hear the cars circling around the parking deck just outside the studio, and an analogue clock ticking somewhere; all of the sounds became oddly relaxing.

"Now as you sit in this present moment, allow every thought that surfaces in your mind to simply come and go—do not attach yourself to the thoughts or accept them as your own. Just let them come, and go, as they arrive. You can acknowledge them simply as the fertile ideas that they are and then…let them go. They are not bad or good in nature, because they are just passing thoughts. They are not your thoughts until you claim them as your truth. So for this exercise let them all pass—just like the credits after a film, let them roll away."

I could feel my entire being surrendering to her words, and my body melting into the floor. It felt like I was becoming denser, yet, I felt lighter at the same time.

"Now lets imagine a light at the very top of your head, and as you breathe in, it draws the light-energy into your body's heart center…"

Slowly, images began to form in my mind's eye. They were a shade of red, or was it green? The more I watched them without trying to analyze them, the less shy they became. Eventually they were so pronounced that I thought I could see the shape of a man standing in a doorway, but before I could really get a sense of what was happening, a voice swept them all away.

"When you are ready, gently bring your attention back to your body —but only when you are ready—then you can slowly open your eyes," she said.

I opened my eyes, and they met hers staring directly back into mine, unsettling my newfound peace. Behind her, stood three people that were silently waiting for her instruction.

"Did you know that you were all meditating for thirty-three minutes," she said.

Waves of resounding surprise glossed over her audience. It was true, thirty-three minutes had passed in what seemed like only three or five. I was impressed, and I'm sure that my face gave that away. She had my complete attention and I was hooked.

"I would like for you to lend your attention to my friends. They would like to share their stories with you," she said, and introduced the three people standing next to her.

Each one was demographically different from the next: varying in gender, race, apparent income, and vocation. In fact the only thing they all had in common, besides their deep admiration and gratitude for the instructor, was their similar yet extraordinary testimonies. One by one they took their turn professing how their lives were miraculously changed from a three-day workshop that the instructor taught—a workshop that was coming up next month and had limited availability.

One of her loyal's claimed that, "The class was filling up quickly and would probably be full by the end of today."

After the guest speakers were finished, the instructor thanked each one individually, before motioning for them to take their place back on the floor.

"So," she began, with her hands pressed flat together at the center of her chest, "if you too want to experience such peace and happiness for the rest of your lives, you can."

She marched over to a giant blank notepad, that sat on a tall tripod off to the side of the room. When she reached up to rip the top sheet off, her red blouse sleeve fell back on her arm. Under the silky cuff, I noticed a brand new Rolex watch. It was gorgeous, gold and silver, with an onyx face, and pristine diamond nodes. Apparently the first sheet on top had been left intentionally blank to conceal the sales portion of the miracle class seminar. The sheet underneath was fully marked up.

She read, "Reach - Your - True - Peace." She pointed to each word as she spoke it. Her voice was still pleasant, but louder, and her words took on a different tone. Her speech became meaningless sound to me as soon as I saw the price listed beneath the title of the workshop— $1,999 dollars. Ironically I felt all of the *true peace* dissipate from my body right after I read the words. I also had a strange feeling of being caught in a trap, that I couldn't shake, like something was closing in on me. They had me where they wanted me. I was a rabbit in a snare— chewing innocently on a sweet carrot—just before the spring was about to snap. The lady continued to pitch her three-day miracle seminar, that promised peace and happiness for the rest of one's life, but I had already tuned out. I was just eagerly waiting for it all to end and for the doors to open so I could slip out without offending anyone. I began to stand up after what seemed like a plausible conclusion in her pitch.

"Tasha, are you going to take the next step in your spiritual journey and join the workshop?" Sonny swooped in on me.

Shit. Fuck. Hell. "You know, I'm going to think about it, and…I'll call them when I'm ready," I said.

I noticed that one-third of the class seemed to be just as inquisitive towards their neighbors as Sonny was with me.

"Sure, sure, but if you sign up today it's ten percent off," Sonny hung both hands in the air in an offering, "but if you leave, we can't honor that price."

I could hear similar conversations happening all around me. Pushy sales tones were met with uncomfortable and reluctant ones. I wasn't getting out of there as simply as I came in.

"Oh, unfortunately I walked here so I didn't bring my purse," I slapped both hands on each of the metaphorical pockets on my burgundy leggings. Thankfully I had left my keys in my car—a habit that Bryan had always considered rashly irresponsible, but that day, it paid off.

"I will make a special deal for you. I will still honor the ten percent discount if you sign up today when you get home," Sonny said, "just give me your number, and I will call to remind you so you don't miss out." He handed me the notecard and the pen beside the blanket, "This class has changed my whole life and I just want the same for you."

I scribbled down my number on the notecard—my real number—afraid that he might call my phone right then and there in order to verify the digits I gave him. The *same phone* that lied face up, between Sonny and I, on that bright-blonde floor.

"Thank you, but I really do need to get going," I grabbed my phone and quickly walked out avoiding eye contact with anyone whom I assumed might work for the boss.

Once I was well into the garage, I walked just past my car. I quickly looked over my shoulder before ducking down beside someone else's vehicle. Then crawled low to the ground until I reached the drivers side of my car. I climbed into my car with a brand new appreciation for my barely legal tinted windows. I felt like a baby gazelle whom just escaped a pack of hyenas. While I was genuinely curious to explore what had happened in my mind, and sincerely thankful for the experience with the meditation, I was not two thousand dollars curious. I needed to *save* money, not give it to a mono-manic sales-pitch, that promised to change my entire life in three days.

The whole thing reminded me of how we would sell packs of water for one-hundred and twenty dollars at Club Daze. People actually needed the water, but damn if we didn't exploit that need for it. On the ride home, my phone vibrated on the passenger seat. A quick glance to the screen told me that the number was from an unknown caller. The second call, only two minutes later of the same number, told me it was Sonny.

7

THE PSYCHIC

Rinnnging
Rinnnging
Rinnnging

I aimed an eye towards the clock on my nightstand; it was nine—no—eight thirty in the morning.

Who the hell was calling me at 8:30 a.m.?

The pitter patter of furry feet grew louder in the distance, and brought a smile to my face as my muscles loosened. Somehow Yumi knew the minute I was awake with impressive accuracy, and her first act of duty was to shower me with affection. The happy beast jumped on the bed, shaking the frame, and flopped her soft body right down beside me. Yumi pawed gingerly at my face. This was her gentle way of asking me to start our day. She mostly just wanted to be fed and walked, but I was happy with the exchange regardless.

The missed call on my phone was listed as, "unknown," with some eight hundred number attached to it. I assumed that it was Sonny—and the gang—trying to recruit me. I cringed. How much longer would I be dodging calls, assuming that they would ever stop? On a positive note, I still had about twelve days of my forced vacation left: referring to my imposed leave of absence as a *vacation* made my reality more palatable each morning. It was also a lot more fun to plan out *activities* on a *vacation* than to face the surmounting pressure to attain a fully functional adult psyche within a hard deadline.

That day my vacation's itinerary listed: a visit to a psychic, a trip to that cute bookstore in the highlands, and a spa-day for Yumi. I would end my night soaking in a hot bath, with an oversized glass of red wine, which I assumed was allowed—on my *vacation*. I couldn't remember the last time I had a full Saturday to myself.

I pulled up Jesmitha's text message from yesterday with the Psychic's contact info, and I realized she hadn't sent an actual name.

I texted the number, "Hello, this is Tasha, I'm your eleven o'clock appointment, I just need your address and I'll be on my way."

A green text bubble appeared with only, "*138 Whindle Lane,*" in it.

When I typed her address into my GPS, the directions said that she lived about twenty minutes from me. I put on a pair of black leggings and threw on an oversized plain white t-shirt. I also grabbed a black hoodie with the words, "Club Daze," printed on it. The lettering was also black, but in a different texture, so the text was only clearly visible in passing light. I helped Bryan design these for the grand re-opening event, that we had shortly after he bought the club from it's previous owners. As I left my apartment and shut the door behind me, I looked down at my welcome mat. For the first time in over three years, I felt the need to remove my spare key from under that mat. Maybe it was the persistent calling from unknown numbers, or Yumi's creepy reaction at the park, but for whatever reason, I didn't want it there anymore.

One hundred and thirty-eight presented in faded gold-foil stickers that were pressed onto the side of an old white mailbox. The mail box's wooden post was stained three-fourths from the bottom with Georgia Red clay. Her driveway was narrow, barely distinguishable from the surrounding yard, and led to a ranch-style house. I parked my car behind a utility truck, and beside a teal Toyota Corolla. The Corolla was about eight to ten years old but looked like it was brand new. The home was a pale yellow with maroon accents. I felt a bit of tension rise into my shoulders as I walked towards the door and I regretted not asking Jes to come with me. I was about eleven minutes late because the traffic was heavy. I took a deep breath and stepped onto the porch. A tiny black spider crawled across my path, inches from my sneakers. When I looked up, a small asian woman was at the door.

"Hi, I'm Tasha."

"Hi Tasha, come in." She waved me inside the house. "Come sit," she motioned me to follow her to a square wooden table, that sat in the very corner of her house, between her living room and a kitchenette. The only light that entered the home, did so through curtain-less windows. Once I sat down at the table, I took off my jacket and immediately put it back on; it was just as cold inside her house as it was outside. In front of me sat a deck of ordinary playing cards. They were so worn that their edges were soft. Behind the cards, sat the psychic…waiting. "Have you had a reading before," she asked, her eyes were sparkling, and her face was thoughtful—her voice humble.

I decided to enjoy this experience regardless of the outcome, "No, not really."

"Oh-kay, first I read your palm, it shows your whole life, from the beginning to end, but the future can change if you will it to," her black eyebrows raised, "your palm can change, when you change, understand?"

I nodded.

"Oh-kay, let me see your hand," she took both of my hands in hers, gently cupping and un-cupping my fingers, so she could see all of my lines. She studied them like she was reading a book, or better yet, a map.

"Tell me if this has already happen to you, so I will know where I am in your story," she traced a line with her fingertip, "your mom, she has already pass?"

I opened my mouth, but only my eyes confirmed her statement.

"How old are you?" she asked.

"I'm twenty-eight"

"Oh-kay, so you already go to hospital for—I'm sorry, but I have to say it—for the drugs?"

"Yes," I whispered. My face burned.

"Do you already have the dreams," she asked.

"I dream all the time," I said, "are you talking about *the* dream, with my mom?"

"I'm not sure what this mean, but I see you traveling a lot…but you sleeping a lot too—I'm sorry let me look again." She blinked a couple of times like she was trying to see a road through a heavy rainfall, "I see you making a big trip, and you will go there often…but this trip is too dangerous for you," she shook her head and her voice ringed out with concern.

"I might be changing my job soon, so yeah, I guess I could be traveling more for that, but I don't have any big trips planned." I smiled, "Although, I'm kind of on a vacation right now."

The tiny lady looked at me with a dead panned face. Together we sat in complete silence for a few seconds. I shifted in my seat, and felt too warm in my jacket.

She lightly tossed my hands back to me like she had just finished reading an article in the newspaper that she disagreed with. "You need a new job, or hobby, something to make you happy and healthy...or a good lover to help you—do you have partner"

"No, no boyfriend now, just an overbearing boss." I sighed. "But you're probably right, it's time to move on—and trust me I know, I've needed a new job for while."

The Psychic smiled curtly and said, "You will have a big choice to make very soon," then tucked her thick, short, black hair behind one ear before she reached for the red deck of cards that sat between us. She handed the deck to me, "Shuffle them in your hand like this." She held them in her left hand and gently rearranged their order with her right. "Think about three things you want to know."

After I shuffled the cards, I returned them to her, and she placed the cards into four piles forming a square.

"Pick one for all of your questions," she said.

I pointed to the top right corner. She put the remaining three piles back in the box, then gathered up the cards in the selected pile and dealt them into three uneven stacks—side by side. There appeared to be about four to five cards in each of the stacks.

"Ask your first question and pick," she said pointing to the cards.

"Do I have a serious relationship in my near future?" I asked aloud, and pointed to the middle group—the one with the most cards in it.

She flipped over each card consecutively, and laid them in a straight vertical line. They read: King of Hearts, King of Spades, King of Clubs, and two Jokers—one of which, was upside down.

"Ah. Oh-kay, oh-kay, yes you do have three serious relationships in your life this year—big role in your life," she said excitingly. "The first man is very patient with you and he really loves you, I like this one," she smiled. "The second one, you must resists, very important that you do not..." she gazed off into the distance, "that you do not...sleep with this one."

She looked up at me for a nonverbal contract of consent before returning her focus to the cards.

"The third is an intelligent man, but he too selfish, and focus too much on work and his legacy, to have any love relationship." She shook her head in disapproval. "You must know that the most important relationship is with yourself. The cards say, that you are being reckless or risky with your life, but you can change your future and have a new life if you choose. You will have a choice to make. One way foolish and one has unlimited potential—next question."

"You said three relationships this year, but it's already mid-October…"

She sat quietly smiling at me.

"Well, I guess if I'm dating three men then I can definitely quit my job right?" I leaned in, and smiled with all of my teeth.

"Is that your next question?" she asked.

"No—I was just…never mind," I checked the time on my cellphone.

"Next question."

"I don't really know how to ask this one," I placed my fist on my chin and looked up as if waiting for the right question to drop down from above. "Are my dreams real?"

"You want to know if your dreams are real?" Her brow furrowed.

"Yes, but maybe a better question is: will I find what, or who, I'm looking for in the next two weeks?" I pointed to the first stack.

She flipped over four cards: Two of Diamonds, Four of Clubs, Six of Spades and Seven of hearts.

"The cards say that what you seek is possible, through balance of your mind and heart—and your imagination. You will have what you desire. What you find could create a new home, and is end of a bad cycle for you, as long as you make the right choice—last question."

"Is my best-friend sleeping with my ex-boyfriend?" I asked not batting an eyelash.

She laid out the last four cards; Queen of Clubs, Queen of Hearts, Four of Hearts, King of Hearts.

"Hmmm, you should talk to your friend—this is a good friend, but she is young. Whatever is happening with her you can work it out. There is *lots of love* here, from everyone involved…sometimes you just have to look at the bigger picture." She grinned to herself as she collected all of the cards and re-joined them to the others in the box.

I paid her twice as much as she asked for, but she didn't ask for much to start with. I left feeling optimistic about my future, but I got the impression from the last question that she wasn't telling me the *whole truth* so help me God.

8

THE HYPNOTIST

Rinnnging
Rinnnging
Rinnnging

I'm going to murder someone.

Okay so probably not the best thought to wake up with on hypnotist day. Sure enough, my clock read 8:26 a.m., and some *unknown* ass-hat was calling me again. I must have fallen asleep reading. I could taste stale red wine in my mouth. While I brushed my teeth, I thought about the Psychic from yesterday. She seemed pretty grounded in her readings, and I saw why Jesmitha's mom liked her. The only thing was, I could hardly imagine myself dating anyone anytime soon—let alone three men! A burst of laughter splattered a mixture of toothpaste and saliva against my mirror. I took a cloth and wiped it clean. I was however, happy to agree with what she said about Jes and Bryan, even if it wasn't complete answer—or if it was total bullshit. My dopamine starved brain decided the reading was to be accepted as sweet facts, in order to get through the next couple of days. After I was fully recovered from my self-induced chemical imbalance, then I would have a sobering conversation with Jes about Bryan.

The Hypnotist appointment would be a completely different experience from the palm reading activity, because it would ether work or it wouldn't. I wouldn't have to wonder if it was real or not—which was comforting. The office was a little far away so I downloaded an audio-book on dreams to listen to on the drive. I was so engrossed in the material, that I hadn't realized that thirty minutes had passed. Before I knew it, I had arrived at Mr. Reynold's Hypnotherapy Office.

The building looked like an old warehouse that was repurposed for economical office space and suite rentals. The tenants all seem to have a similar vibe. On ether side of Reynold's Hypnotherapy: stood Gemini's crystal shop and Leah's Pages (a new age bookstore). Above Reynold's suite, was a trendy hair salon. It was the type of salon that made their clients feel like *they* were lucky to get the chance to spend their money there, and that their hair was only the artist's medium; their locks only belonging to the talent, and their bodies draped in all black to rid of any distraction from the serious work at hand.

I walked through a door that had a wood-burned sign above it that read, "All Ye Who Enter There Is Hope." In the waiting room, a very young receptionist greeted me with a clipboard through a cutout window in the wall. The paperwork asked for any symptoms, previous medical history, and reason for seeking therapy. *My symptoms?* I just circled anxiety, wrote a giant, "N/A," over the medical history part, and then signed my name at the bottom.

As soon as I handed the receptionist the clipboard, she asked me to follow her back to Reynold's office. Once she stepped out from behind the window, I realized that she was maybe only fifteen years old. The floor creaked the entire way, and the hallways smelled like reams of paper. We arrived at the only other room in the suite.

It looked like what I would imagine a typical shrinks office would, except for the stereotypical chaise was amiss. In its place, sat a big royal blue recliner. The vibrant color stood out amongst all of the woods, brown leathers, and golds, that otherwise dominated the office. I sat in the recliner and sunk down, the air escaping the cushions audibly. I was instantly comforted by its give, and surprisingly soft exterior.

Shortly after I sat down, a man walked in. He was very short in stature. He had a solid white head of hair, and a neatly shaven beard. He wore a soft argyle vest in shades of brown, green, and yellow. Underneath the vest, he wore a cream button down, which he paired with jeans and blue suede tennis shoes.

"I'm Harvey," he said, "is this your first experience with hypnotherapy?"

"I've seen it done in Vegas." I said.

"This is a little different. Well it's a lot different actually, in the sense that I won't be manipulating your subconscious to entertain hundreds of drunk strangers...for very little compensation." He straightened a photo on his desk. "Although, the mechanisms are similar."

"Oh. The mechanisms?" I asked.

"I'm simply going to guide your mind into a state of intense concentration, while fully relaxing your body to the point that it is almost asleep. Once we reach that delicate balance, then we can begin the treatment. Which begs the question of the hour, what is bringing you anxiety?"

"Well...I don't know what I want to do with my life. I'm at a crossroads."

He nodded. What specifically are you hoping to achieve in today's session?"

"So I had a dream about my mom, and she spoke the name of a unique book title I had never heard. Then the book appeared the very next day. At first, I felt like my mom was leaving me clues to something bigger—but now I'm not so sure," I stared at my hands, "I also want to know if she's really trying to reach me. I know it all sounds far fetched...but the coincidences are—" a lump in my throat cut me off. I paused to regain my composure. "I'd just like to explore what's going on in my mind. It always feels too cluttered."

"Then, I will realign your jumbled thoughts with more productive ones. Before we start, make sure that you are completely comfortable. Make sure that there are no itchy neck tags, nor any bunched up socks in your shoes. There can't be anything that could take your attention away from my voice, and this present moment. When you are ready, recline the chair to your comfort, and we will begin."

I pulled my hair tie out and let my hair hang loose. Then I grabbed the latch that released the back of the chair.

"Tasha, I would like you to close your eyes and breathe in to the count of five—exhale to the count of six," his voice was a bit softer than before, "now I want you to focus on the air passing through your nostrils. Take special note of the way that it feels. Tiny breezes are pulled in through the small tunnels, and then pushed back out. I am going to take you deep into your mind, which is more vast than any ocean. But you will not get lost, as long as you follow my voice."

I closed my eyes and breathed in through my nose. I could smell a subtle hint of stale smoke.

"Imagine the first house that you called home. You're standing in the backyard of that house. Imagine staring at the horizon. A line where you can no longer see beyond. I want you to start walking towards that line. You are walking past your backyard now towards the horizon. Maybe you are on a magical street, or a bridge. A walkway that carries you across any obstacles. As you continue walking you notice a house on your left. An old house that you used to live in. Pass it by, and continue walking towards the horizon. As you get closer to the horizon, you notice a more recent house on your right. A recent house from your past, but you continue walking. You walk further, and further away, from your past. A brand new house appears on the horizon, one that you have never seen. Walk towards the new house. You open a door to the new house. You are fully welcomed and safe there. There is a descending staircase. Begin to walk down it. With each step, you feel more warmth. The warmth is radiating from below. You are on the correct path. You are safe. The deeper you go, the closer you are, to all of your answers. Down, down, you go. You are almost there. At the bottom, you can rest. You will find peace there. This is your place of peace. You can return here anytime you like. To return here, you only have to close your eyes, and breathe deeply. When I count down from ten, you will open your eyes: ten, nine, eight, seven, six, five, four, three…two and one."

I opened my eyes. He was sitting directly across from me. He was close enough to whisper, but not close enough to startle me. His eyes were hazel—not brown—like I had thought at first. I could definitely smell tobacco.

"When I snap my fingers you will fall back asleep," he said, "*snap*."

I closed my eyes, and sat in silence but I didn't feel—asleep. I did however begin to feel disingenuous, so I peeked an eye open. His disappointment pulled my other eye open to fully meet his gaze.

"I see," he exhaled, "well, we can try again, but I will say about ten percent of people cannot be hypnotized. Some people are too self-conscious, or sometimes the line between awake and asleep is distorted." He opened an ornate carved wooden box, that sat on top of his desk, and pulled out a very beautiful and delicate smoking pipe.

"So, what does this mean, exactly?" I asked.

"It means, that I think we're done for today, but you could come back for another session next week. I recommend some meditation or breathing exercises, before we try again. For the follow-up appointment, I will only charge you if we are successful," he looked me up and down, "but if I had to guess, you might fall into the group of people that are not open to suggestions."

"Okay?" I stood up to leave.

I would rather be home with Yumi watching television on her couch, and I hated television. I was disappointed, but I shouldn't have been surprised. I set this up as a joke in the first place, hadn't I? I quickly turned and walked out of the office. I wasn't any closer to finding out how to navigate my dreams—literally or metaphorically.

I slapped my card down on the receptionist's desk—perhaps a little too hard. The hazel-eyed teen jumped upon impact. She reached the my card timidly, not daring to ask how everything went. The look on my face already said it all. I didn't have a full explanation for the sudden bout of anger that was radiating off of me; although, it could have easily been a symptom of withdrawal.

All of the substances might have finally been clearing my system: my body scrubbing the chemical remnants out of my cells, with the attitude of a single mother cleaning mud out of the carpet for the hundredth time. "This is why we can't have nice things," my body screamed.

Or maybe it was all residual irritation, from my whole life, finally surfacing. My life hadn't been the easiest, yet I made the best of it— hadn't I? I had a well paying job, lived in a nice apartment with the best girl in the world, and I earned a Bachelor's degree in a demanding discipline. If only I would have had the foresight at twenty-four to see that my current job was going to lead nowhere, then maybe I wouldn't be in my current predicament: yes, that was my crime—no foresight. I could live with that.

The receptionist handed me my card, and a receipt to sign for seventy-five dollars. I guess that's not bad for absolutely nothing.

Thanks a lot, Mr. Har-vee-har-har Reynolds, what a joke. I signed the receipt and walked out.

"Have a good day?" The receptionist suggested, right before the door closed behind me.

9

THE THERAPIST

To my delight, there wasn't a single missed call that morning. The clock on my phone read, "8:45." I sighed with relief, and swung my feet onto the floor. Right on cue, Yumi jumped on the bed. My personal superhero in white shiny tufts of fur. She still smelled of lavender from her groom the other day.

"We're going to have company today girl." I scratched behind Yumi's ear. "Unfortunately."

Yumi looked towards the bedroom door expectedly.

"You speak English don't you." I stared at her, "come on, out with it —your schtick is up."

Yumi tilted her head and ran out of the room.

After yesterday's fiasco, I was not looking forward to another intrusion into my mind. But I could never disrespect Jes's mom and cancel; she reminded me a lot of my own mother. Jes's mom had a calming presence and a quiet strength. If she approved of this Malinda-therapist, then I would like her too. Also, Jes said I wouldn't have to leave my home, and that was qualification enough for me.

Per Jes, the therapist encouraged in-home sessions because she believed that people are more comfortable, and more open, in their natural environments. I thought I would show Malinda just how much I supported her theory. So in the spirit of comfort, I barely got dressed for my session that day. Who was I to question her process? I wore a pair of grey sweatpants, with a long-sleeved thermal that was tucked in a few inches along the front of my waist band—sans bra. My hair was piled half heartedly on the top of my head, and my face was void of any makeup. I was in a desperate need of a pedicure, so I slipped on my white fuzzy slippers: they looked like mini Yumi.

Speaking of comfort, I still had ten days left on my *vacation*, so tomorrow I think I should schedule a spa day for me, just to reset: it *was* mind, *body*, and soul after all. Afterwards, I would take Yumi to the dog park. Maybe one of my three men from the Psychic's prophesy would be there—just waiting to swoop us off our feet. My phone vibrated in my pocket—she must have arrived early.

I answered the phone, "Hi Malinda."

A very excited Indian male voice answered back. "Hello Tasha! It is so good to finally get ahold of you, we have been trying to contact you for a couple of days. I was beginning to think that we had the wrong number, but I am very happy to know that this one is correct. Have you considered—

I hung up.

Sonny called almost an hour later than usual—sneaky. I blocked the number, which was probably something I should have done a several days ago. To my dismay my phone immediately rang again. But thankfully, it was just the therapist. Malinda had arrived.

When I opened my apartment door, I was happy to see that she was a little more relaxed than her headshot alluded her to be. She had natural curly hair that sprung out in every direction, and a healthy build. She looked up at me and said, "Hello, I'm Malinda, it's nice to finally meet you," and put out her hand for me to shake, "I've heard so much about you." Then she leaned in like she was sharing a secret, "from Jesmitha's mom."

"You guys talk about me in sessions?" I asked, releasing her hand so that I could bend over to keep a very excited Yumi a respectful distance away from our guest until she calmed down.

"No, she's not my client any longer...because we've become friends. We lost touch some years ago when she moved an hour north of the city. Then we reunited unexpectedly outside the office, when we both attended Dragon Con last year. She walked into a panel on publishing, where I was dressed as Princess Leia—if you can imagine that. It was a very memorable weekend. Did you know that she writes short stories?"

"I can't imagine, and no, I had no idea," I said in awe, warming up to Malinda the longer she spoke, "please make yourself at home and don't mind Yumi, I know she's really big but she doesn't bite."

Yumi was still trying her best to get Malinda's attention without incurring a scolding from me.

"Hi Yumi, how beautiful you are—and such a big girl!" she said, barely having to bend over to address her. "She's not bothering me. I would have one just like her if I could, but I'm never home. So I just babysit my older brother's Yorki when I can…but there's quite the size disparity between the two."

Malinda's mouth took up most of the real estate on her face whenever she smiled. She wore bright fuchsia lipstick which was a stark contrast to the rest of her makeup-less face, save for some mascara. But her hair was so thick and coarse, her lashes could have been naturally that black and full.

Yumi circled her, and then leaned her body against her navy slacks, leaving a hefty swipe of white fur once she left. Yumi seemed to like this lady too.

"Is she a husky?" Malinda tried to pat away the fur from her pants.

"No—well actually…I'm not sure. I found her when she was a baby. She was in a trash bag with three other puppies alongside a highway. When I brought them all in, the veterinarian said: telling from the nature of their injuries, it was likely that they had been thrown from a moving vehicle. I still have a hard time accepting that anyone would do something like that." I grimaced. "But anyway—I just figured that she was a German Shepard mix, maybe even part wolf, because she is a lot taller than most shepherds. Also her fur is like silk." I shrugged.

I looked at Yumi, she was huge. She weighed almost eighty pounds of lean muscle, but her fur made her appear even larger.

Malinda considered my story, "What a shame, I can't imagine the headspace you would have to be in to harm something so innocent and helpless. It makes you sad for everyone involved."

"I guess?"

She looked at her watch, "Let's get started."

We walked to my living room. We sat on the opposite ends of my L-shaped couch, facing one another. I reached for the blanket neatly folded on the end of the chaise, but then thought better of it. I wanted to show her some respect. I wished I would have dressed nicer for our meeting.

"Feel free to use a blanket if it makes you more comfortable," she said, "I'm just going to ask you a few questions. One thing you will come to understand about me is that I believe in being completely open with my clients. It is in this way, that we can move forward with full transparency. Truth has a very specific ring to it, and all of our ears are adept at hearing, whether we are conscious of it or not. The more truthful we are with each other, the more progress we will make: that goes for in here, and out there." Her hands made a ball, before she expanded the shape to open palms. "With that said, the true purpose of this meeting is to see if we're a good fit for each other. If we are, then this session will help me to decide which approach is most beneficial. But please don't worry, there is someone for everyone at our healing center. So if I'm not the right one for you, then I'll find someone who is, and you will not have to repeat this process," her fingers held on to her necklace, a flattened sphere of amethyst on a gold chain.

I nodded.

"Okay great," she grabbed a clipboard, and a thick black pen; both pulled out of an oversized leather tote bag. "What made you seek out a counselor?"

I shrugged my shoulders, and smiled while frowning at the same time.

"There are no wrong answers Tasha, whatever comes to your mind is exactly what I want to hear. Tell me the thoughts that arrive right after the question is asked: What made you seek out a counselor?"

"I didn't seek out a councilor. My friends are making me talk to someone because I made a mistake at work. One of those *friends* is my boss—whose also my ex-boyfriend." My bottom lip pushed upwards upon the top one.

"Can you elaborate on the nature of the mistake," she asked, after she wrote down a few notes on her clipboard.

I sighed. "I accidentally took drugs at work. They led to a bigger problem, which then created an even bigger problem. Eventually the night ended in the Emergency Room—and here we are."

Malinda raised her eyebrows and smiled, "Do you feel that you have a problem?"

"I know I don't have a drug problem, because I was never *trying* to get high, I was trying to...trying to focus."

"Can you explain that a bit more?"

"It's not as complicated as it sounds. The night this happened, I thought I was taking Adderall, but it was actually an ecstasy pressed pill. They are the exact same color, shape, and feel. I take adderall sometimes so I can stay up all night, and do my job effectively. I completely forgot that there were two party pills in my bag from a festival that Jes—UHh-Ca." I paused. "yes a festival that...my friend *Jessica* and I, went to a month prior. The real irony is that they were only in my bookbag because I *didn't end* up taking them that weekend. I quit doing that stuff years ago, and I only considered it." I said with my face on fire.

I hoped that she didn't catch the slip. I nearly incriminated Jesmitha by saying her name. Her mother would probably disown her if she found out that's who the pills came from.

"The second time it happened, I was just trying to contact my dead mom."

"The second time?" Malinda asked.

"Right...because you didn't know about the second time." *Sigh.*

"No I didn't, I know nothing, but what you tell me." Malinda smiled.

"*Well*, during the blackout, my mom gave me a message in my dreams, but I couldn't remember it fully. So, I tried to reach her again by re-creating that night in some capacity."

"And did it work?"

I laughed.

"I see. How long ago did your mom pass?"

"About four years ago," I said.

"I'm sorry, thats a tough age to lose your mom. Do you mind me asking how?"

I sat for a moment, staring at my white walls. I wondered if there was any easy age to lose your parents—surely every age had a unique pain that accompanied it, but easier? I doubt it. I also debated back and forth on how much I really wanted to tell her. People never knew how to respond appropriately. Once I actually shared the details, no response had ever made me feel better. I always left the conversation feeling like I had just made someone feel sad for no reason—for something that had no resolution. But, I guess this is the whole point of her sitting there.

"My mom drove her car off a bridge. She died on impact. Thankfully she didn't hurt anyone else in the process. She had been suffering from Alzheimer's for a couple of years, so I really don't know what happened. If I had to guess, it was probably just an accident... even though sometimes...I think it could have been suicide. But that doesn't match up with her personality. I also can't rule out that the accident could have been caused by the dementia itself. There are a lot of questions left."

"Oh Tasha," she put her fingers over her mouth, "Tasha, I am so sorry, what a heavy experience to carry with you. It is certainly understandable why you would want to know what happened." Malinda's hand found her Amethyst pendant again.

"She's gone and nothing will change that," I said, "but I don't think she was trying to tell me about her death, I think she was trying to tell me about my life. It wasn't like Mom to dwell in the past, she was always looking forward. If she really came to me with a message, it would be about something that was happening right now. After I woke up, the dream slipped away so fast. The harder I tried to hold on to it —the quicker the memory disappeared. I imagine if Mom were still here now, she could relate to that feeling." I reached down a pulled the blanket over me. "So thats why I wanted to go back, I only wanted to know what she was trying to tell me. It was never about the drugs."

Malinda jotted down some notes on her pad. She flipped the page, and tucked it behind her hand on the back of the clipboard. "On a scale, from zero to ten, how much do you think your mom's death is affecting your life right now?"

"Right now...an eight? I'm not depressed every day, but I feel disconnected from the world. She was the last family member that I had. It feels like I don't really belong to anyone."

Yumi's head popped up from her tightly curled body, that laid outside the dog bed a few feet in front of us.

"Besides Yumi." I laughed. "I also worry all the time that I might have the same fate as her, which is why I'm incredibly picky about what I put into my body. I don't use aluminum, fluoride, artificial sweeteners, processed food, or take drugs normally—prescription or otherwise."

Her honey brown eyes locked with mine, and nodded in understanding. "Okay switching gears a bit, how would you describe your personality?"

"Nice...I think."

"What is your biggest life accomplishment?"

I felt really tired all of the sudden.

"Are we almost done? It seems like you should know by now if we're a good match or not." I avoided making eye contact.

"Yes, nearly finished—and also yes—I believe we will be a good fit together. I'm just getting a few more questions for our first session. Just bare with me a few more minutes," she said, with almost an air of laughter lifting her words up, "How do you get yourself out of a bad mood?"

"Exercise or sleep," I said.

"Ok, last question Tasha, if I could wave a magic wand and make everything perfect for you, what would your life look like? Take your time."

I looked at the photo of my mom and I. It still laid on the coffee table. "My mom would be alive, I would have a mentally stimulating career...a perfect body, and maybe a family?"

"So what I heard was, that you want to work on creating a sense of family and belonging in your life, finding a career involving a deeper purpose, and invest in a healthy self-image. That we can do."

"Sure."

"You don't seem so convinced and that's okay—one step at a time," Malinda clicked her pen closed. "You know, I have a friend of the family that you might be interested in meeting with. He would be the perfect person to talk to about accessing your dreams in a deeper and safe manner. I know you have some unanswered questions and curiosities there, and I don't want you experimenting on your own anymore."

"I've actually been reading a little bit about that. There are real professionals that specialize in dreams?" I asked.

"Yes, and he's the best there is. And even if you don't find a direct line of contact with your mom, Lucid Dreaming is a wonderful way to access your subconscious mind to heal any past traumas, or find untapped or repressed potential."

"Repressed potential?" I asked.

"Sometimes people are not afraid of failure, they're afraid of success, but that is another lesson—for another day," she said.

I nodded. "Let's do it, what do I have to lose?"

"You always have something to lose, but you assuringly won't lose anything in seeing Dr. Joe." She smiled.

Malinda happily clapped her hands.

Yumi was scared from a sleeping position. She went straight to her feet—fully alarmed—with no noticeable in-between stage.

"Great, I'll set up an appointment with him. I think this will be a perfect match. He doesn't like to call it therapy though—he calls them workshops."

"Oh no, workshops?"

I thought of Sonny, and of him shaking the blank notecard at me for my phone number, like a street performer with his tip-hat.

"These workshops aren't two grand are they?" I asked.

Malinda laughed, "Not at all, he is very passionate about and dedicated to his cause. I doubt he will charge you at all." She stood up. "So we can continue to meet if you'd like, which days work for you?"

"Friday at eleven would work better, I usually work Thursday nights," I said.

"Sure I can move some things around and make that work for this month."

She put her clipboard and pen away in her oversized bag, and miraculously pulled her phone out in one solid movement, without even looking down.

After only a few minutes of texting, she said, "Can you meet with Dr. Joe, this Wednesday afternoon?"

"I sure can—I'm on vacation."

10

WEDNESDAY'S WORKSHOP

I stood two feet away from a loud, turquoise door. I could see my twisted reflection in its golden knob; more notably, I saw the look of distaste on my face. The door smelled of the fresh paint that smothered its wood. This color was not some calamity from an outdated trend, but a recent offense. Just standing in front of that obnoxious door, made me doubt the sincerity of my efforts. I *should* be looking for legitimate ways to re-direct my life; not wasting the day with an imaginary mom. Bryan was literally *paying me* to grow up. What if he was testing me to see if I could handle more responsibility in the future, and this is the best I could do—a dream doctor? *Pathetic.*

I turned around, and headed back towards my car. My time would be better spent taking Yumi to the dog park. Yesterday, she overcame her fear of the sway-bridge, and that achievement seemed more productive than anything that could come from that ridiculous door.

"Ms. Price?" An English voice called from behind me.

I froze en route to my car. When I turned around, I saw a well groomed man standing in front of the silly door. He was about fifty years old, had unnaturally white teeth, and very smooth skin for his age.

"Hi, you must be Dr. Joe? I'm just going to grab a pen and paper from my car. I'll be right back."

"Perhaps you could record our session on your phone, as not to distract—come inside, won't you?" He held the door open.

"Right." I said, slowly closing the distance between me and that door. A door that now seemed to mock me as I walked into its mouth.

Once inside the townhome, I was pleasantly surprised. I wasn't optically assaulted in the least. For starters, there was no more turquoise in sight, save for a few delightful moments in the colorful wall art. The art pieces sat above—and on either side—of a fireplace, in a sitting room to the right of the foyer that we stood in. The paintings were set in antique-gold and ornate frames, that effectively punctuated the muted cream couches and wooden tables. A sparkling crystal chandelier pulled my gaze upward at least fifteen feet high. I noticed that the ceiling was outlined with an intricate crown molding, that also bordered the floor, and continued uninterrupted around the fireplace. This place was, *dare I say, exquisite.*

"Nice place," I petted a rich mahogany stallion, that was fiercely galloping through water—or was it mud?

The mustang sculpture rested on its own podium in the foyer.

"Thank you," he said, "so, Malinda tells me that you are interested in learning about Lucid Dreaming."

"I mentioned to her that I spoke to my dead mom in my dreams, and she passed me off to you."

He chuckled. "Brilliant! Yes, that would be my department indeed. Everyone could benefit from Lucid Dreaming: a heightened creativity, enriched problem solving skills, healing from past traumas, and sometimes, it can just be entertaining—which is an underrated need. The most important qualifier of efficacy is whether or not the client is open to the practice, otherwise it's a fool's errand to try and teach them. Do you believe in Lucid Dreaming Ms. Price?"

"I don't dis-believe."

"Very well," he said, unclasping and clasping his hands that were held in at his chest.

"So how does this work…do I take some DMT or something?"

"Ehm," he cleared his throat, "no, we want to remain in our bodies for this exercise. In fact, the more pure your body is, clear of any dodgy substances, the better Lucid Dreaming will work for you." He must have noticed the fear in my eyes, "wine is fine, but anything over two drinks a day will hurt your progress. You'll also need to abstain from *all* drugs. A little melatonin can help in certain situations, but that's it."

"Got it," I said, "ironically that is kinda the theme of this week."

His face lost it's expression, and his eyes looked towards the exquisite sitting room, "Let's have a seat shall we."

We walked into the room, which was really for sitting as it were. Once I sat on the couch, I saw a wooden bookshelf in my direct line of sight. It was packed with dozens of books written by Dr. Joseph N. Wells; whom I assumed was the same *Joe* that sat before me. There were also hundreds of other authors keeping Dr. Wells company on the shelf. I noticed one book in particular, that was of special interest to me: a lime green spine with the words, *This world is made for you, by PhD Lim.*

"That's so weird," I pointed to his bookshelf as his eyes followed my hand, "that book on your shelf, the one by Lim is very much the reason why I am here." I sat staring at the book as if it was about to sprout legs and walk to me.

"That's a very special book, the author is actually a close colleague of mine. She's a wonderful and bright woman. You can take it if you like—consider it yours."

"No. No, thank you. I already have it—*that book title* is the one that my mom spoke in my dreams; it's the same title I heard on the radio a day later!" I ran my hands through my hair. "And…now it's right there. I know I sound crazy, I'm sorry."

"No need for apologies Natasha," he stood up from an ivory, throne-chair, and walked over to the bookshelf to retrieve the book, "here, sometimes there's no substitute for the real thing."

I accepted the book. It was heavy. I turned it over in my hands and traced the outline of the tree. "Thank you," I said.

He sat back down in the chair across from me. "Lucid Dreaming is a simple concept, although people love to complicate it. It is at the very core of its ideology, just an awareness of your experiences. An awareness that is held in the present moment, without being carried away by the story, or the emotions that come with the story. In other words, controlling the narrative within the dream. Understand?"

I nodded. "Sort of."

"Lucid Dream *Therapy* is the *practice* of perfecting the observer in you. The observer is your higher self, and it is always present, whether you are conscious of it or not. The goal is to observe what is happening in your reality, with the clarity of calmness and without judgment. This is difficult enough for people to do in the waking world, so you can see why it is quite the chore for most people to achieve while they're unconscious—when we have more faculties against us. However, if you're successful, and you can master the role of the observer while you're dreaming, then you can become a creator."

"A dream creator?"

"Correct, once you really comprehend that you are in control, your possibilities are endless. It's your world and you make the rules. You may do anything you wish, go anywhere you want, and speak with anyone you so choose. Furthermore, if you can awake in your dreaming body, then one day you might be able to awake from the master dream as well." He eyed me like he was revealing some ancient and profound knowledge.

"Okay, so how do I become…the observer," I edged closer to him.

"Motivation or intent is the biggest factor in the ability to achieve lucidity, yet there is no shortage of technical methods."

He stood up and walked back to the shelf. He pulled off a blue, landscape-oriented, workbook from a row of hundreds of identical copies. He handed the paperback to me.

"The first thing you must do is buy a programable recorder, so that you can record your dreams immediately upon waking. This step is paramount. For some reason, the physical body's mechanisms shroud our dreams; it's as if, we're not meant to fully remember everything from our dreamlands. We Oneironauts—

"I'm sorry what?" I said.

"Oneironaut, a scientist that studies Lucid Dreaming. We've found that if you do not move your body and keep your eyes closed—or if you return to the same position quickly—then you can re-enter a dream, or recall it. Instead of searching for pen and paper, as the dream slips away from you, you can program a recorder to start every morning at a time that you normally arouse. So you can speak your entire dream aloud without even opening your eyes. The less you move, the more clarity you will have. Sometimes you can record your entire dream without fail. This brings us to the first—and most important step—to Lucid Dreaming: dream recall."

"Dream recall, so I just have to remember my dreams?"

Dr. Joe wagged his finger in the air, "The second step is identifying symbols that repeat in your dreams, which are typically: dead people, animals, places, or specific actions. You'll find these by transcribing your dreams from your recordings into a journal and highlighting anything that made you *feel* odd. Even if you can't explain the emotion right away. That unexplainable feeling is precisely what you are looking for—you will get better at recognizing it. These stirring images are your dream cues. Eventually you will use these exact cues to signal to your observer, that you are dreaming, so you can become lucid within the dream."

"I can do that. I might already know one—I dream about crocodiles all of the time," I said.

"Crocodiles? Remind me to tell you about their symbolism, and be sure to record them from here on out."

I agreed.

"After about a fortnight's worth of journal entries, you should be able to identify a few dream cues. From there, the most straightforward method to attaining your first Lucid Dreams, is through simple repetition. Relentlessly, remind yourself throughout the entire day that when you see said cue, you will *know* that you are dreaming. There are *many* other methods, but this is the simplest one."

"Let me see if I understand. I'm supposed to remember not to move and start recording myself babbling each morning. I write down all of the dead people that show up in my dreams. Then talk to myself throughout the whole day. And all of this for what again? So I'll wake up inside of the dream? It sounds a little crazy."

Dr. Joe chuckled. "Agreed, it's not for everyone." He stood up and walked out of the room.

"Oh, I'm sorry...Joe—uh—Dr. Joe? I didn't mean to offend you. I was just a little overwhelmed—I want to hear the rest," I said into an empty room.

The townhome became completely quiet and still. After several minutes of waiting, I walked over to the fireplace to get a better look at the photos sitting on the mantle. In the biggest frame, there was a picture of him and another man with a Yorkshire Terrier. It appeared to be taken at a European cafe.

"Care for some tea or water?" Dr. Joe offered.

I jumped. "Yes—thank you."

On the coffee table between us, sat a white porcelain tea set. It had bright reddish-pink roses painted all over, and was trimmed in real gold. The set was complete with matching little bowls, full of sugar cubes, and a tiny pitcher of cream. In addition to the tea, he brought out a small gold tower with cute sandwiches and teeny desserts.

"Please help yourself to the biscuits, have you any experience with meditation?"

"Yes, well sort of," I grabbed a mini sandwich off of the tower, "is this—

"Egg salad—I ask because meditation plays an important role in Lucid Dreaming, it relaxes the body and does so while keeping a specific type of concentration active; a pointed, yet non-arousing, focus. This type of concentration distracts the ego, and lets the higher self take the lead. Meditation is an advanced method, but it is my preferred way to enter into a Lucid Dream. I can fall straight into a Lucid Dream this way, sometimes with the aid of hypnagogic images."

I took a long sip of tea, wishing it was wine. "I don't mean to be rude, but I still don't get the point of all of this. Even if I use cues and repetition, or meditation, or hypna- whatever...what's the point to all of this?"

"The point is Natasha, that outside of being introduced to a new reality, that readily bends to your will, you will also come in contact with dream figures. *Most of them* are animated symbols of your subconscious—your primordial substrate. When you are allowed this type of intimate proximity with them, you can interact with and ask them questions. They will help you learn about your true self and unlock answers that spur deep healing and promote growth. You'll also extend your life immediately—living whilst asleep—doing whatever you please. You'll discover new colours, so to speak, and you'll build entire worlds to dance in," he said.

"Oh...kay, but what about my mom, are you saying that she was just some dream figure of my...imagination?" I asked, choking on the last word. I cleared my throat, and quickly wiped away any moisture from my eyes.

"Ah, yes, your mum."

Dr. Joe sat his rosy teacup down on the table. The cling-clang of the tiny golden spoon, and the saucer against the cup, was oddly satisfying.

"I prefer to stay within the lines of scientific text during my workshops; but off the record, it is my personal belief, and experience, that other beings can access your dream realm. I have, on more than one occasion, asked some of my reoccurring dream figures questions, in which their answers have turned out to be correct in waking life; but these are answers that I would have no way of knowing. And this is coming from someone who is rather familiar with the subconscious."

"When you say, 'beings,' you mean people right?"

Dr. Joe smiled, but it didn't reach his eyes. "This is another reason to keep a consisted dream journal. In my personal recordings, I have stated that I've met the aforementioned dream figure quite frequently. It is noted that he is quite the character. He's much different from all of my other dream figures. There are things that we have discussed that I do not remember now as I speak them. I can only reference them from my journal. Luckily, because I have captured the memories in that precious moment each morning before full arousal."

"You don't remember him? So you can only read about him in your journal? That's gotta feel weird—like having amnesia."

"Yes, that is true for the most part. I do remember somethings vaguely. I think you will come to fine out that memory is just another form of perception; and that perception my dear, is *extremely* malleable."

"Have you ever had a parent visit you?"

"I have—my father." Dr. Joe warmed his hands. "I believe it is more than plausible that you spoke with your Mum."

That's all I needed to hear…to stop fighting them. I let them come. I cried big toddler tears, in that beautiful room. I let all of the sadness pour out of me like a Florida storm—intense but brief—and he let me. He handed me a box of tissues, and after I finished, there was a pile of them on my lap. Dr. Joe grabbed all of the weepy tissues with his bare hands, and took them around the corner to throw them away. I squirmed at the motherly gesture, and pulled my hair back. While he was gone I ordered the recorder off of Amazon, and sat in silence until he returned. I felt uneasy in his presence for crying so hard.

He returned with a new glass of water, a teal leather-bound journal, and a book he wrote on Lucid Dreaming titled: *Leaving the Lights On.*

"Here's a little gift from me to you, a proper journal, and the first book I ever wrote." He handed them both to me.

"Thank you, it's all too much though, you've given me a small library now."

"The pleasure is all mine dear. Once you have a lucid dream make sure to write those down. When you start becoming lucid regularly, give me a ring so we can move onto deeper techniques and theory—but everything we covered today—is in this book." He pointed to *Leaving The Lights On.*

"What do I owe you?" I said, sniffling against my will.

"Only to keep trying, even when you don't succeed at first. When you finally do, because *you will*, just promise me that you'll follow up."

"I can do that." I thanked him, apologized for crying on his nice sofa, and gathered my things.

On the way out, Doctor Joe watched me leave from his door. "I also find it helpful to speak to the person you want to meet in your dreams."

I smiled, and nodded, before ducking into my car.

* * *

STRAWBERRY ROSES

When I got home, Yumi greeted me with her usual happy-waggly-self. Her joy inspired me to take her on an extra long walk through the park —she deserved it—she always deserved it. Along our stroll, an autumn bouquet of honey and scarlet greeted us over and over again, like a young and eager suitor. The air outside was comfortably cool and energizing. I felt like we could have walked all night, and Yumi wouldn't have minded. She was busy investigating all the old bushes and lamp posts that we hadn't visited in a while. Soon the street lights buzzed on, and the sun set behind the buildings. When the temperature dropped, I made the decision to return home. The sidewalk leading back to our apartment appeared dim orange, through a silhouette of hanging trees up ahead.

I felt the cold wind on my teeth, and realized that I was smiling—a genuine grin had crept up upon my face and taken residence all by itself. I thought about my new direction in life. I was hopeful for the first time in a long time, and even a little restless to get started. I visualized myself thriving with my new therapist's guidance, and mastering Lucid Dreaming. I imagined having all of my affairs in order, running Club Daze along side Bryan, and coming up with new and creative ideas to boost our revenue.

The wind picked up a few fallen leaves from the ground in front of us, giving them life for a moment. I was also ready to turn over a new leaf. I remembered that Joe said that he could fall asleep directly into a lucid dream, and something about Hypnagogic images. He also said I should try and talk to Mom before bed. As I considered what I would say to her, a little streak of excitement ran down my spine. The thought of finally being able to speak with her, one more time, was motivating. I tried to picked up the pace, but Yumi was dragging; as she often did, when she realized we were heading home, and she wasn't ready to turn in. I turned and pounced on Yumi's fluffy butt with both hands in claw formation. She jumped back with surprise, and reciprocated my play by rearing on her hind legs. She gallop-swatted at me with her front paws and chased me all the way home. We collapsed on her couch, both panting.

I showered, and got ready for bed. Once settled, I closed my eyes and tried to picture a motherly image, but my eyes were persistent in remaining apart, so I unplugged my phone and looked up *Hypnagogic Images* on the internet. Laying in my bed, with a pale blue glow on my face, I digested bouts of knowledge.

One website stated, "segments of your brain and your body fall asleep individually, and in doing so cause you to dream (or hallucinate) in a semi-conscious state."

I read that you could use the images to carry you into a full-blown lucid dream. I also learned that my previous methods at trying to reach my mom were so far from effective, that it would have been laughable, had it not been so sad. I stayed up a few more hours reading, trying to get into the encouraged *extra drowsy state*, in order to see the images— but they never came. Finally, I put my phone down when I was too tired to read any longer. I concentrated on my mom. I hoped that she would do the rest on her end.

"Okay Mom, if you can hear me, please come back. Even if it's just one more time, please give me guidance on my future. I love you Mommy, I miss you." I whispered to my ceiling in the darkness.

I saw the outline of Yumi's head pop up and stare at me for a few moments, before she re-curled her body to be closer to mine. I closed my eyes and tried my best to combine everything I had just learned, with what I remembered, from the meditation class. I focused on my breath. I breathed in to the count of six, and exhaled to the count of seven, a few times.

The first image of my mom floated into my minds eye, and I held it there as calmly as I could. I saw her soft strawberry blonde hair, that she was always trying to condition smooth. Yet, her hair always remained a billowy cotton-cloud, just the way I liked it. I could still feel it in my memory, and see it webbed between my fingers like I was ten years old again. I smelled white roses. Her fragrance that wafted in the air, every time she moved: when she talked or threw her head back to laugh.

11

LUCIDITY

Hair webbed between fingers.

Roses in the air.

Her mom threw her head back to laugh.

They both chuckled together as if they had just closed a big business deal.

Tasha and her mom embraced.

"You're so beautiful mom, I hope I look like you when I'm your age," Tasha said.

"Thank you darling. Come inside, I have something for you!" She pressed her back against a turquoise door, pushing it open.

Tasha followed her mom into the apartment, through a long and dimly lit hallway of photographs. The frames that hung on the wall held photos of family in various places around the globe. The people had no faces. From the hall, they emptied out into the kitchen. It smelled like warm vanilla birthday cake. Her mom had been baking in preparation for Tasha's arrival. A fluffy chicken, named snowball, greeted them with excitement. He bounced up and down until he eventually sat on top of Tasha's feet, at the kitchen table, where they all sat.

"Natasha, can you hear me?" her mom's voice echoed. Her face became abruptly serious.

"Yes, I'm right here," Tasha said, her voice sounded like it was traveling through water.

"Wake up! Wake up!" Her mom slammed her fists down on the

table. "You still have roots here on Earth, Natasha!"

Someone knocked at the door and both of their heads snapped towards the sound. Tasha and her mom were now traveling along a narrow and dilapidated bridge, with incredibly high peaks, and low valleys. It appeared as if the bridge was once a roller coaster. The road crossed over a grand canyon filled with crocodile infested waters. In their very exposed Jeep Wrangler, they could clearly see hundreds of snouts, surface and submerge.

"Slow down." Tasha pleaded to the back of a Driver's head. She looked at her mom who was hanging out of the open car window, "and put your seatbelt on mom!"

Tasha reached over her mothers lap and tried to buckle her in to no avail. The car sped up. The straps were all tangled together. The buckles wouldn't connect to the clasps, no matter how hard Tasha tried to force them in. The hectic jerks of the vehicle slid both their bodies towards the drivers side of the Jeep. Tasha's mom was practically in her lap—in *more* danger of falling into the crocodiles snapping below!

"I don't want to lose you again!" Tasha cried.

"I'm not lost, Natasha." her mom said calmly, placing her hand over Tasha's, and gently pushing down until they both heard an assuring click.

Tasha sat back into her seat, and took control of a steering wheel, "But I did lose you," she looked at her hands that were driving and grasping the wheel with white knuckles, "that's right, I've *already* lost you." Tasha stopped the car.

She looked into the backseat at her Mom's kind face, and her eyes seem to encourage her, while she donned a sympathetic smile.

"I must be dreaming," I said, "Mom, we're in my dream aren't we?"

I looked at my hands again, they were my hands! I had become lucid in my dream.

I felt the scenery around me shake as my excitement grew with my lucidity. I tried to remain calm by returning my attention to my breath. I closed my eyes and counted: one, two, three...

I looked up. "Mom—wait, my mom should still be here."

Mom was right there before I closed my eyes, but when I opened them, I was in the backseat again. In front of me—was the Driver. He watched me from the rearview mirror with familiar eyes.

"Where is my mom?" I asked.

"She is still within reach, we can say goodbye now, if you would like," he said.

His words came out slowly, each one carefully selected. There was something like surprise tinting his every word.

"Over there." He pointed to an ivory couch. It sat the middle of a pale grey space that extended to every visible corner.

On the couch, sat my mom in a peaceful stillness. I stepped out of the car and walked over to her. She faced forward with her eyes closed, and she did not acknowledge my presence. I sat down next to her on the couch.

"Mom, I'm here, I did it—we did it!" I waited. "I love you."

Nothing.

"Thank you for all you fought through to take care of me. I know it wasn't easy, and I know you would have never left if there was any way you could have stayed." My heart broke all over again. "What do I do now?" I pleaded.

Her head did not turn, and her mouth did not move, but a voice that had only ever belonged to her said, "My darling Natasha, please do not harbor any fear or pain in your heart. I'm at peace and you are on the right path now. Never forget that time is a gift. Appreciate the infinite potential of every present moment, so that you do not squander them. You will find your roots and do great things. This life is the womb to eternity."

Tasha became lost in her mothers words. The next thing she saw, was the back of the Drivers head again. She kicked the back of his seat as hard as she could.

"Damn it! Where is she?" Tasha demanded.

The Driver studied her in the rear-view mirror with amusement in his eyes, "you're good—a little unbalanced to be that lucid—but not bad."

Tasha sat back in the seat."Where are we going?" she huffed.

"Well, I guess thats up to you now, isn't it?" he said, with his eyes still smiling.

"I want to go wherever Mom went, so take me there—you dream thing,"

Tasha pressed her forehead against the side window. She watched the heat from her nostrils fog up the glass, as her inhales cleared it.

12

TWO FOR THE SHOW

Rinnnging
Rinnnging
Rinnnging

My hands searched for my phone in a silver sea of sheets: *unknown,* again, at, "9:10 a.m.."

Was Sonny calling me from a different number?

I managed to read the alert through the ridiculous amount of hair that was tangled in my face and restricting my view. I must have tossed and turned all night.

My dream. I remembered!

I might have reached my mom last night—or something like her. The journal that Dr. Joe gave me was sitting on my nightstand. I opened it and scribbled down everything that I could remember: the couch, my mom, the car, my hands, the bridge, and the crocodiles. The dream was fading fast, like sand through my fingers.

What did Mom say?

Beside *Mom,* I wrote, "my roots are here on Earth," and also, "this life is the womb to eternity." Then I wrote the word, "Driver," and circled it aggressively three times. I felt like the point of lucidity occurred directly after realizing that she was no longer living, so I noted that as well. I couldn't really remember anything else of importance, except possibly, something about a chicken-cake—or chicken-pie? But, that seemed very wrong.

I heard two quick, loud knocks at the door.

"Ah! A tiny *pet* chicken, thats right—fluffy and white just like Yumi, I remember now," I said.

Yumi perked up, straight from a deep sleep, and vaulted to the front door. She pressed her wet nose as hard as she could against a crack that allowed her senses to reach the outside world. She violently blew air from her nostrils into the crevice, sniffing up all of the loosened particles that her gusts had created, in order to maximize her investigation into our mystery guest-knocker.

I opened the door and saw a yellow padded envelope leaning on the exterior wall. My tape-recorder had arrived. The sky was grey-green. It was pouring down rain. My weather-app said that it was going to storm all weekend. It wasn't ideal for shopping, especially not in the hellish Atlanta traffic, but I needed to get Yumi's dog food. I figured I could pick up some dream-supplies while I was out. I also had an intense craving for vanilla birthday cake.

I made a giant coffee, and sat down on the couch to make my shopping list: a white-noise sound machine, maybe some new pillows, a few more books on Lucid Dreaming couldn't hurt, vanilla birthday cake mix, a couple more bottles of wine, some fresh roses for the apartment, melatonin, and maybe a box of Tylenol PM. Joe said no drugs but surely he didn't mean Tylenol.

After Yumi and I had breakfast, we went on a soaked and rushed potty break. Neither of us were happy with each other's performance. Then I left to the store. I arrived home with my treasures about three hours later. I would force a nap to try out my new tools. I poured a glass of wine and took some melatonin. Then I set up the white noise machine that came with some interesting options other than the mock-sounds available, such as, *fan* or *thunderstorm*. The sound machine's booklet called the new options: Isochronic tones and Solfeggio tones.

It explained, "*All frequencies ranging from 2.5-20 Hertz, were called Isochronic tones, and 174 Hz-852 Hertz, were named Solfeggio tones. The tones affect the brain by aligning it to the waves and frequencies that are being emitted. Isochronic tones were classified further into the names of the specific waves: Delta waves (2.5 Hz) are for the deepest portion of a sleep cycle and are beneficial for a dreamless sleep. Low and High Theta waves (4 Hz and 5 Hz) help with dreams and meditation respectively. Low and High Alpha waves (8 Hz and 10 Hz) help with transitional states of sleep and relaxation respectively; and Beta waves (20 Hz) assist with alert concentration.*"

I didn't bother to read the Solfeggio tones section, since it seemed like the Isochronic tones were exactly what I needed right now, and I could research the other ones later. I turned my new sound machine on to the Low Theta at 4 Hertz. The beat was a little off putting at first. It reminded me of all the MRIs I had done when I was little, but for what, I couldn't remember now.

I got comfortable on the couch, and began reading Joe's intro book on Lucid Dreaming. After a while the beat became hypnotic. Once I felt drowsy enough, I closed my eyes. I looked for any of the hypnagogic images discussed in the book, but the only visuals I could see were little red dots, maybe thirty or so. They swirled around and seem to play together. Slightly disappointed, I briefly considered picturing my mom again to try to reach her, but something felt inherently wrong about it. It felt selfish to summon her; like I could be disturbing her peace. I had enough messages to sort through anyway, without adding any more to the mix: *my roots are here on Earth*? Whatever that means.

I gently watched my dots chase each other for a while. Slowly they began to form a circle. The circle then split into two circles, and then into three—still remaining red in color. I kept a soft focus on my diaphragm, rising and falling, just as I was taught. I let the images continue to play in the background. I noticed that if I gave them too much attention, they seemed to fade or stop moving. It reminded me of trying to remember a word on the tip of my tongue. The harder I focused, the more evasive the word became; but if I relaxed, it would returned to me.

The three circles merged into rectangles and continued their charade. At one point I thought they might have formed a bridge, but the last image that I remembered was a rear-view mirror.

13

THE INDIGO VEIL

"You again." Tasha glared into a rearview mirror.

"Natasha, you remember me, I'm honored," the Driver said.

"Who are you—exactly?" Tasha asked.

"I'm an old friend—

"Thats nice, how do I get out of this car? I seem to be stuck in here." she said.

"You are the only one keeping yourself here." The driver raised his eyebrows.

Even though she had been in the car before, this is the first time she'd ever taken a moment to look around. In doing so, she recognized the patterns on the soft blue-gray seats. They were tiny, thin, and hollow: geometric shapes of neon red-orange and green-yellow. She looked down at her feet and recognized her shoes.

"These are the shoes I begged my mom for, the week before I started my Junior year in high school."

Tasha looked around the cabin once more.

"This is the car, that I learned to drive in...and—and it's the car that she...died in!" Tasha shrieked.

I must be dreaming—yes, this is all just a dream.

I was able to become lucid, but the emotions were so strong. They threatened to pull me back out into the dream with the tide. I tried to calm myself—to stabilize. It didn't help that my surroundings were more vivid than ever.

"I want out of this car now." I demanded.

"That is perfectly fine with me, where do you want to go?"

I looked around us, there was nothing in sight. There were no colors, nor shapes, to point to—just a solid blanket of white.

"I want to go to my mom—she needs me," I clawed at the door handles, but the doors wouldn't open.

"I assure you that she doesn't *need* you. She is at peace. It's also a bad idea to visit there, with such wild emotion."

"*You* said I can go anywhere, well that's where I choose, so let me out. I want to be where my mom is!"

"It's true, *I* won't stop you, I am only here to guide you," the driver's eyes studied my reflection in the rearview mirror.

I was tired of this man and his riddles. I pinched myself and tried to wake, but it didn't hurt. I was *more* tired of being in this car. I hung my head in surrender.

"Natasha, if I show you that she is at peace—prove to you that she is safe—will you leave her to rest?"

I looked up, "Yes I promise, thank you. If she is resting then I won't wake her."

He began driving to what appeared as a tiny black dot on the horizon. It grew larger as we approached it. Once we were closer, it took on the shape of a tunnel. We drove through the opening, into the darkness.

Black out.

I could no longer see the hands in front of my face. It was eerily quiet. I thought maybe I had woken up—that I was laying in my bed.

"Yumi?" I whispered with staggered breath, not sure if I was really awake.

"Yumi isn't here." A voice in the darkness said. I recognized it as the Driver's.

A pale bluish circle, like the color of the moon, appeared on the horizon. As we continued towards it, I was eventually able to make out the shaped of my hands against the darkness—if I strained my eyes. Soon I could see an outline of the Drivers head. As we drove towards the light, it grew from a pale blue, into a vibrant silver. The circle grew and the road—if you can call it a road—now led into nothing but blinding light.

The light flooded the vehicle. There was so much light that vision was, once again, nearly impossible. We approached what looked like a thin indigo veil, or net, of some sort. It stretched outwards infinitely—no beginning or end in sight. The veil appeared like it would block our path, but our vehicle pushed through it, with only minor resistance.

* * *

THE SUBTLE REALM

I'm not prepared for what I see on the other side of the indigo veil. We are no longer in a vehicle at all, but standing outside in a park. The area looks like, what I assume Earth did, before it was adulterated with our industries and waste. I can see a few structures though. The ones I can see the clearest, are still very far in the distance—and they look... wrong.

It takes me a long time to realize where I am. And that I should already be very familiar with the area that we are standing in. It's the lake I recognize first: its unique triangular shape with a lonely tree situated directly in the center of it. There is also a steep hill to the left of the lake that I recognize; but, I could have sworn that was supposed to be on the right side. But we are indeed in my neighborhood park, the one right outside of my apartment. We're standing exactly in the spot where my apartment *would be* located at if it were...here.

Where am I? Am I still dreaming?

There are some *things* moving around in the distance as well, they're close to the structures. They appear to crawl like animals, but they could be other people? It's all very difficult to decipher what I am actually seeing. Because the most shocking aspect of this new world is the visuals.

Everything that I see before me, is more or less translucent. I can see every side, of everything, all at once. The exterior of every object is slightly more bold in its lining, but the insides are completely visible; being only slightly fainter in imagery. It didn't take long to figure out, that the longer I stare at an object, and the more I fixate upon it, the more particularized it becomes.

Under my gaze, a rock's surface quickly dissolves into distinguishable compounds. The molecules break down into the interior of their atoms: electrons, protons, nuclei. It doesn't stop there; inside of them there is a whole new system as well: a mini universe, opening up right before my eyes.

I quickly make a point not to stare too long at any one thing, or in any particular direction, so I can keep some sense of focus. Everything here seems to draw you into it, like it has its very own psychic gravitational pull. I can get lost in the depths of a simple rock for an eternity here, if I'm not careful. When it comes to the flora, there are higher levels of complexity that I can't even begin to understand. Worlds, within worlds, exist inside the most basic of plants.

I pull my attention from the ground, with some difficulty, and turn to look at the person standing in front of me. He looks like a normal human for the most part, but his body is blue. He is also outlined in layers of varying substances and colors. The layers are all unique. Most of them look like emitted light. In some layers, the light appears particularized—like a fine powder; other layers look like a gel.

After almost getting completely entranced by a rock, I don't dare try my new superzoom powers on him; nor do I care to look at my own body. I'm afraid of what worlds I would possibly disappear into there.

"What...is this place?" I ask the man in front of me, whom I still know to be the Driver, but in a less fleshy form. This is the first time I have ever spoke with him face to face.

"Welcome to the Subtle Realm Natasha. You can think of this place as running parallel to the Physical Plane—that you're familiar," he says.

"Like a dreamworld," I say.

"Well no—not really, you're awake and conscious. This isn't a dream in the way that you mean it to be. We're—passed that."

"Passed a dream." I echo.

I'm looking at my hands. They seem to grow bigger and shrink as soon as I think them to do so. Although, I am unable to decipher which comes first, the thought or the action.

"So that net—

"The veil is a bridge, or more of a gate really. It connects to the Subtle Realm to the Physical Plane."

"I'm sorry," I say, peeling my focus away from my hands, "are you saying this isn't a dream?"

He smiles. "Correct. The Subtle Realm isn't a dream, anymore than the Physical Realm is a dream." He's speech increases in speed. "unless of course," he's speaking more to himself, "you consider the Physical Plane just a part of the Master Illusion, then I guess it's all a dream manifestation by the Creator himself." He laughs, and a layer of colors change around his body. A second layer around him, yellow, pulses with light.

"I'm sorry, what?" I ask.

"You my dear, are in a neighboring realm, some refer to it as the Astral Plane. And by *you*, I mean your conscious material is here—it has passed through a dream gate." He looks at me like this one statement explains it all and when it obviously does not, he adds, "the mind is the atmosphere, between the Flesh and the Spirit."

"Ohh okay, well when you put it that way—yeah no—I don't understand, Dream Thing."

"You can call me Nathan."

"Okay Nathan."

I walk towards the park's lake, led by my curiosity. I want to know what the water looks like. I was still too afraid to look closely at his body—or mine—and it is getting harder not to stare. The water seems like a safe place to get acquainted with my new microscope and X-ray vision. I look up and notice that the sky above me is a swirling a velvet black and blue. There are tiny moments of neon pink and purple, but it's neither day nor night. There are what might constitute as stars blinking in above. Nathan follows me to the lake.

"Nathan, why am I here?"

"Memory is funny isn't it?" He grins. "And it doesn't get easier when you're distant from your physical body—you probably won't remember the details of this conversation—if you recall this conversation at all. Yet, that's still a good question to ask though. Why did you want to come here?"

"I don't know, I think I came here to find something, but I can't remember what it is anymore. Why do most people come here?" I ask.

"That all depends if they're still tethered to their bodies or not. The recently deceased come here to process their life, and try to shed their heavy-ego energies, along with any other low energies, before ascension. The physically-bound—well there are lots of reasons—but hopefully the bodied are accessing the Subtle Realm for their own spiritual growth, or mentorship."

My feet stand at the edge of the Earth's crust where the water meets the land. I crouch down to see the water with my new eyes, and I accidentally catch a quick glimpse of my own reflection. Thankfully, I am spared from any existential crisis as it is still very much my own face as I know it—just now with a bluish-grey tint. It might even be a bit translucent. However, I have a sneaking suspicion that if I want to, I can dive into the sum of my parts: of which I absolutely do not want to.

The water is probably the most familiar component of this new world because it's already transparent on the Physical Plane. The only major difference is that I can see the hydrogen and the oxygen; the little mickey-mouse shaped compounds, dancing within the matrix as clear as day. There is also a golden light source of some sort. It's radiating from within the depths of the water.

"I love it here. It's so peaceful, and I don't have any pain in my back anymore…actually I don't feel anything in my body at all." I pat myself down, but there's not much of a physical sensation.

The only things I've felt, since being in this place, have been in terms of sight, sound, possibly smell, and emotion; but, the emotion is so tangible, that it might as well be a physical sensation.

I look up from the water and there's a man that I recognize standing in front of me, "I'm sorry, who are you again?"

"I'm an old friend," he smiles at me, "I'm glad you've had a positive experience here, but that's probably enough for now."

"But wait, how do I get back?" I ask.

"I'll be around for a little while longer. I can help you return." his hands reach forward and gently push my shoulders back.

I fall back.

Backwards I softly tumble,

—falling through an indigo veil.

Backwards I fell.

I floated down into my body.

Back and down, down and back—into sleep.

Tasha relaxed back into her dream.

14

THE CHECK UP

I jerked awake with a sensation of falling. My awareness extended to the mattress underneath me, and the support it provided to my flesh, muscle, and bone. I remembered not to move and laid there in the dark, inert, with my eyes closed. I hoped that the recorder was recording. I spoke into the darkness, "In the car—again, but taken to a new world this time, a violet veil separates the physical and subtle world...everything is visible. Microscope-eyes. Intended Earth. Colorful bodies of light. No pain—Mom is safe...and Nathan."

I sat up, and rubbed my eyes. That was an intense dream, yet it didn't feel like a dream. It felt so...tangible.

My head ached. *Where was Yumi?*

"Yumi? Yumi Girl?"

I moseyed out of my bedroom and across the hall to a half-bathroom —where Yumi likes to hide when it storms—but she wasn't there. I walked back into my bedroom to check my bathroom and the closet— no luck there either.

"Yumi?"

I went back out into the hall and turned to quickly scan the living room, but I saw no sign of her. A spurt of worry rushed me past the kitchen, to the front door. That's where I found her. She was huddled in the corner of the foyer—sulking. Her large ears, normally fully erected satellites, were now flat against her head. Her eyes were steady averted to the floor.

"What's wrong girl?" I crouched down to console her.

Knock Knock Knock

My heart skipped a beat. I looked through the peep-hole. It was Bryan. He was standing about four feet from the door, but staring directly at the other end of the peep-hole's lens, as if he could see me standing there behind it. I quickly undid the deadbolt, and opened the door.

Bryan rushed in, his clothes soaked from the rain.

"Hey, I've been calling you all night. Are you all right—Why wouldn't you answer?" He was breathing hard. "I couldn't get ahold of Jesmitha either, so I felt like I needed to stop by...considering last time. I didn't know if..." He looked around the apartment. "Anyway, I just wanted to check up on you as promised—Jesus, what's that smell?"

"Sorry, I just woke up, and I couldn't find—oh no..." I smelled it, just as Bryan did, and walked back towards the living room.

Sure enough there was a steaming pile of dog poo on my silver shag rug. It was a mere two inches away from being on the hardwoods, which could have been easily been cleaned up. But no, there it sat, marinating in the fibers: brown play-doo mingled in the shag for eternity.

"I guess I need a new rug."

Bryan pointed to the fridge. "There's also a puddle—never mind—make that a small lake, of pee over here too. Tasha is she okay? Are you okay? Did you forget to take her out or something?"

It was as if Yumi had been comprehending our entire conversation, word for word, and that she knew that this was the optimal moment to punish me for my misdeeds. As Bryan's last words left his lips, she sauntered over to her empty food bowl. Yumi picked it up and shook it back and forth vigorously, and let the momentum take it spiraling through the air. It landed between our feet. Bryan looked down at the bowl, and then back at me.

"Don't start, please," I said, bending over and picking up the stainless steel bowl.

"Look, I said I would stop by in a week, it's been a week." He took the bowl from my hands and filled it with water. "And I need *you* to take a test—before you say anything, I'm not going to fight with you Tasha. You can pee, or be set free." He gestured with a free hand in the air like he was releasing a dove.

"We're rhyming now? Also you said check in—like as in a phone call—not stop in—like in my apartment," I said, to his back as he placed down the bowl for Yumi.

She sniffed and kissed his face in appreciation for the water service, consequently twisting the knife in.

"And what do you mean by, 'set free,' exactly?"

"I mean we can go our separate ways…in business. I need my staff to be clean, especially my management, Natasha. I can't have employees overdosing in the bathrooms, or in your case, on stairways," Bryan said.

"For the last time, it was a mistake!" I said, with the last bit of patience ringing out of my voice.

"Well, if it was just, *a momentary lapse in reason,* as you like to say, then you shouldn't have any problem pissing in this cup," he jingled it only inches from my face. The cup had twelve colorful assays built in into it.

After a considerable moment of silence, and an intentional glaring into his soul, I snatched the cup out of his hand. "Fine, I'll pee in the damned cup, but that means you get to clean up Yumi's shit and piss. One demeaning act for another…if you would be *so* kind." I ran into my bathroom before he could respond.

That man's nerve. He barged in my house at what—nine p.m.? What if I had company over? *Unbelievable.* I had the right to be mad. I should be furious. *Right?* Yet, I couldn't find those emotions anywhere. I was barely even annoyed, if I was being honest. The only thing I felt was a little static electricity of excitement from his presence, and any of the irritation I expressed to him was all theatrics.

After I filled up the little white cup, I placed the cap on it, and cleaned off any piddle-splashes from the sides. Then I took a second to add a tiny bit of concealer, mascara, and lip balm; but nothing overtly obvious, nothing that would look like actual effort. I applied deodorant, and sprayed some purple body spray I'd had forever. I met him in the kitchen, with the drug-test kit in hand. Bryan was sitting at the kitchen bar, patiently waiting for me. He had cared to Yumi and had all of the mess cleaned up. She was napping under his feet, her body expanding in peaceful intervals. I placed the warm little cup on top of the counter, and leaned against the bar, directly beside Bryan.

We watched the results form slowly together. We looked like a couple hoping to conceive, only, we were exes, watching for lines to *not* show up. In hopes to prove that I'm *not* a drug addict—just as romantic.

"Hey, would you look at that…you are clean," Bryan said.

"Your flirting skills need work," I said.

"How about, you look beautiful and I'm proud of you." He smiled.

"Umm, how about, I can come back to work now, and you'll pay me double for doubting me," I moved in between his legs, with one hand on each knee, and batted my lashes.

"Well, now that you mention it, Jes and I are planning…a sort of… welcome back party, on Sunday, before we start the Fall Fest concert. Only if you're up for it. Jes has been working on it for a couple days now. She's pretty excited about surprising you, but I wanted to make sure you wanted to be there—so don't tell her I said anything."

"You and Jes, right," I got up, walked around the bar to grab my water bottle out of the fridge.

"You can still take this weekend off to regroup, but I thought Sunday would be a good transition back into the work environment, before the following Halloween weekend. If it's too soon let me know?"

"It's definitely not too soon, like I said, I never had a drug problem. I don't know how many times I will have to repeat myself before everyone accepts that as a fact. It was an accident, and a *really* bad night, all *rolled* into one—no pun intended."

"Okay," he said thoughtfully, "good, because I need you around— and we definitely need you to work Halloween weekend."

I rolled my eyes. "Ugh Halloween—you know, on second thought, I think I'm going to be sick that weekend."

"Yeah right, nice try." Bryan said.

"No, yeah actually…I feel a craving for the bath-salt-drug coming on…what do they call it again? Flacka! Yeah that's it. Yep, sorry I can't make it in to Halloween on account of my bath-salt addiction." I teased. "You don't want me streaking and attacking our patrons." I grinned.

"That's not funny." Bryan got up from the barstool and walked over to me. "This is going to be our biggest halloween weekend since we opened, especially since we weren't fully open last year, with the renovations—and everything."

"I know, I just like to hear you tell me how much you need me," I whispered.

Bryan leaned in for a kiss. I let his lips press against mine. We shared a breath, in that intimate and familiar space, but just for a moment.

I interrupted our trajectory with a sobering request. "Do you think you could take Yumi for a couple nights?" I took a sip of my water. "I'm doing a sleep therapy thing that Jes's mom suggested."

Bryan drew in a deep sigh. He rested his forehead against mine. "Sure Tasha, I love keeping Yumi. But sleep therapy...is this for real?" his eyes studied mine.

"Yes, Bry-an," I grabbed at his ribs beneath his olive green thermal shirt. His abs contracted under my hands, and he jumped back. Bryan hated little less, than to be tickled, which naturally meant that it was an irresistible past-time of mine. Plus, it worked like magic as a deflection device, anytime that I didn't want to broach a subject with him. A comfortable quiet hung in the air after our laughter trailed off into silence. We stood there holding one another, waiting for the other to bear the conscious of that night's decisions. I might have asked him to stay, in fact, I know I would have, but I wanted to be alone with my dreams.

Instead, I said, "I guess I should get back to bed, you know, so I can keep consistent hours for the therapy work."

"Right, I should let you get to that then." He released me. "Yumi! Come on girl, it's just you and me tonight." She sprung up like she had been waiting for that very moment all along. She circled Bryan, before following him out the door, trotting along without so much as a glance back at me. "Bye Tasha! Yumi say, *bye mommy*," he said, as the door slammed behind them.

"Bye!" I yelled after them.

I sat there for a moment wondering if Yumi was holding a grudge against me for sleeping through her dinner and afternoon walk—of course she was—or if telling Bryan to leave, was the right thing to do. We really made a perfect little family, the three of us. I imagined Bryan and I running Club Daze as husband and wife. Maybe one day we would open a few restaurants, or flip houses, we worked so well together. We communicated without words. More and more lately, I found myself trying to remember the real reason why I ended things between us. I felt like my independence was threatened, and I hated my boyfriend telling me what to do, *as my boss*. But, I think the breaking point, was that I couldn't stand watching him get hurt over and over again. Part of my job was to generate, and maintain, a high-profile clientele. That was impossible without fraternizing and flirting. If I did my job well, then my clients would come in to see me, just as much as they would anything else.

Yumi's leash and food!

I ran to the door, and sped down the flights of stairs, but it was no use. They were already gone.

When I finally crawled back in bed, it was past eleven, but I was wide awake from my extensive mid-day nap. I decided to have a glass of wine, and take a few Tylenol PM, so I could sleep through the night. I waited patiently for sleep to come, watching my faithful red dots act out their show. They really seemed to have a personality of their own. They masqueraded across their dark stage, and I appreciated their creativity. Every now and then, new colors like blue or green, would peek into the production for a moment. Tonight, instead of focusing on the rising and falling of my ribcage, when I counted my breaths, I narrowed my focus on the tip of my nose; specifically, the way it felt when the air was drawn in, and pushed back out. A trick I learned from the Hypnotist. It took a bit more concentration, but it helped me stay more aware, yet remain fully relaxed, so I could follow my faithful dream-pixels into their full masterpiece.

15

DANCING CROCS

Three monstrous playing cards marched by, all Kings of different suits. They towered over the buildings as they paraded down the street. Tasha sat on a curb in front of her old apartment at Dogwood Park. She watched the show, fully entertained. She enjoyed the lively music. Two Jesters, juggling, followed behind their two-dimensional Royalty; both dressed in matching motleys, that only differed in color. The first Jester's outfit was green and blue. It was stitched together with mismatched fabric. The second one donned a red and orange version. The leading Jester juggled golden chalices, and the other—wands of fire. They both smiled at Tasha as they passed her. Yet, on closer inspection, the last Joker's smile was actually sewn onto his face, a grin forced upon him, and his eyes spoke of a darker truth.

Behind the Jesters, danced a pair of pink Crocodiles. They stood upright on their stubby hind-legs, and carried sparklers and bottles of liquor in their forelimbs. The sparklers and bottles pulsed above their heads to the beat. After the parade ended, a long and pearlescent limousine slid up to the curb. The Driver stopped the car right in front of Tasha, and she stood up to greet him.

He seemed very happy to see her, "Enjoying your *dream* Natasha?"

"*Am I dreaming?*" I looked down at my hands.

There they were, my old faithfuls. The world blinked. When it came back, I was in the limo. I sat in the passengers seat. I was sitting beside Nathan—not behind him. He was easy to look at, and appeared to be a few years younger than me. His symmetrical face had soft features, but it wasn't round. He had a smooth jawline, void of any stubble. He reminded me of the type of men whose images were only captured in sepia-toned photographs. The attraction towards him caused a surprising shift in my temperament.

"Can we go back again?" I asked shyly.

"To where do you refer?" He asked, with an air of coyness.

"I want to go to the Subtle Realm again."

Nathan's eyes narrowed. He looked at me, possibly considering my ask, but maybe contemplating me as a whole.

I got the feeling that Nathan was about to decline my request, when the entire cabin of our vehicle began to glow a brilliant ultraviolet.

THE SUBTLE REALM

We pass through the electric indigo curtain. Once the mist fully clears, I'm disappointed when I realize that we are still in the park.

"Isn't there another place we can go?"

"We can *go* anywhere. This is where we *are*."

My blue hand finds my chin. I try to think of my personal heaven, "Lets go to a place with champagne rivers, where dogs can talk, or where money grows on trees."

Nathan laughs. "You must not remember, or you simply don't understand, what this place actually is."

I shrug at him.

"This realm is just as varied and magical as the Physical Plane, but it isn't a mirage for entertainment. There are no candy-lands here—*unless of course*…you were to create them yourself." Nathan stops speaking *to me*, and talks to himself, as if he is swept away by a train of thought. "But then that would take an incredible amount of energy: in memory, visualization, *and* will power." He's counting on his blue hands, and isn't even looking at me anymore. "You would be better off creating that world on Earth, with the gross physical elements—

"I hate when you do that…"

"Sorry." He shakes his head as if to clear the clutter.

"Like really hate it."

Nathan smirks. "What I mean is, even though our conscious matter is existing in an alternate reality—this is a metaphysical place. It's real, its just a lot lighter in density than you are used to, and I can't emphasize the word *a lot* enough here. So while we're not bound to *all* of the laws of Earth's Physics, a lot of them still exist in some form in this realm as well."

I look around at the surrounding terrain. It was, more or less, the same. There are some differences though, and some new—*things* moving about in the distance. The creatures loitered around the structures. They are still too far away, and blurry, to recognize. What's stranger, is how they never seem to approach us. It's like we are invisible to them.

"I want to know more about this place. You said I would forget you, and our conversation, but I remember everything—I mean—I *think* I remember." I look at my hand. I made it grow large and shrink back to size, just by thinking it to be so. "It's difficult to be sure because, you don't know, what you don't know."

"What else do you remember?" he asked.

"I know that I forgot that we came here for my mom last time, and you failed to remind me on purpose."

Nathan frowns and studies me, "You have a natural talent for navigating these waters for sure—to say the least."

"Is this Heaven?"

"No, not Heaven, although I can easily see why one might think it is —especially at first. Souls come here with such heightened desire for a break from the aching, ever-wanting, and needy physical body. There is certainly a more direct access to Universal Knowledge here, but Heaven, or what I think you are referring to as Heaven, is in another, *much higher* realm."

"I'm sorry but your princess is in another castle," I say in a strange cartoon voice. I laugh at my own joke.

Nathan stares at me.

"Its a Mario joke, you know the little Italian man…and his pal Luigi?"

"I'm afraid not."

"Really? He loves mushrooms, and makes his cash from bricks— which actually makes him sound like The Godfather—but it's completely different."

Nathan stares.

"Never mind, it's not important. So if this isn't Heaven, then why was Mom here—and where is she now?"

"Your mom spent considerable time watching over you as a Spirit Guide in the Spiritual Realm with me and a few of your other guides, but now she's continuing on with her path of enlightenment. She's ascending, and her connection is a little distant for now. There might be a few times, where she will be able to communicate again before she fully transitions into the Celestial Realms."

"And then what happens?"

"I can't say. I'm no Angel. I've never been beyond the Transitional and Spiritual Realms. I'm not certain, and I wouldn't want to guess at something like that." Nathan reads the confusion on my face. "The Transitional and Spiritual Realms are higher planes, between here and the Celestial. The Angels inhabit the Celestial Realms…mostly."

"Where is *your* body?"

Nathan blinks at me.

"You don't have one do you?" I gasp, "you're dead—sorry, that's rude—is that rude?"

"It's really okay. I've had a few lifetimes to come to terms with being body-less, but I'm no more *less alive* than you are. I chose to become a guide. and stay for a while longer in the in-between. It's a choice that not all are honored with."

"You're a Spirit Guide…whose guide *are you*?" I ask, immediately point to myself, and my eyebrows raise in surprise by the obvious answer.

Nathan nods.

"So if there are Spirits here, does that mean that there are Demons here too?"

"You have a lot of questions," he says.

"That should make you happy, since you love to teach so much, and besides I imagine most people have a lot of questions."

Nathan's blue eyebrows raise, "Most *people* aren't able to keep their physical bodies asleep this long, nor are they able to maintain so much clarity, nor can they access this plane with such ease as you do." Nathan pauses. "I have to admit, it makes speaking with you innately pleasant although strikingly curious. Typically my communication is preformed more as a duty—a responsibility. I pass on knowledge and I guide where I am needed. But it's never easy like this. I've only ever heard of conversations like ours, between Spirit Guides and highly skilled souls; souls trained in deep meditation techniques: such as the Buddhist Monks, or natural mediums."

A low rumble shakes in the background.

"Do you hear that?" I ask.

"I don't hear anything."

"So no Demons here?" I ask, now creeped out by the sounds that only I hear. The noises sound like someone took a metal pole and dragged it over a storm drain.

"Demons are not Spirits, they're a class of Angel. My experience has been that they're more concerned with visits to the Physical and Spiritual Realm, not the Subtle Realm, but I never say never."

I relax. "Okay so nothing to be worried about then," I pick up a rock to play with my superzoom eyesight, zooming inside the tiny universes and back out again to my current life-size one. I feel like I'm getting a handle on this place's quirks.

"I didn't say that. There are plenty things to be worried about here, outside of my protection: lost souls, Shades, Astral Corpses, and worse, that roam about in the Subtle Realm, but we need not go into that. It's best not to speak of them, lest we attract them to us."

I look up at him, "Can I die in here?"

"No, you can only die in the Subtle Realm, if your body dies on the Physical Plane...but trust me when I say: there are entities in here that can, and will, make you wish you were dead, if you give them the opportunity to influence you."

The rumble is louder now. But it can no longer be classified as a rumble. Now it's a steady elongated beeping. It's distracting me from what Nathan is saying. I throw the rock in my hand as far as I can. It lightly floats only a few inches away, before gently landing on the ground. It's like I threw a dryer sheet, instead of a stone.

"You really can't hear that...ringing?" I put both hands over my ears, but it does nothing to dampen the sound. The noise had evolved into a high-pitched ring, growing louder and sharper, by the moment.

The lights around Nathans head blink in a yellow-orange color, before returning to their standard mix.

"I'm sorry, I'm afraid I do not. It's possible that if it's coming from the Physical Plane, that I won't always be able to perceive it. It depends on the frequency, the source, the intention, and a few other variables—"

"Wait, did you say, Astral Corpses?"

A devious look washes over Nathan's face. "Ah...yes you did. Let me ask you, have you ever had a dream that you were running, but you couldn't move?"

"Yes, I think everyone has, I'm usually being chased by something," I say looking at him, "do I even want to know?"

Nathan folds his hands, "I'd want to know if I were you, it's very interesting."

"Okay?"

"They happen you accidentally fall into the lowest subdivision of the Subtle Realm. In the space where the densest layer of this realm, overlaps the lightest layer of the Physical Realm. This space is what some nightmares are literally made of."

Nathan snickers at a joke that only he gets.

"It's where all of the Astral Corpses lay, decaying—rotting Astral bodies."

I stare at him with heavy eyelids. I'm not sure what's more annoying right now, Nathan's explanations, or this internal ringing.

Nathan continues, "When you're stuck running in place in a dream, it's really because your consciousness is stuck in the dead-ego matter." His chin turns down, and he grins from ear to ear.

"Oh my God, ew, that's horrifying. There's no way that's true." I cover my mouth.

"You're right I'm kidding—only I'm not."

He laughs hysterically, and looks proud of his execution.

"It's in the pits of the Subtle Realm, which are perpendicular to the dream veil. So if you pass through the gate, and sink, you'll run into the ego-sludge right below. Do you want to go see it?"

"Absolutely not." I put my hand up.

"Come on, it's mostly harmless, and it's not living any more. It's just low-energy matter shedded from past souls—awaiting its time to be recycled into new personalities. It's innocuous in its undisturbed form —unless of course—someone tries to perform black magic on it..." Nathan's eyes slid to the left in thought.

"I'm good, but thank you for the nightmare."

"It's fascinating really, the cycle here is similar to how a decaying physical body returns to the soil on Earth to be reborn into nutrients that will eventually build and nourish plants and embryos; your Astral Corpse will also return to the core of this realm. There it breaks down into basic Astral elemental forms, so it can be recycled into a new soul's ego—is this bothering you?"

My hands are pressing into either side of my head again; not because of Nathan's nasty obsession with Astral Corpses, but because of the sound—that only I could hear—was now so intensely resounding in my skull that it is hard to focus on *anything* else.

"Yes, Nathan it's incredibly disturbing, but I still have this piercing sound in my ears. I can't concentrate. It's like the noise is literally coming from inside my head!" I crouch down on the grass.

Nathan walks toward me, "Oh, I see now—

16

ROCK THE BOAT

That wretched sound penetrated through every layer of existence, like a needle pulling through fabric; my consciousness—the floundering piece of thread. The sound was coming from my phone. It was ringing incessantly right beside my ear. I opened my eyes and shut them immediately, the light outside was scoring. I must have overslept. My head was throbbing and my throat was burning raw. I tried to clear my throat, and started coughing. I stood up to go get a glass of water from the kitchen, but my field of vision quickly recoiled into a small circle before going completely black. I fell back, luckily against my bed.

I laid there, not moving, conscious of my surroundings but weak and blind. There was not much else I could do but wait it out, and so I did. I heard my phone ring a few more times, but I couldn't move to reach it. After a few minutes, my sight returned to me. I remained still, too afraid to spook it away again. Slowly I sat up, carefully, using my arms to support my weight.

Okay, sitting up is good, sitting is living.

Next up, would be standing. I pushed off from the side of the bed and rose to a vertical position as slowly as I could. Thankfully the lights stayed on upstairs. I felt otherwise okay, if you didn't consider the pounding in my head threatening to pulverize my skull into powdered chalk; which actually might have been merciful at this point. I gingerly made my way to the kitchen. The sun was painfully gleaming and reflecting off of all of my stainless steel appliances: the fridge, the oven, the microwave, the toaster—punishing me further. I downed about a liter of water and swallowed two ibuprofen.

On the way back to my bedroom, a picturesque bowl of fruit that sat on my island, mostly for looks, became prey to a sudden bout of voracious hunger. I inhaled a banana, bit an apple for the hell of it, and ravished a clementine. While gorging on the innards of that little orange cutie, with its pulp splattered on my cheeks, my eyes were instinctually drawn upwards. Viewing the packages from under my brow, I spotted a bag of everything bagels, popcorn, and tortilla chips huddled together on the counter. They were nestled comfortably in the corner between the fridge and the stove. I launched forward, ripped into the bag of bagels, and ate two. Finally satiated, I burped, and returned to my den. My phone was ringing again, but this time I was able to answer it.

"Hello?" I answered.

"Tasha? What the fuck is wrong with you! We've been trying to—"

"What? Jes, slow down what are you talking about…" I sat down on my bed and rubbed my forehead, it was beginning to ache again.

"Are you high, like are you on drugs *right now*, where tha' hell have you been?"

"No Jes, I'm actually doing really well *right now*, but I guess you wouldn't know that, since I haven't heard from you since the cafe."

"You're doing well? Thats a whole laugh! YEAH, you're doing so great,'Sha. So tell me, how was your therapy session on Friday with Malinda, huh? Tell me about it?"

"Oh shit, that *was* today! I overslept Jes, I'm so sorry, I know your mom set that up for me. I get why you're pissed—mostly. I still think you are overreacting a bit. I mean, you could have at least checked in once? I don't need a baby sitter, but it's a little hypocritical to be this upset don't you think?"

Jesmitha sat silent.

"Jes?...Hello?"

"What day do you think it is Tasha?" Jes asked.

"Friday…it's Friday."

"No, Tasha, today is Sunday and it's after 3pm."

"What, how—

"Yeah, so we're all here at Daze now, just waiting on you! We've been trying to get ahold of you all weekend. I've been telling Bryan to take down the *Welcome Back* sign for hours. Girl, you need to get help." The tiny click of Jesmitha hanging up felt like a gunshot to the chest.

Could it really be Sunday? How could Tylenol PM be that strong? It couldn't be. I looked at my phone, it corroborated Jes's story, it also said that I had twenty-two notifications: eighteen missed calls, two unread messages, and two voicemails.

Jesmitha DAZEGIRL: 8 missed calls and 2 unread messages.

Malinda Brown: 3 missed calls and 1 Voicemail.

Bryan <3: 5 missed calls and 2 Voicemails.

Unknown: 2 missed calls.

I took a deep breath, and then one more to stall, before hitting play:

Call From, Bryan less than three, on Friday at October 22, at 10:11 a.m.: "Hey, I ran out of there without her food or leash last night. I have a little in a ziplock from the last time I watched her. I can pick up some more before I head into Daze tonight, I just need to know what brand you use. Also, did you want me to keep her for the whole weekend? I don't mind, but I just need to know. See you Sunday!"

Call From, Malinda Brown, on Friday October 22, at 12:35 p.m.: "Hi Tasha, I think maybe you forgot about our session today. I'm at your place, but the lights are off, and you and Yumi appear to be gone. Anyway, please call me back to reschedule. I hope all is well."

Text Message Jesmitha, Saturday October 23 at 11:12 a.m.: "Hey, Tash. Mom said you bailed on a meeting with PhD Brown? What happened there? Oh and she told me not to tell you that I know you missed a meeting. Text me back!"

Call From, Bryan less than three, on Saturday October 23 at 12:21 p.m.: "Jes told me that you're not showing up to your therapy meetings, and has no idea about the sleep therapy thing that you were talking about. So obviously I'm worried. I stopped by and no-one answered the door. The door is locked, and it doesn't look like your home. Are you still planning on coming tomorrow? If I don't hear from you, I'll be calling the police. So this is serious Tasha. Please let me know you're alive."

Text Message From Jesmitha, Sunday October 24 at 10:35 a.m.: "yeah, so if you're not already dead, I'm going to kill you."

POUND POUND POUND

I jumped, and my phone flew far from my hands. It tumbled onto my hardwood floors with a series of hard thuds.

Oh my God, the police—blood fled from my face to save my heart.

I was paralyzed, once again held captive on my bed, but this time with embarrassment—not from any physical ailment.

POUND POUND POUND

There was nothing I could do but face the music. I left my room, pausing at the doorway for just a moment, before I forced myself to move. I crept through the apartment, and slowly approached the front door. I reached for the knob like it was a loaded gun, and after a deep breath I turned and pulled it towards me. When the door opened, there were no flashing lights, no sirens, and no men in uniform. The police and the padded wagon that were ready to whisk me away, existed solely in my mind. In their places however, was Bryan. His eyes locked with mine and I felt something stir in my heart, that I've never felt from him: I felt threatened. He looked me up and down before pushing past me, brushing my shoulder, and almost knocking me off balance.

"You look like hell, when is the last time you've eaten anything— actually don't tell me, I don't want to know because I officially don't care."

"If you don't care, then why are you here." *Not the right move.*

Bryan looked at me like I stabbed him in the heart and was standing over his body laughing. "You know I put a lot of money into the party because of you, we looked like real idiots Tasha! I was *proud of you*, and for what? For not being a drug addict?! For being a functional adult? It's my fault, for setting the bar so fucking low."

He looked around my apartment, just like he did last time he had barged in. It was like he was searching for something, but he didn't know what he was looking for, and it set me off.

"What are you looking for!" I stepped inches in front of him, and waved my hands in his face.

"It doesn't matter—don't come in this week—or ever."

My mouth hung open in shock.

Bryan walked towards me, and for a moment, I thought maybe he had realized he had taken things too far, and that he was about to retract his words, but no, he was just heading for the door.

"Wait, Bryan don't leave—where are you going?"

"To get *your* dog out of the car. Her name is Yumi, remember her?" He said, his pupils were needle-prick points, "Tell me why I feel like it's a mistake to leave her here? We're going out of town for few days. If you can't handle the responsibility let me know, and I'll gladly come pick her up for good," he said, before storming out of my apartment.

His stomps carried two flights of stairs down, until they faded to what resembled regular steps. He's never been this angry, or this careless with me. Things have never felt this final. There was no telling what he believed I was doing for three days, and I was hard pressed to explain otherwise. I was afraid anything I'd say would only make it worse. He returned quickly, barely stepping in the door to return Yumi, before he was out of sight again. I heard his tires screeching all the way down the road.

He can't fire me before Halloween weekend, he's just heated right now. That has to be it, he'll calm down.

I sat down on the floor, buried my face into Yumi's fur, and wept. She panted harshly. Her coat smelled like lavender, which of course meant that Bryan must have had her groomed as a surprised for me. I cried harder.

"I'm so sorry Yumi, I love you my sweet girl."

I was so close to getting everything back to normal—no not back to normal—better than normal. I was really starting to see a glimmer of light at the end of the tunnel, and now I had just lost everything. They had all given up on me. Did he say, *we're* going out of town: as in him and Jes, going together—alone? The thought of him and Jesmitha leaving out of town for a few days, near the anniversary of their All-Hallows-Eve-Hookup, ripped at my heart.

I can't deal with this right now.

"I can't, I can't breathe," I sobbed. Each breath escaped my control.

I found my way to a water bottle in the fridge. In the process, I saw both melatonin and Tylenol PM sitting on the counter. *Sleep.* I wanted, *needed,* to be anywhere but here. If I could only escape this moment for just a little while. *Nathan,* I needed him. He was the only person I had and I didn't care if he was real or not. He was helping me.

I knew I couldn't sleep again without some type of sleeping aid, but I didn't want to accidentally stay in too long. I needed a safeguard of sorts. I decided I would only take the natural melatonin, not the Tylenol PM, and that I would also set an alarm clock—sound seemed to bring me back before. I looked at the fruit-basket crime scene from earlier. I also should force myself to eat a real meal before bedtime too, so that my body wouldn't be so weak. I set up a little emergency kit, and placed it on the nightstand for in the morning...just in case. With everything in place, I climbed back in bed, and I threw back a couple of melatonin with the water. I let them flow gently down the stream—merrily, merrily, merrily...

17

THE SUBTLE REALM

"Nathan I missed you." I fling my arms around him. A heavy sense of peace penetrates the core of my being. "I couldn't get back here soon enough."

"You seem upset," Nathan says.

But I'm not sure if I *hear* his words, or if I *feel* them.

I pull back to look at him. "No, I'm fine, really, let's go to the Pyramids today, or the Mayan Ruins—oh, actually, can we breathe underwater here?"

Nathan stares at me like he was scanning a piece of text.

"What are you looking at?" I ask.

"There's no point in hiding your feelings from me, I can see your emotional-vibrations, almost as clearly as I understand your spoken language."

"Huh?"

"I can see your energy field, and I can read the different colors in your emotional and Astral layers; I can even read your mental energy field most of the time." Nathan traces his hands half way down my body, starting from my head. "I know you're upset, because of the colors emitting from you—and your root chakra's vortices are barely spinning."

"You can see all of that…right now?"

"Sure, every emotion and thought you engage with, carry with it, a specific energy. The wavelengths produce these light according—

"Is that what all of these colors are around your head and body?" I run my hand through them but they don't part or scatter.

The colors stay contained within their respective layer, for the most part. The layers stack atop of one another and overlap, mingling a bit, before they extend out further into differentiation.

"They're beautiful, why aren't some of these colors on Earth?"

Nathan gently pushes my hands away. "The colors you've never seen before, are produced by thoughts—the highest frequencies of all. But they're ever-present, even on the Physical Plane."

"No, I've never seen anything like this on Earth—I would remember."

There are no words in the English language to adequately describe the new colors. I guess that's why people resort to the phrase, 'you have to see it, to believe it,' when their spoken language fails them. All I could do is liken the new colors to a bioluminescence—a color emitting its own light; and also a tone, that brings an emotion along with it, a feeling strong enough to overshadow the or visual aspect completely.

"When you're in the Subtle Realm you're no longer under your brain's governor—so to speak. Your field of perception is wider here, so you can perceive the *entire* spectrum," Nathan looks upwards pensively, "at least the *entire* color spectrum in terms of the Earth, Astral, and Spiritual Realms...so really, as much as we can perceive on *these* realms," his hand finds his chin, "but I wonder if the angels can see more—you know, I bet they—"

I snap my fingers, "Bring it back, Steven Hawking."

He laughs. "Sorry."

"What I'm trying to say, is that all of the colors do exist on Earth," Nathan pauses, holds both hands in front of him as he tilts his head. "How do I say this...there is a very large part of the brain, dedicated solely to *restricting* vast amounts of sensory input, sort of like a gauge."

"So when they say we only use ten percent of our brain..."

"Your intuition already tells you that's incorrect. There *is* a lot of insulation, for lack of a better term. The human brain works diligently, around the clock, to protect its user from a daily deluge of information," He gestures an explosion, with both of his hands on either side of his head.

I nod.

"Thus, all of the 'new' colors are invisible to you: in the same way you can't hear a dog whistle because the frequency is too high for you—"

"—but a dogs brain can," I say, taking it all in.

"Right. It's *all perception*."

"This is kinda like the brain in the box theory," I pause, "only my brains the box, and my conscious is the brain, in this scenario."

I began to play in his field of color again, although I can't *feel* any physical sensations on my hand, the different colors of light leave unique impressions on me emotionally. I can feel the bluish colors, and experience the reds. Some them even produce their own subtle smell.

"This place is wild."

Nathan bats my hands away again. "I've never thought of it that way, but I'm not sure I like your analogy. You should just imagine a higher plane that is hinged its foundation on largely non perceivable frequencies and densities. This is an integral part of how the Subtle Realm is able to exist in tandem with the physical and not cause too much friction."

"So the Subtle Realm has been here the whole time. That means that the Physical Plane is right here as we speak."

I twirl around and imagine bumping into people as they pass by, and freaking them out.

"Can we touch people?" I grin.

"No—yes, you shouldn't…but technically—you could. It would be *incredibly* difficult and complicated for you to do so. You'd have to possess a powerful amount of will or passion, and even then, you would only be successful manipulating the pure elements with synergistic energies: like electricity, water, plants, minerals, or even pendulums."

"This is so fun, I miss learning. I feel like a child again."

"I know," he says, looking me over smiling.

"That's right, you can read me. Have you been reading me this whole time—my whole life?"

"Well yes, when permitted, the longer you do this sort of work the better you get at it. It's a science and an art, as is everything, but I can teach you too."

"Really? I would love that…but first, I want to learn how to spook people."

Nathan shakes his head.

We walk through the park and study all of the minerals and flora. He points out the Divine Love light within all of their auras, which exists within all of the elements.

"I didn't realize there was Love in rocks, or that they were even alive; although, it does explain a lot with all the crystal fanatics out there," I study a stone in my hand, noticing a glowing pink hue coming from inside it.

Nathan takes the stone from me and pulls it apart with little effort; the beautiful Rose Quartz now clearly exposed. Then he takes half of the quartz and compresses it into the shape of a heart. He hands it back to me.

If I still had blood and flesh, then my cheeks would match the pink crystal heart. "I wish I could take this back with me."

We walk for what seems like for miles, but I never get tired, or hungry, my back never aches, and I never get bored. At one point, Nathan shows me his ability to manifest Physical Realm objects from memory. He projects a simple bench for us to sit on, using the elements around us, existing in the environment. Some of the materials he uses look familiar to what I would see on Earth, but the majority of them are new: elements that are specific to the Astral Plane. Nathan wills them all together by the vibration of thought. Together we sit on his will-chair, talking about life and purpose.

"I don't think I want to go back to the Physical Plane for a while, it is so much more peaceful here—euphoric even. How long can I stay?"

"You must be careful not to idealize this place. Many have mistakenly come here with the idea of a Nirvana, but that is not so. Please, take it from me, you'll begin to miss your body." Nathan wrings his hands. "You'll miss the small things in life: like feeling the wind on your face, or sitting under an Oak tree's cool shade—in refuge from the scorching heat—or sex. Sometimes I even miss pain. This is not a place of pure bliss, this is a place of knowledge, and teaching, and duty; but most of all, this is a place of refinement and transformation. For the recently deceased, this is just another womb, or cocoon, before the next phase."

"It doesn't seem that bad to me though."

I look at the sparkling water in front of us: it's an invitation into serenity, with its deep navy-blue ripples, that spread over the etherial golden light within.

"What if I prefer it here, what if I didn't want to go back—what if I wanted to stay here with you?"

"No Natasha, I think you have gotten the wrong impression, and it's my fault. Right now, I have you protected, you're in somewhat of a projected bubble of imagination. But if I were to release the glamour… then I think you would have a very different idea of this place. I don't reside here naturally. After you return to your body, I return to the Spiritual Realm."

"Nathan you're scaring me, what is this place really like then?" I think of the things I've seen crawling in the distance, and although they're too far away to be anything more than silhouettes, their movements appear jerky and unnatural.

"It's a complicated realm that comes with a lot of responsibility—a vantage point that grants access to unlimited power over the Physical Realm—to whomever learns how to manipulate it. This is why its best that your understanding of it be a slow and natural one."

"Why can't we meet in the Spiritual Realm then?"

"You aren't permitted there yet, or I would surely take you." Nathan turns his body to face mine. He strokes my hand.

I softly pull my hands back and fold my arms. His touch makes me uncomfortable.

"Most people are not able to exist here as you do, so I know there is a higher purpose for you. I'm going to teach you as much as I can before I go."

"Before you go? What do you mean? Please don't go."

Nathan seems to be reading my energy again, and appears to be staring towards my crotch of all places. I put my hands over my lap, and cross my legs.

"I'm only here for a finite time, just as you are on the Physical Plane for a finite time." He looks sad, "I don't know exactly when my time will end here, but I do have a sense of it, just like most physical beings on Earth have an idea of their natural cycles coming to a close."

"The more you speak, the more this place just seems like it's some trippy-extension of the physical world. It's not the paradise that I thought it was." I contemplate the blue man in front of me. "Maybe I've lost my mind and you're not real at all."

"*The Physical Realm is an extension of the Subtle*, but yes. Especially in the lower subdivisions of this realm, you'll notice that there are a lot of similarities, which is to be expected as it has the same designer." Nathan takes in a deep breath, and places his right hand over my heart, "Natasha no-one ever leaves you, we are always together, at all times. I know it's a very hard concept to grasp—it's the one that took me the longest to understand too."

My chest tingles. "How much time do we have left together?"

"Time, like memory, is another figment of perception. Depending where you are on the Subtle Realm, one day here could be like ten days on earth. In the higher subdivisions, one day could be more closely perceived as a hundred earth days. Even further still, in the Celestial Realm one day can equal a thousand, and eventually time isn't linear at all. So I don't know how to answer that for you, because I travel between the Subtle and the Spiritual Planes." Nathan stands up from the bench and pulls me up from it as well.

"Where will you go after you leave?" I ask.

"I'll finally enter the Celestial Realms. I'm immensely curious to find out what it's like there." As the bench dematerializes back into multiple sources, he seems more energized. "While I am here though, I'm willing to teach you whatever you'd like to know. Especially if there is anything that you want to know about your life, your past lives, or any questions you may have about your moms passing. I can also help you uncover your gifts and talents, or reveal any inner blockages."

"I want to know all of it," I say, distracted in my attempt to make my own chair, at which I am failing miserably.

Nathan helps me with my sad chair, and I can't help but have images from the movie *Ghost*, pop into my mind—my very own Swayze behind me.

He teaches me how our thought-vibrations manipulate the minuscule particles of unfathomably light densities, and how they penetrate every single thing in the Subtle Realm, as well as on Earth. He explains the power of Astral Sight in detail, and how to read the seven main energy centers, or Chakras that I can see clearly with my Astral Sight The Chakras generate the first seven energy fields around our Astral bodies: the blue body, the Emotion Aura, the Mental Matrix, the Divine Love, the communication and manifestation center, our Intuitive Higher Self, and finally, our direct pathway to the Source.

"I want to address the damage to the vortices in your Root Chakra. They're being degraded by persistent negative thoughts," Nathan pauses, "why don't you feel safe?"

"I don't want to talk about it. Can you teach me how to fly next?"

"While I can't force you to face this—Free Will is a law here as well —the Creator is really big on that one." Nathan laughed to himself, "Although if you ask me, *Free Will* is piss-poor nomenclature, as it's incredibly expensive to most people—

"Did you ramble this much in your carnal life?"

Nathan frowns, "Your root chakra should be addressed soon, trust me."

"*Soon*—sounds good—so flying?" I flap my arms up and down with my hands tucked into my underarms.

Nathan sighs. "Flying, traveling, or projecting anything here in the Subtle Realm, is done through the power of thought coupled with the energy of intention, or will rather. It's helpful to speak where you want to go too, because sound waves are a part of another, more expansive discipline," he takes on that teaching voice that I am starting to despise, "just consider that the Universe was created by *one-word* or a, "uni-verse."

I stare at him unimpressed.

He sighs. "If you want to fly, then you must have a crystal clear image of where you want to go in your mind. You have to imagine yourself as if you are already there, and you have the energy available." A smile creeps up on his face. "Which comes from having unblocked, open, and balanced chakras Natasha, so it looks like we have come full circle."

Nathan mimics my chicken wing-flaps, and is visibly pleased with himself. He crosses his arms at his chest.

I cave, "I don't feel safe because my dad left us, my mom left me, and every day since then seems like an opportunity for more good things to escape from me too."

Nathan studies my field. "That's a start: truth has a very unique and powerful cleansing vibration. Here is another truth: none of those things: family, career, money, beauty, social-status, will ground you. They are only symbols—or conduits—that are supposed to help us find our way to that root energy *of being grounded*. Those things are helpful in the right environment. However, it's a dangerous mis-step when we confused those physical things, people included, for the very grounded energy itself."

The truth resonates within me. The profound beauty of the statement impresses on my spirit like a therapeutic massage—working out any deep rooted energy knots. I look down at my body. Something I was afraid to do since I first arrived here. I halfway expected to see blood and guts, or worse, an exposed vulva staring back at me. Yet, there is no such horror or embarrassment. There is only a discrete bluish-grey mold of my familiar body structure.

I also see, four of the seven, energy centers that Nathan just described. They're spinning mini-tornados that form along the center of my being. The first, and lowest center, is clearly generating the light for my blue body. The next center, or Chakra, is emitting the pretty colors that swirl against my blue-grey mold. The third Chakra is contributing to the patterns of a pulsing yellow light; and the last energy vortex that's visible from my perspective, is situated at my heart. Its center is a clear green light that radiates out into multiple sets of colorful clouds. These colors are different in texture from the emotional layer's, and there's a pink hue that hovers over them all. The colors from my heart seem to shift much slower than the emotional aura, if at all.

"I can only count four," I say, looking at his astral body.

"The blue body *is* the first layer, it's called the Etheric Template. I'm sure you can easily distinguish the colorful emotional aura from the yellow mental layer by now; you may even be able to perceive the astral layer, but I doubt you can already see the three outermost layers. Those generated by the fifth, sixth, and seventh chakras. It takes time for your astral eyes to adjust. Just as it does, whenever the light changes drastically in your environment."

I walk up to Nathan. My face is only a few inches from his. He backs away.

"I'm trying to see where the layers stop and start, they blend into each other—some indistinguishably—I don't think I can see the outer most energy fields." I say, still squinting.

"It will come when you're ready, don't rush it. And just so you know, the outermost layer is a couple feet out from your template. The seventh layer holds your past earth experiential energy, or your karma —I call it the DeJa-Vu energy. I'm afraid even I'm not that skilled at reading that layer, but I can count the past lives, they're clearly visible —like rings on a tree."

"You can tell me if I *had* a past life?"

Nathan looks at me for a moment. He seems to be considering the weight of the knowledge he possesses. "Do you want to know your natural gifts?"

"Oh come on—you know more than you say...tell me."

"It would be more beneficial to focus on the present for now."

"Why do I feel like you're lying...can Spirit Guides lie?"

"I didn't lie to you," Nathan looks down.

He looks sad, and I wonder if I am being naive in wanting to know such information with such nonchalance. "What is it?" I gasp, "Was I a murderer or something? Oh my God who did I kill—

"No, you didn't kill anyone." Nathan turns his back to me. "You were my wife in another life, your name was Bellany. We were in our early twenties when we parted. We were only married for three months."

I walk around to him.

"But I loved you all your life. Now you know."

The look on his face...I feel awful. This is how people must feel when I tell them how my mother died—and why I never did.

"I don't know what to say."

"It's best if we move on from this subject." Nathan creates a fire in his hand. "Did you know you can create almost anything you want to in the Astral field? You can project your childhood home, your favorite movie theatre, even an apple. It's not permanent of course, but as long as you focus your thoughts, and spend your energy on it, it will exist for you and those around you—just as real as anything else I suppose. Let's try something easy...like a playing card."

Nathan changes the fire into a playing card right in front of me, and holds it out. I don't take it.

"I'm sorry you had a shitty life, I hope your next one was better?"

"Right, too easy, let's try an apple. Food is tricky because of taste, you *can* experience the apple in your mind though if you remember the taste clear enough, the trick is to lead with smell...do you want to try?"

"You *did* have another life right, you didn't stay here for me?" I hang my head, praying he hasn't been stuck here as my glorified baby-sitter.

"I didn't have a bad life, but yes, I remained for you, or rather I waited here for Bellany—your soul's past personality. I died a sudden death, from a bullet that I never saw coming, nor did I feel much pain from. I wondered around the Subtle Realm for a while, because I had trouble fully accepting that I was dead, or that I would never return home to you." Nathan pauses to change the playing card to a green apple with a concerted effort. "But I had help from my own Spirit Guides, my grandfather, and an older brother who died two years prior in the same war. They helped me process my physical death, so I could begin the ascension process."

Nathan hands me the apple, and I bring it to my mouth. I look for permission to take a bite. He encourages me with a smile and a nod. It smells like a Granny Smith apple, and the skin feels smooth and waxy under my hand. I press my teeth into it, and the skin succumbs to the sharp pressure; the apple breaks off with a loud chomp. It's wet and juicy—but it tastes like my grandmother! It tastes like her perfume, and the smell of her house! I spit it out with disgust. "Gross."

The apple dematerializes and Nathan laughs. "I guess I should have warned you about memory associations."

"Yes, you should have." I scrap my tongue. "but you're trying to deflect, I want to know what happened, why didn't you pass on when you had the chance?"

Nathan sighed lightly, "Once I passed through the Transitional Realm, I was given a choice: continue to the Celestial Realms or stay as Bellany's spirit guide and remain in the Spiritual Realm. I was more than happy to stay. There are a lot of beings in the Spiritual realms. It has communities of its own, it's not crude like this place. This place is more out of necessity, and nature, than Love: although it encompasses all three."

"What happened to me—or Bellany?"

Nathan eyed me. "I watched over her as she grieved for me, and I guided her to another husband; which ironically helped me in my ascension process as it healed Bellany too. She fell in love again...and started a family," Nathan pauses, "I met her baby before she was born, and assisted her daughter into a physical body. I helped Bellany crossover, and I was waiting in the Subtle Realm to meet her—the first time you *died*."

"Nathan I..." I was too overwhelmed to speak. The emotion that typically proceeded tears came, but none fell.

"All in all, I helped you just as my Spirit Guides helped me. When we were finally reunited here, it was my happiest days in memory. It's one memory that this place will never take from me."

"I don't understand, if you and I reunited already, then why are you still here with me again? "

"I wasn't ready to say goodbye to you—or our memory. Memories are a lot harder to give uo when you have the choice. I wanted to stay, and help you in your next life, from start to finish—really protect you —and give you the life you deserved. A life without such deep grief or struggles. So, with permission, I was allowed to oversee your next incarnation. I helped you into your body, and I watched over your mom when she was pregnant, while I waited for you to be born again. I wanted so badly for you to have a life without such heartbreak and loss; but there are tough lessons that we both had to learn, necessary for our evolution. I wasn't allowed to intervene." Nathan pauses and lets me take in everything.

"My Mom." My eyes find the lake. I want to jump in.

"I helped your mom, along with her own guides, while she was suffering from dementia. We eventually helped her cross all the way over."

I nodded slowly.

"I like your mom: she was full of proactive love—such a nurturing soul. I got to know her well. Especially during the time that her consciousness was stuck partially in this realm and partially in the physical realm—when her brain was losing its ability to filter out certain input, or how to differentiate the two."

My eyes widen, and it hits me all at once what he's saying.

"My mom would sometimes talk to people that I thought weren't there. It scared me, but it gives me peace to know that she was talking to you, or her other guides." I hug him tightly, "Thank you Nathan, I wish I could remember you, but all I know is how I feel about you when you're around."

"Like I said, memory is a funny thing." He took a deep breath. "As soon as I enter the Celestial Realm, I doubt I will remember any of this, which is why it was so hard to leave. I didn't want to forget you, or us. I wanted to make sure someone was there to take care of you."

My head is still on his shoulder. "You literally waited a lifetime for me…does it feel like you've been here a long time?"

"It doesn't *feel* long. I only feel like I'm ready to move on to the next phase. Like I said, time is a lot more useful on Earth."

I step back, "Do you know how long I've been here?"

"I can sense that you've been here longer than any bodied-soul that I've come in contact with, but I don't know how long that is in minutes or hours. I can seek out an actual clock through a medium, and then maybe watch it through them, but I can't tell Earth-time passively, which is probably for the best"

"But how long have I been asleep?" I say nervously.

"You're not asleep, but your body has been at rest on the Physical Plane. Again, I can only see in the Realm I'm in, just as you can't see me when you are on the Physical Plane."

"I should go."

Nathan suggests that we fly home. We both concentrate on the location of my body like we are all ready there, he tells me to imagine the room, the temperature, the sheets against my skin, and the smells around me. Then we use the vibrational energy from our thoughts to propel our conscious matter through the realm. Once we arrive back to my body, Nathan looks at me with Love in his eyes. My Astral eyes may be finally adjusting to this place because his features are clearer.

"I don't know how much you will remember when you awake, so I'll say goodbye now." Nathan moves in to press his chest and forehead to mine. His hands interlock with my hands. I can feel all of his vibrations more powerful than ever before. It's as if they were apart of me—as if he's a part of me. My energy lifts to match his own. *This* is ecstasy in the truest form.

18

LIVING NIGHTMARE

The smell of urine flooded my nostrils. I sat straight up, as if re-animated from the dead—rising up out of a coffin. I'm not sure I could have felt any worse if I *had* just risen from the dead. Ammonia stung my eyes. I flung back the duvet, revealing the source of the stench. To my dismay, there were several outlines of urine varying in shape and dampness on the bed sheets. The patterns also decorated the crouch of my pink, silk pajama shorts. From the looks of it, I had wet myself at least four to five separate times. *Gross.* I reached for the giant water bottle, vitamins, meal replacement bars, and pain relievers, that I planted on my end table the night before in preparation. I consumed them all. My phone sat amongst all of the other items. It was just where I thought it should be, but it was dead—no longer able to send an alarm—an overpriced paperweight.

I slithered off the bed and corralled the soiled sheets, wadding them up in my arms. I threw them into the washing machine. Then I stripped naked, added my pajamas to the load, and hurried to the shower as fast as my weakened state would allow. I caught my reflection in the bathroom's panoramic mirror. It shocked me. My body was looked sickly. My skin was as pale as it had ever been, and my flesh was starting to sink in between the negative spaces of my bones. I needed to start eating more. I was past the point of an attractive-thin, and edging on the side of, don't-stare-too-long-at-her-thin. My slightly skeletal frame welcomed the warmth from the water. I poured shampoo into my hands, and massaged it into the heavy, water-logged mass of hair. A citrusy blood orange saturated the humid air—a scent I was undecided on. I rested my sudsy head against the wall and tried to replay the events of yesterday in my mind. I had to figure out the best way to explain all of this to Bryan and Jes. I needed to fill them in, on what was going on, without looking clinically insane. I hadn't ruled out that I might actually have a sleep disorder, and it that possibly was brought on from the fall when I hit my head. I saw Bryan in my mind's eye, looking uncomfortable and embarrassed at the welcome back event they threw for me. The staff already teased him about me, and there he stood looking like an idiot in front of them all. I get why he was so mad, but he didn't give me a chance to explain myself—and poor Yumi—she was so frightened when he was shouting.

Yumi.

Bryan brought Yumi home...

Yumi should be here.

"Yumi!" I shouted, turning off the water to listen.

There was no pitter, or patter. I flung open the glass door, not stopping to rinse out the shampoo from my hair, and grabbed a towel from the wall hook. I scoured the apartment for her. I rushed inside the walk-in closet connected to my bathroom, tripping on a basket of clean folded close that sat on the floor. I searched for her under the massive pile of dirty clothes, but she wasn't there. I ran back through the bathroom and into my bedroom. I dropped to the floor to look under my bed. There was nothing underneath but a framed diploma and a preserved graduation gown. My heart was thumping in my throat. It was so loud that I couldn't hear anything else, only the alarmed thuds echoing in my ears. I scrambled to my feet. I had to stand up slowly so that I wouldn't black out. I turned into the hall to check the half-bathroom—nothing. A quick survey of my open living room showed no signs of her either.

Did I only imagine Bryan bringing her home? Was yesterday a dream? Am I just getting my days mixed up? I felt so out of touch with time, and in some ways, out of touch with reality.

"Yumi?"

I walked into the kitchen. I looked around the kitchen bar wall, and there it was. When I walked further into the kitchen, I looked down and confirmed my fear. The garbage had been strewn out across the floor. I saw remanences of a banana peel, a shredded pizza box, and pieces of apple core. Everything that was even semi-edible, had been devoured. Her dog food bin was intact and full, but that's only because it had a special top. It was impossible for dogs to open. The lid however, was chewed up all around the interlocking rim. An obvious attempt to reach the food inside. There was dried blood, the color of rust, all over the white bin.

No. Not a dream—where was Yumi though?

I looked around the house. I spun slowly in a circle. Something white caught the corner of my eye—the tip of a tail—peeking out from behind the television's entertainment center. I ran to her. I found Yumi in the dog bed. She laid crumpled in the corner—a lifeless pile of white fur.

"Yumi!" I screamed.

She didn't stir. Not an inch. Not a single shutter. I collapsed down beside her motionless body. Her fur looked like a blanket—a white pelt —that hung loosely on still bones. I was terrified to touch her. I was afraid that her body would be cold, and that my heart would stop right alongside hers.

"Yumi please!" I wailed.

Nothing. Even the air around us was inert, heavy, and unyielding. I glided my hand lightly over her body. My hands were shaking wildly. Yumi's bones were jolting out of her skin. They looked like they might pop through, if I pressed on her too hard. Her fur was dull and flat. It fell out in clumps in my hand.

"She's dead," I whispered.

A screamed escaped me, something inhuman, something only a soul could decipher.

An eye parted, for just a second: a gaze unfocused, the whites of her eyes were the color of blood.

"Oh God, oh Yumi," I whimpered between sobs.

I clamored to my feet: I rushed to my bedroom to grab a robe and to find my purse. In the time that I was away, I could feel the light in her dimming. I wasn't even sure if what I saw was really life at all, rather than an involuntary and cruel reflex. I reached my arms under her bones, and lifted her up. My heart splintered again at how unusually light she was. I carried her to the car, and sat her gently in the backseat.

The nearest hospital would only take me ten minutes to reach. In the last mile of the trip: traffic slowed to a halt. My car made a ping sound. Through all the chaos, it took me awhile to realize that the sound was a gas alert on my dashboard. I was running out of gas. The labored breathing in the backseat, was a visceral reminder that there was no time to stop. I turned around to check on Yumi, she was taking in air awkwardly. It was like each breath was only granted through great effort. Any one of them might be her last. My vision blurred with grief.

HONNNNNNNK!

My eyes reached the road just in time to slam on the brakes. I stopped inches from a red Dodge Charger in front of us. I heard Yumi's body slide forward. I looked in the rearview mirror to check on her, and I saw the driver behind us flip me off. I began to feel dizzy. What little vision I had left, was now pulsing grey at the corners. I had only a small window in the center of my sight that I could see out of.

"We are almost there, Just a few more turns Yumi, hold on girl!" *Only one more light to go. I can do this. I have to do this...for Yumi.*

My tires squealed as I turned into the animal hospital's parking lot. I couldn't lift Yumi up anymore, so I stumbled into the hospital's lobby.

"Please help me," I cried. I broke down on their gritty checkered floor.

A red-headed receptionist came running out from behind her counter. A plump freckled arm helped me sit up, "Are you okay?"

"I'm okay, my baby—my dog is dying in my car, it's the black one... with the doors open," I said through frantic gasps.

The blonde receptionist, waiting behind the counter called for help, while the first one, "Rhonda," stayed with me. "It's okay, help is coming, we're going to do the best we can for her. Let's get you in a room. Can we call anyone for you?" Rhonda asked.

"No, please just save my girl," I begged.

Two vet technicians whizzed past me with a teal bed sheet. Rhonda helped me up off the floor, and into a room. They returned swiftly with Yumi incased within it, like a cocoon, and carried her to the back. I watched through swollen eyes, for any signs of life from her. I prayed for any signs of hopeful struggle from my girl in that sheet, but there were none. Rhonda brought me into an examination room and offered me a seat. Minutes later, she returned with a cup of chamomile tea, along with some paperwork to fill out, and collected my ID.

While I waited for any news on Yumi, I distracted myself with all of the posters on the wall. Most of them showed, with microscopic illustrations, what *could* go wrong with your pets. My mind wondered over how much science would benefit from having Astral sight. I imagined all of the advances we could make with superzoom and x-ray vision, especially in diagnostics. We could read the emotions and thoughts of the animals too. A pang of guilt and shame washed all of those thoughts away.

How could I even think of that place right now? The place that brought us here.

I picked up a jar on the counter with a dog heart submerged in formaldehyde, it was full of worms.

"Hello, Ms. Price." It was one of the technicians that had been carrying Yumi, he entered the room. "I Just need to ask a few questions about your dog. How long has she been sick?"

"She's not sick, at least I don't think she is," I said, putting my hand to my hair and realizing that I still had matted sudsy shampoo in it. I did not like this citrus scent.

"Okay…what problems has she been having, any vomiting, diarrhea, anorexia—"

"She hasn't been having any problems! She's a perfect dog! I'm the one with all the problems!" I screamed at him, half crying.

The tech looked up from his clipboard, "I'm going to let you calm down a bit, then I'll be back."

I covered my face in my arms on the counter. It smelled like bleach. I wept into my house coat. After what seemed like an eternity, left alone in that ever-shrinking square room, I heard someone pick up a chart that must have been hanging on the other side of the door. The door swung open and a short, very muscular doctor, entered the room.

"Please tell me she's not dead. Please, I'll never forgive myself," I begged.

"Hello Ms. Price, I'm Dr. Rue…can you help me understand what happened?"

"Is she alive?" I asked.

"She is stable for now. The next 24 hours will be telling. It's very important that you explain to me exactly what happened to her to your best ability. How did she end up in this situation?" The Doctor's sleeve fell back to reveal another sleeve—one made completely of ink.

"I fell asleep for too long. My ex-boyfriend dropped her off at my house, but I forgot that he did, because there was *a lot* going on. I didn't mean to hurt her, I would never hurt her. She's all I care about and everything I have."

"Ms. Price, I always want to give our clients the benefit of the doubt, but it's hard to believe that someone fell asleep for a week or longer, and just didn't realize their dog was home. I'm sorry I just can't buy—"

"Did you say a week?" I asked.

"Or longer…" Dr. Rue said. There was no emotion in her face.

I stood up. I sat right back down. "I think I might have a sleep disorder." The shock from her words almost knocked me out. "But I'll get help, I won't ever let this happen again."

"I see," the veterinarian looked at her chart, "Yumi will definitely need to stay here with us overnight. As I'm sure you already know, she was suffering from starvation and severe dehydration. Thankfully, it seems that she did have access to some sort of shelter and possibly even water, because she's still with us," she said.

"She lives inside with me." I said, trying to help my case, "It might be important to know that she was already very lean to begin with: I know German Shepards have problems with their hips and I didn't want her to get fat and suffer when she's older."

Dr. Rue looked me in the eyes, "She's not a German Shepherd."

I failed miserably.

Her face was square and intimidating, she continued, "Yumi's G.I. tract is inflamed, and she has an opportunistic infection in her mouth from several cuts and a compromised immune system," the Doctor flipped back a page in her clipboard, "we will start antibiotics, and of course will keep her overnight on fluids and introduce solid food slowly. One of my techs will call you in the morning." She paused, "I need to ask, are you okay to drive home? Is there someone we can call for you?"

"No, no one. Just keep Yumi safe. Thats all that matters to me," I said.

She nodded and left the room. When she turned around, I saw a tattoo on her neck. It looked like the Golden Gate Bridge, but it was placed on a rainbow backdrop with tiny sets of black puppy paw prints.

The other receptionist came in through the open door—not *nice Rhonda*—but the other one. The one that sat behind the desk. She looked like she did a lot of sitting. She was blonde, with a fake tan that concentrated aggressively around her hands and elbows in shades of mud-orange. She rambled down the list of charges that my carelessness incurred. Then she ultimately named a price over three syllables long. I hadn't actually heard a word she said, just sounds coming from her direction. I hadn't even looked her in the eyes, since she walked in the door. I pulled out a random card from my wallet and handed it to her.

How could I be this blind? I should have known this could have happened. I should have been more careful, there were warning signs everywhere. Now I could lose Yumi forever.

"Ma'am…Ma'am," The bad tan said.

"Yes?" I looked up, stars were clouding my vision. I hoped I could make the drive home.

"Your card." Her orange arm was outstretched with a card in her hand. She was wearing purples scrubs. They were covered with tiny pumpkins and cat-witches flying mid-air on their brooms.

"What time do you open tomorrow?"

"Eight a.m., but there will be someone here around the clock to watch her tonight. Don't worry, we will call you tomorrow with an update. regardless," she said.

Regardless? What does that even mean? "Okay."

I left the animal hospital. I arrived at my apartment entrance. I do not remember the drive home—the in-between—I only remember looking up and seeing the black stone sign at the entry. When I opened my apartment door, the smell of shit, piss, and rotten garbage punched me in the face. My stomach knotted. I frantically opened all of the windows, and turned on all of the fans. I sat down to catch my breath, exhausted from the slight increase in energy uptake. After nursing my body back to some form of homeostasis, it was time to clean up my mess. I grabbed two bright lilac rubber gloves from under the kitchen sink and slid them up to each elbow. I collected three full rolls of paper towels, a trash bag, and a very large bottle of the citrus cleaner that I stole from Daze. I pulled my shirt over my nose and mouth, got down on my hands and knees, and began scrubbing the floors—cleaning up my tears as they fell.

19

THE VOICEMAIL

Brown, everything was brown.

It took me a minute to orient myself and realize that I was laying on the floor. I must have fallen asleep cleaning. If my consciousness went anywhere last night, it was an empty and desolate place, void of anything or anyone. My back constricted with vibrations, in hopes of generating any warmth left in my body. I was stiff and sore, especially at the points where my bones trapped muscle and flesh between their knobs and the hardwoods. I looked around. At least my apartment was clean, but my mind and my conscious, that was a different story.

The birds were still asleep, and the sky was a deep navy. It would be a while before the sun made an appearance in the sky. In all of yesterday's chaos, I'd forgotten that my phone remained dead next to my bed.

What if Dr. Rue tried to call me last night?

I crawled to my room as quickly as my body would allow. I was too weak to stand and walk normally. I reached for my phone on the nightstand. Then I crawled back to the kitchen on all fours, in awkward movements, with my phone in my hand. I felt like a wild creature—not fully part of this world—and not fully part of the other. I held onto the counter, plugged my phone in to charge, and grabbed a meal bar out of the cabinet. I gummed the processed protien as I stared at the black screen, anxiously waiting for the bitten apple to appear.

I dropped to my knees to pray, "Mom, Nathan, Creator of the Universe, Dad?...or any Angels listening? *Please* don't take Yumi from me. If you let me keep her I promise I'll get help. I respect our lives! I love her so much. Please don't let her die—not like this."

A soft ping alerted me that my phone was awake. I stood up slowly and began to read my notifications: there was not a single missed call from Bryan or Jes. There was only one missed call from Malinda, and a missed call from an unknown number. Only one voicemail awaited me.

Call from, 1-888-112-9660, November 2, at 11:11AM: "Hello Natasha. I am not quite sure where to begin, or how this will be received. I can only hope that as my blood runs through your veins, that you will have the intuition and the foresight to accept my words at face value. I have thought of this moment many times, and each time there is always sufficient justification, real or imagined, to prolong the inevitable. Alas, now as fate would have it, this life has given me very few avenues to choose from. Yet ironically, I am grateful. For now I can finally out-rationalize my ego on this matter—the matter being, clearly, contacting you—my daughter. I know that might come as a shock, but there are things that you need to know, so please try and—

I slapped my phone on the counter. *Could it really be him? Dad? After all this time? Right now?!*

It was if the universe had been preparing me for this one phone call. It let everything else in my life go to hell, so that when I received his call it wouldn't break me. It's disorienting to think that if I would have received this call—*only three weeks ago*—it would have been the biggest moment in my life.

I could see the alternate-reality-show play out in my mind's eye now. Jesmitha and I would be at Club Daze chatting in the dressing room about what I should do for hours. We'd get trashed throughout the night. Then I would probably hook up with Bryan in a reckless attempt for familiar comfort. And I would justify it all on my wacky childhood—as if I had no choice over my actions. That of course being the best-case scenario. That Tasha seemed like a stranger to me now.

But now? My life had been flipped inside out, folded seventy times, then cut in half and sprinkled out of a car window, going ninety over a bridge—crossing an alligator infested swamp. There *was* no going back to normal, and because *normal* no longer existed as a standard, then *abnormal*, as an outlier, couldn't either. Infinite possibility of the present moment, *was* the new-normal. Sure, I'd call him back, what did I have to lose?

Besides Yumi.

I called the animal hospital back first.

"Thank you for calling TNC Veterinary Clinic, this is Rhonda, how can I help you?"

"Hi Rhonda, it's Tasha from yesterday, with Yumi." I swallowed, "Is she...okay?"

"Oh hey Tasha, one moment dear," she said, placing me on hold.

I recognized their playback music. It was a song that blared through the house on Saturday mornings, when I was a small child.

"...*Up ahead in the distance, I saw a shimmering light,*
My head grew heavy and my sight grew dim..."

"Hi, Tasha?" Rhonda answered.

"Yes?"

"Okay, so Yumi is doing well, she is recovering nicely."

"This is great news! Thank you!" I took in my first full breath since the day I thought she might be dead. "This means so much to me you have no idea."

"Yes, okay then, well I hope you have a good afternoon dear."

"Wait, when can I pick her up?"

There was a beat of silence before I heard unintelligible noise in the background, she had her hand over the receiver, "One moment, dear."

"...*Last thing I remember, I was running for the door,*
I had to find the passage back to the place I was before,
'Relax,' said the night man, we are programmed to receive.
You can check-out any time you like..."

"The Eagles, Hotel California." *That's right,* I remembered.

Dr. Rue picked up the phone, "Hi Ms. Price, listen, we don't want to cause you any more pain, as you look like you are already in a very precarious...situation. However, I cannot in good faith promise you that we will be able to return Yumi to you. I want to be straight up with you, as to manage your expectations."

"What...no, what do you mean...she's mine, you can't keep her— can you?"

"Please try and calm down Ms. Price, as of right now nothing has been decided. I promise you we will do what's best for Yumi, which is ultimately what we both want—correct?"

"Of course, but—

"She's still in treatment and we are making sure that she recovers fully, she is doing so well and she's a fighter and that is all we can say...for now."

"What do I do now?" I asked.

"Focus on your health, we're taking care of Yumi's. She's a very good girl and I promise she is safe. Have a nice day, Ms. Price."

I hung up the phone and screamed as loud as I could, as long as I could, until my lungs gave out. Then I took another breath, and I screamed again until the rage exhausted itself into tears. My life was a carcass, left on the side of a desert highway, and fate was a giant buzzard plucking away at it until there was nothing left but a shell of ribs picked clean. Grief was heavy in my heart. It had been sitting dense and stationary for far too long, rubbing raw like a bed sore. But there was something else there too—something festering in the wound — irritating. I was a live wire, ready to electrocute anyone that touched me. Luckily, I had just the target.

If Mikael could casually drop a voicemail-bomb into my life, then I could respond with even less effort. So I texted Ol' Daddio. Maybe it was the sheer exhaustion: the lack of food, dehydration, or my state of shock, but I felt intoxicated, even though I hadn't touched so much as a drink in almost a month.

I pulled out my weapon of choice and proceeded to text him, in all caps. "OH HI MIKAEL, WOW. It's so great to hear from you. You know, I was just sitting here thinking: man, I wish my deadbeat dad would drop in my life randomly, and impart his wisdom on me—and here you are. Crazy right? So how is life oh wise one? I hope it's just super. Mine (you've never asked)? Well it's the best it's ever been, everything is going perfectly to plan, so I don't need anything from you. But, if you would like to reconcile the last fifteen birthdays for your own soul, you can send funds to @TashaPriceDazeGirl. Yes, I changed my last name to mom's maiden name, because I didn't want anything to do with you!"

I hit send, and realized that my twenty-ninth birthday was coming up next week—November eleven. *So make that sixteen birthdays Mikael.*

I wandered aimlessly around my house for hours, not knowing what to do with myself. I wanted to call Bryan, or even Jes, but I knew they would just prod me for answers. I was in so much emotional pain that I wouldn't be able to communicate anything well, I would end up making things worse. Instead, I looked for a bottle of wine to accompany me to a movie in my living room. I reached for a bottle that I was saving for quite some time. It was one that Bryan and I bought in the North Carolina Mountains—again because I liked the label art— but this one was special. It was a bottle that we had kept as inspiration for our own wine one day. The glass was black, or maybe a dark green, and the label was also black but only at first: the heat from your hands transformed it into a beautiful yet muddy rainbow—like an oil spill on the concrete. We had never seen anything like it before. The wine was called mood liquid. It reminded me of the color-changing pencils I had when I was in middle school, or the popular mood rings from the nineties. It was our *muse bottle*.

How far we had fallen from that day.

I slit the neck on the bottle with a golden blade from a corkscrew that an overzealous client gave me for my birthday. At first I thought the gift was obvious and embarrassing, like giving ties for father's day or apples to a teacher, but I ended up treasuring the little piece of hardware. It didn't hurt when I found out that the corkscrew was solid gold. I removed the capsule, it too changed color under the warmth of my finger tips. I pushed the worm into the center of the spongy head. It pierced the surface, and I twisted it down deep. The sharp metal tip dug further into the cork until it had enough grip to go to work. I pressed the beautiful shining leaver against the base of its neck with my thumb and held it there. Pulling back and out, I removed the cork in one fluid motion. I brought the red stained cork to my nose, just out of habit, not actually expecting the wine to be corked—but of course it was.

"Why are you punishing me!" I screamed to my ceiling.

I abandoned the tainted bottle on the counter, and surrendered to my couch. I was surprisingly tired. Even though a large portion of my recent life had been spent unconscious, I didn't feel rested in the least bit. I went on social media. I was immediately met with everyone's largely uninspiring halloween costumes from the past weekend; most of them followed the tired format of sexy-blank for the girls, and ironic-blank—or hyper-sexualized-blank—for the guys. There were also some pop-culture niche costumes, exhibited by their doters, whom overestimated their cleverness.

As I scrolled down I felt a growing sense of sick-anxiety, like the feeling you get right before you run into someone you didn't want to see in a public place. It didn't take long before I saw the reason for the prophetic feeling. There, on my feed, sat a glowing image of Jes and Bryan smiling in their halloween costumes at Club Daze. I might have been reading too much into things, or maybe it was just wishful thinking, but I thought I recognized one of those forced smiles—that I so often wear at Daze—right there on Bryan's face.

From the looks of things, Jes went with the theme of aliens—and it was done well. There was a banner in the background that read, "Area

51." Bryan wore an orange haz-mat suit. Jesmitha was in a tiny, holographic, two-piece set, paired with light up tennis shoes, and a glittering antenna. Her long nails were glowing hot white in the dark, and her skin was covered in green-to-gold shimmer.

I felt an unsavory brew of guilt and grief in my gut; they both looked exhausted, regardless if their smiles were genuine or not. I didn't want to see anymore—nothing else that my brain had to dissect. I clicked on, and scrolled through Yumi's page: "@mylilYumi," who was not so little any more. There were so many precious moments captured there, but this stroll down memory lane proved to be a dumb mistake. I threw my phone across the floor, and covered my head with a pillow. There was nothing I could do to escape from my pain—it wasn't going anywhere. I just had to sit with it, and get acquainted.

TURN FROM HERE AND GO

Nathan stood in a doorway with his back to her. He wore a military uniform, and his hair was styled with a slick, exaggerated part.

"Nathan!" Tasha called, as he walked through the doorway into darkness.

She ran after him, but only found herself alone in a room with five orange lockers. Above her, were bright stars in an open sky. They reminded her of the cool, calm nights that she used to spend by a crackling campfire, in the Georgia southern mountains, with her parents as a child. The lockers in front of her were labeled: Elemental, Mineral, Vegetable, Animal, and Person. She turned around to leave back out from which she'd came, but the door she'd passed through vanished. In its place, was a dense forest that was too dark to distinguish any one shape from another, save for the light Spanish moss, softly reflecting the starlight from above.

Tasha opened a locker—this one labeled people—to see what was inside. A breeze coming from the depths of the locker took her by surprise. The interior was so deep that she could not see the back of it. She stepped inside.

Once she was fully inside, the metal door swung shut behind her. She was left in complete blackness. Her curiosity powered her steps, and she continued through the narrow passageway. The opening was just wide enough for her to walk straight, but her shoulders would occasionally scrape against the walls. She could sense a downward slope underneath her feet, as the temperature dropped around her. Tasha walked in blindness for a while, but soon her eyes adjusted to the lack of light; she could barely visualize her surroundings. Perhaps there was a subtle light entering the passageway ahead—a few more steps confirmed this to be true. The tunnel led to a small Earthy launching pad, with seven bridges extending out from it—all in different colors.

The furthest bridge to her left was a bright lavender; its neighbor was a deep indigo, and next to that one was cyan in color: then green, and yellow, and orange. The last bridge to her right was a deep red. Tasha walked straight onto the green bridge. As she walked across, it swayed a bit, but was steady and secure. On the other side of the crossing was a green door, and at that door was Nathan's silhouette. He was singing to her, but she couldn't make out his words. She ran to him. As she reached the end of the bridge, she heard his lyrics clearly.

"…and I have loved you wild," Nathan sang.

Just as her bare toes imprinted on the cool wet ground, he vanished through the door once again. Tasha chased after him. As soon as she stepped passed the opening, her feet landed on nothing, and she fell into the darkness. She tumbled in the air—not fast—more of a slow float than a fall. The further she went down the brighter her surroundings became. She could see her hands and feet stretched out in front of her as she fell—a little leaf in the wind.

Tasha looked down, over her shoulder. There was a reddish-orange glow emitting from the bottom of the tunnel. As she continued, she saw that there were millions of lockers surrounding her, billions even, all with various people's names embossed on them. She could have, at any moment, grabbed onto one of the lockers if she so chose to. Finally, with no end in sight, she reached out to the closest one, halting her momentum, and pushed it open. She pulled herself up into the locker with moderate effort, like pulling her body out of a shallow pool.

She took a few steps into the new locker before she began to float down once more—yet again in *another* cylinder of lockers. But *these* were all labeled as major body parts! "Left Leg, Stomach, Arm." She grabbed the closest locker and repeated. Now she was falling in a cylinder of lockers labeled with the parts of a leg specifically, "Femur, Patella, Meniscus." This could go on forever, into infinite particles, she knew this truth intimately. She should find a way back out.

Instinctually she tried to swim upwards. It worked! She was quite buoyant in this strange world. She retraced her steps back to reach the seven bridges. She stood, swaying in the center of the green bridge, distracted by a familiar sound coming from beneath her. It's a melody she knew well, one of bass, laughter, and drinks clinking—the sound of a party. She jumped off the bridge and allowed the soft gravity to caress her down to a black mirrored surface. Once she had a solid foundation under her, she looked along the path that led to thousands of iridescent pulsing lights. It was Club Daze, or some form of it. Nathan was standing at the entry waiting for her.

"Hi honey, care to dance while I have the time?" He said, with his hand extended for hers.

THE CALL BACK

My eyes were swollen shut. I pressed a warm washcloth over them, while I played some soft music. I waited patiently for the vet clinic to call; I was afraid to pester them as it might lessen my chances of getting Yumi back. She had been there for two nights already. I'm sure she was frightened. I wanted to comfort her and tell her that everything would be okay. My sleep has been terrible, I don't think I've had a single dream since the day I lost her. If I couldn't find a way to get her back, I may never sleep soundly again.

I called my therapist and apologized. We spoke for a while, and set up our next meeting for Friday; thankfully she understood, or she pretended too. I think it's kind of her job to be understanding, or at the very least, be convincingly sincere.

I stared at my phone. Then, with bated breath, I swallowed the only grain of pride I had left. I texted Bryan and Jes in a group message, "Hey guys, I'm sorry for missing the event that you planned for me. I know you put a lot of time, money, and effort into it. The last thing I wanted is to embarrass you, or make you feel like I take you for granted. I promise it wasn't anything drug-related, and I didn't blow anyone off on purpose. I've been having some sleep disorder...or health related issues. I think they could be from my fall. I'm trying to get a grasp on what's going on. I'm trying to get better. I hope Halloween weekend was a success, and I'm sorry I wasn't there to help...oh and I hope you guys had a good time on your trip together."

Then I deleted "together," and hit send. I didn't like that word there. The last line was the hardest to write, because there wasn't an ounce of truth in it. In no way did I hope their trip was enjoyable, but it needed to be said, even if I'm the only one that needed to hear it. *I broke up with Bryan. I should let him go.* After my apology tour, my apartment's silence became insufferable. I tried to watch television but it was of no use. I couldn't bear waiting around to hear back from Yumi, so I did the only thing in the world that could have possibly distracted me from her. I called Mikael, for the first time in fifteen years.

"Hello," a voice answered with guttural familiarity tugging at it.

"Hi," I said.

"Natasha, it's nice to hear your voice…I'm glad you called."

I sat silent.

"I'd like to meet with you. I know it's brash, but time is a luxury that I can't afford." he said.

The irony was overwhelming. I didn't know where to begin, so I didn't.

"Would you be willing to meet?" He continued.

"You're dying, you can just say it, I've seen this movie before," I blurted out.

"Well…yes, Natasha, we all are," he paused, "but I happen to know my date now, within a very narrow margin of error, and there are things that I need to share with you, before I leave this world. Things that *you want* to know. If it's money you want, I have that as well, but I think you will find that what I have to offer is much more satisfactory and fulfilling than some imaginary value construct created to maintain power and order—"

"Okay—okay, let's do it." *Why the hell not?* I didn't care anymore. "But since you want to meet up, then you'll have to meet me at Leaf N' Bean Cafe in the central park in Midtown, tomorrow at eleven a.m.; it's the only time I'm free for the rest of my life. Oh and there's a chance I might have to pick up my dog from the vet last minute. So if I don't show up that's why—but I'm not bothering to call you and cancel. Other than that, I'll probably meet you there, sound good?"

"That sounds great," he said.

I could hear a smile through his tone and it irritated me. The more blatantly immune he was to my sarcasm, the more he made me feel like a small child for employing it.

"If I feel like at any time you're lying to me, or if you ask me for so much as a pen, I'm gone." I paused. "Coffee is on you—and no hugs." I hung up.

Either he shows or he doesn't. I surely wasn't getting my hopes up for stranger-dad. He could be insane for all I know; fifteen years is a long time. I couldn't exactly remember what he did for a living, but I knew it was something with science—like Mom. This is one of those moments where it would have been helpful to have *anyone* in my family to call—but no. Mikael remained a complete wild card for now.

THE MEETING

If I wasn't already in a sour mood from waking up alone in a joyless apartment, sans Yumi's pure angel-like affection, then the icy temperatures assaulting my face along the walk to the cafe were sure to do it. To make matters worse, Atlanta's bipolar weather wasn't the only thing disrupting the usual serenity of the park. The assholes who ruin halloween each year had also defiled, that otherwise, beautiful piece of Earth.

There were bits and pieces of discarded costumes scattered all over; cigarette butts and vapes speckled the land like confetti. Large sections of grass were stopped on, murdered, and drowned, under the influx of foot traffic: leaving ugly brown holes—like liver spots on the lawn. And every so often I'd walk past massive piles of trash, that the park committees had been relentlessly trying to clean up for days: beer cans, tiny liquor bottles, and all of the plastic containers from the shitty food they'd shoved into their gaping mouths, after they were done desecrating their bodies. I zipped my coat all the way up to my chin. It was freezing for November, but then again, what was normal any more.

I was going to wait until I secured a table by the fire inside the cafe, but I couldn't stand to. The pressure was surmounting, like a dusty cinderblock on my chest, so I called the clinic. "Hello, thank you for calling TNC veterinary hospital can you hold please, or is this an emergency?" A female voice answered.

"It's an emergency, I need to know about my dog Yumi?" I said.

"Oh, one moment please."

"…this could be Heaven or this could be Hell…"

"Hi, I'm sorry, we will call you back this afternoon Tasha." she snipped, right before she hung up.

"Oh, Come on!"

My shouting stopped everything in their tracks. There were pink-nosed joggers, little kids on bikes, and squirrels that were frantically collecting their last bit of food before the winter set in; they all paused for a tick before politely continuing along their day.

I approached Leaf N' Bean, but the warm welcome it typically provided me was amiss. Instead it was replaced with a strange caution —a feeling I wasn't expecting. I regretted sharing this space with *him*. It was a sensation of suspecting that your house was bugged; a space that was once so comfortable—now infiltrated by the enemy. I didn't expect to feel so prepared for battle. I was sweating profusely despite the low temperatures.

I scanned the cafe, wondering if Mikael had shown up early too. Maybe one of the men in line at the counter was him. I looked for pieces of myself in strangers. I looked for my eyes, or my gait, or my hands, but I saw none. I sat at a table in the back corner with a vantage point that gave me a full view of the main door: the big red door that most entered through. Patrons who weren't regulars were never sure if the small purple side-door was actually an entrance for them or not. It was mildly entertaining to watch them through the giant windows, while I drank my morning beverages: one after one, they contemplated the violet door, with such novice hesitation.

Over the next hour, several paternity contenders walked in. Each one held against a test that they hadn't any knowledge of. Some of them I mentally battered, giving them horrible backstories for any phenotypical attributes that I perceived as a shortcoming. The figurative attacks grew in brutality, the more likely I thought the victims to be Mikael.

About five minutes before our arranged meeting time, a frail man walked in. His towering frame was supported by cane. His shirt, and pants that were tourniquet-ed around his waist by a belt, engulfed him; like he had suddenly dropped fifty pounds overnight. He wore sunglasses, although there was no sun outside. His movements were slow and arthritic. I didn't insult this man. *If he had* deserved any punishment, it had clearly already came to fruition. I listened carefully to his raspy conversation with the barista.

"Just a black coffee, please." He puffed out.

"Yes, sir...may I have your name?"

"Lonny."

"Okay Lonny," she smiled sadly, "and here's some fresh Pumpkin bread on us."

I was relieved that this man was not my father, because I felt a penetrating sorrow and compassion for *Lonny*, and I never wanted to feel that for Mikael. I waited patiently for Mikael to join the circus of his not-Mikael counterparts. After a few more bodies passed through the door, and the time ticked to ten minutes passed our arrangement, I began to think that he wouldn't show. The disappointment I felt was vexing.

A man entered through the purple door, and slightly bowed his head under the frame like he might hit it. This—this was him. He was in good shape for his age, which I assumed to be about sixty, save for a small circular pudge in his mid section. Otherwise he was lean with a full head of dark black hair. He had a strong brow bone, and the same sharp, angular features in his face as I did. His mouth was a straight line. He wore a heavy black pea-coat with jeans and white tennis shoes. He ordered a drink, and walked towards me without any need or guidance. His eyes, wintergreen, appeared wet, but did not leak. When he sat down, I recognized my nose. His likeness to me made all of the previous contenders a joke.

"You look just like your—

"Don't," I said, "obviously, I look just like her, I'm her daughter. Let's not reminisce please, we're here on business. You have things you want to tell me before you die, probably to make yourself feel better, and I'm trying to figure out if what you have to say is even worth my time."

"Oh the cost of time," he sighed, "you are more like me than you would ever care to admit."

I rolled my eyes.

He smiled. "You see, I under—then over—estimated the amount of time I had available to me on Earth. I was not able to accomplish all that I wanted, in the time that I was allotted."

"I'm so, so sorry, to hear that," I said cleaning my fingernails.

"Natasha, I know that in your mind your anger protects you, and that's okay for now, but I do love you and your mother. One day you will understand that I had a bigger calling than being a husband and a father. As it were, I couldn't do both. I had to choose," he took a sip of his black coffee, "and I didn't abandon you as a child, I fulfilled my duty to raise you into a young woman. Yet you were still too young to understand the grey areas of choice, the circumstances, the stakes, and thus me leaving. I told your mom to tell you whatever she felt comfortable with, and I promised that if I accomplished what I set out to do, or if—when you were old enough, then I would find you—

"And what exactly was it, I am dying to know, what is so God damned important that you would abandoned your family and...," my lip began to quiver but I stiffened it, "...and not even show up to mom's funeral?"

"I *was* there, and I have been checking in on you ever since, but I lost track of your whereabouts shortly after she died."

"You've been *spying on me* for the past fifteen years!" People in the cafe started looking at us.

Mikael leaned in, "Spying is a strong word, and it would be more like twelve, not fifteen," He took another sip of his coffee, "Natasha, I didn't want to disrupt your life, unless I knew I could be apart of it, or for good reason."

"You're insane."

"I have considered it." He smiled, and set his mug on the table. He looked at his watch, then readjusted the mugs handle so that it pointed in the same direction as the hour hand on the clock: eleven. "As you know I have cancer, or how you so eloquently put it, I am dying...but the reason why we're having this meeting is because of a much greater matter."

"Bigger than dying?"

"Yes." Mikael looked at his watch again. "You, see, I'm the CEO, founder, and majority owner, of ChudaPharma: A biotech company that houses a cause that I have sacrificed everything for. I need you, my blood, for multiple reasons, to continue to run this company."

"That is a horrible name," I said, " and I wouldn't know the first thing about a biotech company. Sorry, but my education stops at an undergraduate degree in science. My post-Bachelor years weren't exactly the most fertile ground for grad-school."

"We can change all of that now." Mikael winced in pain and settled back down into his chair. "I think you'd be surprised by your innate abilities. There are things I haven't told you about your genealogy, and I have several weeks, if not months, to teach you. You'll have an entire team, and my trusted assistant, at your disposal. I just need you at the head of the table."

"Why me?"

"I *want* to give this to you. I need to pay some karmic debts, and believe it or not, there are some things only you might be able to do there."

"I need time to think about this," I said.

"That's the only thing I don't have."

"Then some things never change I guess."

"You're skeptical. Why wouldn't you be? Come see the company tomorrow? I'll pick you up, show you what we do—why it's so important."

I stood up, my chair legs grinding against the floor. "I need to go pick up my dog from the vet," I said, my head spun.

"Meet me here tomorrow, at the same time, you will not regret it," he said.

I left him there, without so much as a nod, and walked in the direction of home. Lately my life made more since as a dream. Maybe I would wake up at any moment and have Yumi back in bed snuggling with me. Just like one of those low-hanging fruit dramas where the actor just wakes up at the end—with no harm done and no worse off from his decisions. My luck, I would be in a dream-within-a-dream and wake up again in a more hellish scenario. Those thoughts turned unnerving quickly.

I should just call Mikael and tell him to fuck off and let his precious empire rot, but then again, wouldn't that be the dumbest thing I could possibly do right now? Isn't this the exact scenario that all little abandoned girls and boys *dream of*? Ew, no, there's that word again, *dream*. No, I wouldn't squander this opportunity out of spite. Even I'm not that stupid, despite the recent mounds of evidence stacking up against me. My pocket vibrated, and then again, *my phone*.

"Hello?" I answered.

"Hello Ms. Price this is Dr. Rue, I'm just calling to let you know that we've decided to place Yumi within a temporary foster home. Her profile is currently up for adoption at a no-kill shelter. Before you get upset, please try and remember she is safe, fully recovered, and doing well. We've all discussed it amongst ourselves, and we see this as the best avenue for everyone involved. We will not be charging you for the rest of the bill, it's been generously covered by her current foster home family. We sincerely hope that you get better soon too." After a long empty silence from my end, the doctor hung up.

I had not a word to utter. My face was numb. My entire life was finally gone: my proverbial cup did not over-flow with anything—it was empty. The last bit of liquid sucked clean, through a giant straw—torturously—from the unskilled mouth of a bratty demonic child. Her wild eyes glaring into the bottom, laughing, snarling, as she made obnoxious slurping noises from her feed.

20

REACH FOR YOUR DREAMS

Water surrounded her—she was wet and cold. She was in the open sea. The ocean stretched on for eternity in every direction. Tasha sat wading in waters the color of ink; she bobbed under a deep maroon sky. There were no stars, only a full moon. A solid circle above her head glinted. Something darted across the dark waters, only inches in front of her. She was frightened. Tasha pushed the water away as to wade backwards, but she didn't move.

She began to sink—sucked down. Further and further, she fell into fabric. A maroon velvet was soft against her skin. She was entangled. The material constricted around her body and face, restricting her view. The sheet snaked itself around her neck. She was suffocating. Right when she was out of air, the fabric thinned, just enough for a tiny, life-saving, inhale.

The cloth thinned again. She could breathe a bit easier now. Thinning once again, she could now see through the individual threads that laid tightly over her face. She recognized her city—it was the aerial view of her city! She was suspended in the air!

The threads, now thinner than butterfly wings, finally split in some areas. She could push her hands straight through the sheets of fuchsia if she wanted to. She grasped at the cloth so she wouldn't crash into the jagged buildings below her; and she might have been able to save herself, but she was carrying too much weight.

Tasha looked down with horror. She saw a terrified Yumi clinging to her legs. The weight of them both was ripping the cloth. Yumi dug in deeper. Her sharp claws split the bonds of Tasha's skin, and then her veins—spilling out their contents. Blood poured onto Yumi's face. The thick liquid covered her eyes, blinding her, and painting her a bright red. The fabric shredded into two parts, swinging violently. Tasha clung to one half of the split cloth. Yumi clawed at the other, yelping; she was about to plummet to her death.

Tasha looked up and saw her father: a giant version of Mikael. He was wearing a crown. He held each of the cloths, separated in each hand; the cloths on which Tasha and Yumi so desperately clung to.

"Why are you doing this?" Tasha screamed to the heavens.

"You're giving me too much power," King Mikael said.

Maybe this is a dream? Tasha felt a slight shift in focus; like when someone changes the camera in a movie—it's subtle but it's there. It might even go unnoticed, unless someone points it out.

"I am dreaming!" I said, taking back my power. "This is a dream, and Yumi is safe. She's playing happily beside me on the soft grass." As I spoke, we both floated back to the earth. We were in a lush green park. Yumi played with a ball at my side.

"Now, you!" I pointed up to the hovering dream-dad over me, "Why are you trying to hurt me?"

"I am not trying to hurt you Natasha, I'm trying to elevate you. Here, let me give you a better view," he said.

"A better view..." I repeated.

The dream-dad brought out a new bedsheet, this one was teal in color, sturdy, and intact. He carefully wrapped up Yumi and I in the sheet and carried us safely across the dawning sky. Bundled together, like a stork's priceless cargo, we rose to the top of the highest building in the city. Together all three of us enjoyed a large feast at a crystal table. The full moon shined above us. When we were finished eating, Mikael brought out a folder with seven documents. He asked me to sign them.

An old friend watched the whole scene from afar.

21

A NEW LEAF

I arranged to meet my therapist at Leaf N' Bean before the company visit. I figured it would be a healthy flow of events: a little session to prepare me for the internal mini crisis that would inevitably follow after Mikael's show-n'-tell of a swan-song.

There was a cool autumn breeze, but it was warm enough to sit outside. I needed the fresh air. Once settled outside the cafe, I checked the time. I noticed that I had an unread message from Jes; it was from three in the morning.

"Hey babe things have been crazy! I care about you too and I'm sorry about how I handled everything I'm just leaving wrk I'm exhausted it's ben rly tough without you here def not the same we need to talk call you as soon as I get a breath."

I felt a little weight lift off of my shoulders. It was the first communication I've had with either of them, since the welcome back party turned into the firing squad. I also knew Jes well enough to know, that if they had repeated any mistakes from last halloween, then she wouldn't be contacting me at all.

Malinda arrived right on time. She was wearing jeans, a white t-shirt, with a long beige cardigan-duster. Her hair was pulled back tight. She looked less friendly this time, or more serious; or maybe she looked exactly the same, but I saw what I was expecting to see. *Has it been two, or three weeks?* I braced myself for a verbal reprimand, but there was none.

"Hello Tasha, how has your week been?" she asked.

"I'm really sorry again for missing our meeting…twice?"

"Yes, twice," she confirmed, "would you like to share what's been going on?"

"I think I might have a sleep disorder? I keep sleeping for extended periods of time, I'm not quite sure what is causing it yet."

"Have you been taking anything or drinking when this happens?"

"No, nothing more than Tylenol PM or melatonin," I said.

"Okay," She jotted down a few notes, "let's switch gears for a bit, what do you expect to get out of our counseling sessions?"

What did I want from them? "At first I just wanted to appease my boss, but now I think I really could use some help; my world has changed so much just within the last time I've seen you. I'm not entirely sure what's real and what is only in my mind. Sometimes my days feel like a dream, like I'm just going through the motions, or I'm just watching everything happen to me."

I told her everything that's taken place since I'd seen her last: the multi-day *dreams*, the broken relationships, Yumi, and how I was supposed to be meeting my long-lost father here in this very cafe so I could visit his company. A company that he's trying to impart to me, before he dies. I left out the part that I believed the Subtle Realm to be a real place because I wasn't trying to be carried away in a straight jacket.

"Have you explained to Jesmitha and Bryan that you suspect this to be a medical problem, and that it has nothing to do with drugs?" she asked.

"It's complicated, because I'm not quite sure it's not entirely my fault, or that it's not something I'm doing. I don't know that they would believe me anyway," I said.

"If you really think that this is some form of Sleeping Beauty Syndrome or Narcolepsy, then you should tell Dr. Joe about it. You shouldn't blame yourself for physical issues, any more than you should blame yourself for mental ones…guilt doesn't serve anyone, it only impedes progress and growth. We need to focus our energy on the root of the problem." She said, her hand grasping the same amethyst pendant she wore the first time I met her.

"I don't know what the root of the problem is though" I said.

"What is your attitude towards change?" she asked.

"Thats a funny question to ask me right now don't you think? My whole life has just turned upside down."

"I think it's the perfect time to ask," she said.

"Okay—I fucking hate it. Nothing ever changes for the better, life's little adjustments just corrode your spirit until you die, is that what you wanted to hear?"

"No, but I'm glad you told me. What specifically is inviting your anger out right now?"

"This conversation," I said.

"Tasha, I want you to be able to let out your anger in a safe place, so that it doesn't build up inside and come out when it would be harmful to yourself or others. Think about it. What keeps happening that repeatedly frustrates you?"

I looked at the cafe, and at the door that Mikael had just walked through; less than twenty-four hours ago, "I never win for long, every time I think I find something good, it's gone and something worse takes its place."

"That's useful. What we tell ourselves has a tendency to become true, so let's rebuild that thought. If we're aware of the negative things we're telling ourselves, then we can counter their low energy with something that's productive and powerful. All thoughts are powerful, but truths founded in love are the strongest of them all."

"You sound like someone else I know," I said. I couldn't help but smile, when thinking of Nathan.

Malinda smiled. "This is your homework," she pulled out a pen. On a piece of paper she wrote down two things: 1. Change is good, it helps me learn, grow and evolve, and 2. I attract only better things into my life. "I want you to wake up each morning and say these things aloud in a mirror. Then repeat them again at every hour on the hour. I also want you to use one of them as a mantra as you meditate for a minimum of twenty minutes. Alternate the mantras each day until I see you next Friday."

I accepted my assignments. I noticed over her shoulder that Mikael was pulling up to the cafe. He was impossible to miss. He had the top down, and drove a bright cerulean blue, metallic sports car. It had shiny black rims. *Embarrassing.*

"He's here, I guess it's time for take-your-daughter to work day."

Her eyes widened over a smile. "I'll see you in a week. Please, please try to monitor your self-talk. It's very important." She stood up and lingered for a while. She added, "I'll see you soon, Tasha." It was like she was prolonging her goodbye, as if to get a better glimpse of the man I called Mikael, in hopes of corroborating a sane person's story.

* * *

THE VISIT

"You ready?" he called from the drivers seat. His pride the only thing shining brighter than the paint on that car.

"What? Is the lime green Lamborghini in the shop?" I said, sliding down into the slick, bucketed seat. He grinned, and shifted into second, before the door was closed all the way.

Our drive was mostly silent, and through back roads. Yellow leaves freckled the brown ground—little instances of joy—amongst the beds of soggy straw, and decaying plant matter. I loved this part of Georgia: the rolling hills and the black wooden fences that glided right along with them. The prestige gates protected all of the livestock—keeping them inside the fence where they were readily nourished and protected.

We passed by old gas stations, where the pumps looked like movie props, and by old, small houses that looked like you could knock them down with a few swift kicks. Butterflies were everywhere. Small ones, that were bright blue—like the color of Mikael's car— and big ones, that were yellow and black. I have never seen this many in the City, it's as if they were too gentle to live there.

We drove for about forty-five minutes outside of Atlanta, in what direction I couldn't be sure. If I hadn't shared so many facial features with the man in the drivers seat, it would be right about then that I would have started to panic, wondering if I made a deadly error in judgment.

He looked peaceful for a sick man. His eyes were still white, and his lips were pink, but his skin was slightly golden; if you didn't know he was dying of liver cancer then you might think it was a bad tan.

We pulled up to an office park with three large buildings that formed a semi circle around a cul-de-sac. The buildings themselves were massive, and all made of glass. In the first building there was a small cafe on the ground floor, that opened to an outside patio. It was full of people enjoying breakfast. The cafe reminded me of the ones in Europe. The chairs and tables were made of hard cast iron, but were softened with pale yellow cushions. The umbrellas hanging overhead might have been the same butter-color at one point, but now appeared to be white. The sports car growled to a stop in front of the center building. A young man behind the valet kiosk jumped to take care of Mikael's car.

When we walked inside the middle building, I suddenly felt underdressed. With the exception of Mikael, everyone else we encountered wore slacks, button downs, blouses, or lab coats: that sophisticatedly supplemented the aforementioned. I looked down at my gray, raggedy sweatshirt, thrown over a pair of black leggings, with black flip flops. I felt like I was transported back in time as the new kid in high school, coming in mid-school year, only to realize that kids dress like full grown adults in the rich neighborhoods, and it was too late to undo the damaged that my wardrobe had already caused.

"You could have told me to dress nicer," I snapped.

"Yes, because that would have went over so well," he said, "besides it doesn't matter, you're with me...you could be in a chicken suit."

"Do *you have a* chicken suit? I'd prefer it," I said.

"You're fine."

Once inside the building, it took a moment to acclimate my senses to the spectacular visuals. It wasn't only the exterior walls that were made of glass, but the entire building. *Every single* wall, sky bridge, ceiling, floor, table, chair, stapler, and pen was made of glass—or some transparent material—save for a few structural places that were constructed from only a semi-reflective metal. It was fascinating.

There were also some walls made of simple mirror, but they were few and far between. As we walked through the building, I realized that some of the mirror was magnifying, and some of it portrayed it's reflections in a wide-lens perspective. It was like you could see *everything*, at all times. It reminded me very much of the Subtle Realm.

"It takes a moment to get used to, but it's beautiful isn't it," he said.

"It's amazing." I gaped at a wall of iridescent chiseled glass.

It was a pane of diamonds shapes. From one angle the carved glass reflected an indigo-violet, and from the opposite angle, a champagne-peach.

"How do you keep it all clean?" I asked.

"Ha, now thats your mother talking. Come on I want you to meet someone." He walked in front of me and led me to an all glass elevator.

I followed behind him like an excited child, I couldn't help myself. This place had already exceeded my expectations, and he really wanted to give it all *to me*? Would this whole place be mine or would I share it with others—and who?

"I see why no one wears skirts here," I said as we ascended up the elevator, staring down at the people shrinking beneath me.

The elevator doors opened, but before they did, I could already see a small round face behind them. Her expression was content and welcoming. Her whole face smiled when she did, and she dressed smart. She didn't wear a lab coat, but she did wear a name tag that read, "Dr. Moon Lim." Dr. Lim looked too young to be a doctor. She put her hand forward for mine. The hand wore no nail polish, but it was remarkably soft and pristinely manicured.

"Tasha, this is my right hand, and she will soon be yours," Mikael said.

And apparently that soft hand belonged to Mikael. I recognized a sadness in her eyes. She was genuinely sad that Mikael was dying... when I felt nothing. I pulled back my hand, and averted my eyes to the floor.

We walked down the hall to the very last office. This was the biggest office on the floor. I could tell because I could see all of the other offices, and everything in them. Although this wasn't the first time I had experience sights in this likeness in the Subtle Realm, it was still disorienting. I had to continuously ground myself, because in the everything is so vivid and tangible; my brain had so much input to process at once.

"Nice to meet you, I've heard so many promising things about you," she said, without any hint of the accent that I expected her to have.

"I doubt it," I started in, but was interrupted by Mikael.

"Okay well let's get started, we shouldn't waste anytime on... pleasantries," he said, "I've already told you that we're a Biotech company, that specializes in several selective fields of cognitive sciences."

I nodded.

We all stood in his office, in front of miniature models of the company's three buildings. The little structures were exact. The trees and landscaping were all in the correct spot. The little cafe was present, only the umbrellas were yellow, not white. The valet kiosk was included too, and there was even a little blue sports car parked out front. Although, the car wasn't attached.

Mikael continued, "What you don't know is that my company is composed of three divisions; which you see, represented in their respective buildings here. The first, is the pharmaceutical company. It's this sister company that we use to fund the other two-thirds of operations. One of our most successful drugs there, is a synthetic and therapeutic version of DMT—

"Is that even legal?"

"So you've heard about it, good, yes, but only under very strict guidelines. We can discuss more about later. We also manufacture drugs for insomnia, narcolepsy, and some endocrine disorders that relate to the Hippocampus, Pineal gland and Pituitary."

"And Cannabis sir," Moon piped in.

"Yes, and that," he said, moving on quickly, "in the second buildings we commit our resources to non-pharmaceutical R&D. The third building is mainly for academic, diagnostic, and therapeutic practice." Mikael checked his watch.

I noticed that his was very old. I wondered how a man could own all of this, and still wear an old watch.

"The third building is composed of seven departments, each with the three, aforementioned sub-departments active on every floor." He pointed to the third building in the model. "They are as follows; Philosophy, Meditation, Onieronautics, Altered States of Consciousness, Neuroscience, Psychology, and Memory." Mikael walked over to his transparent desk, and sat down.

Moon followed suit, taking one of the clear open chairs that sat in front of the desk, leaving just one more available. She asked me to sit in it.

"What do you research and develop in this building?" I asked.

"Why don't you come sit down, Natasha," he said, with excitement pushing out his every word. It like he was about to hand me the keys to my first car—the one that he never did.

"For a dying man you've got a lot energy," I said, regretting it as soon as the words left my lips.

A small gasp escaped from the left of me, but my dads expression remained unchanged.

"I'd have to agree with you, there are days I almost forget...almost, but something eventually reminds me," he said.

"Would anyone like some tea?" Moon asked, standing up from her chair already heading for the transparent door. "I'm going to go get some tea."

"Yes, please and thank you," he said, "Natasha, these buildings house my life's work, and today this building in particular is complete for the first time since it's genesis...because you *are a part* of my life's work. Your mother and I met in grad school. We fell in love, and we always planned on having children—starting a family. We meant to bring you into the world, but what I didn't expect is to discover a calling in my work that could be greater than husbandry or fatherhood, or to come face to face so abruptly with my own — mortality. Furthermore, I could have never presumed that the very organ that your mother studied would turn on her."

I looked away.

"It was not an easy decision in the least to leave my family, but the work I needed to accomplish takes more than a life time, *much longer than I had*, so if I was going to make any solid contributions I had to choose: be great at one, or fail at both. Your mother understood a scientist's brain and my hope is, that maybe you can too…in time."

"You've dragged me out here, you have my attention. I want to know what it is that you chose over us."

Mikael's eyes looked weak, "I didn't choose it over you, my intention was always for you to be part of it."

I looked at him suspiciously.

"Just bear with me, this will seem like a lot at first," Mikael turned his computer screen so that I could see the image on his desktop; it was a structure that mathematically mapped out multiple planes of reality. "What we are perceiving right now, all around us," his hands spanned the air in front of him, "this is called the Physical Plane. It runs in tandem to the Astral Plane. It exists all around us, at this very moment, but you aren't wearing the right lenses—so to speak—to see it, or to perceive it, thus interact with it—"

"Wait, this is too much," laughter exploded from my chest.

Mikael looked disheartened, "I know it's difficult to consider, but there in lies the point behind my work. I aim to prove its existence, by materializing Astral-specific elementals into the Physical Plane. I'll create favorable conditions in which they can exist here, even if only for a moment."

I laughed even harder, partly from relief, partly from confirmation that I wasn't crazy, and if I was, then I wasn't alone. I had a multimillion dollar empire of crazies right here along with me. I guess the apple didn't fall too far from the tree after all, even if the tree was rooted in an illusionary Realm.

"Whew, that is good!" I said, keeled over in my seat. My face was warm with blood from the happy convulsions, and my eyes watered from the strain.

"You don't trust me, and that's fine, I can prove it if you give me time."

"Oh pops, I believe you. I've been there also…so we're both nuts," I said.

A wide grin, spread across his face, "I'd hope so, I was about your age when it started happening to me. Do you remember that we share a Pineal Gland abnormality? I believe that's what aids us in our access of the Astral Plane."

"Really?"

"Yes, we both have congenital tumors. They're benign, but from what we can tell from *my* tumor, it has helped me access the Astral Plane easier, have better vision and clarity while I'm there, and it might be responsible for the improve memory recall when I return."

"I remember the MRIs." The laughter dried up. "This is why you need me —for my tumor," I said.

"Natasha, there are many reasons why I want you here. Yes, your genetics will help continue my work, but even if you didn't have the tumor, I would still want you here. We are physically, and mentally, likeminded—we always have been. Let me pay you back for the years I couldn't be there for you."

"You said you had proof of the Astral Plane?"

"That is the goal, and we're closer now than ever before. I have a lot of promising hypotheticals, and I believe that we're only months away from actual proof. I have enough evidence to spur curiosity in the hearts of any humble scientist—enough to make them at least consider its existence. If I can get enough momentum, then I can finally get funding for this project *specifically*, so we don't have to keep getting… creative." Mikael walked to the acrylic door."Let me take you on the tour."

The elevator went down to the ground floor and stopped. Mikael took out a different key fob, and pressed it to the pad. The elevator began to descend down further to an unmarked floor. When we stepped out, the air sent chills through my body. The space smelled like damp earth.

He offered me his coat and I gladly accepted. On this floor, all of the walls were still glass but that was it, everything else was of normal materials. On our right, there were three main rooms. The first room looked like a serene and peaceful yoga studio. There was something similar to a hospital bed in it. From the cut outs on the wall, it was obvious that the bed could be folded up completely, so that the whole space could be used if desired. There was surround sound set up in that room as well. The middle room was what looked like a Physics laboratory, with typical equipment, nothing quite out of the ordinary. The third room had some computer equipment, and a giant, cylindrical structure in it. I can only likened it to a massive centrifuge, although that didn't seem quite right. To the left, an observation deck with rows of desks.

"This is my favorite place to Astral project," it's the original lab we started with and it's the one I still use, although a bit outdated."

"A bit? I hope this isn't your proof," I teased.

"No, but, when the Astral elements materialize on this plane, it will most likely happen in that very room—the vibe room." He pointed to the giant archaic-looking machinery in the third room.

"Gotcha," I said.

"I can see you are underwhelmed," he motioned for me to follow him into the center laboratory.

He walked up to a whiteboard.

"Let me ask you a question. What would happen if I were able to take a colossal piece of ice in one room," he drew a cube on the board, "and rapidly covert it into steam through millions of inconspicuous holes in a glass wall that separated an adjacent room, where it then, refreezes on contact in the second room."

I looked at his completed image; A cube, a vertical line, and another cube. "It would probably look like you made the giant ice cube go through the glass wall—like magic."

"Exactly, but the elements are still the same, they only changed in density, just long enough to allow it to crossover to the other side."

"Have you ever considered a method for bringing Astral people to the Physical plane?" I ask.

"No, Natasha…are you following my logic," he asked annoyed.

"Yes, it's pretty straightforward." I said.

He looked at me pensively before continuing, "The Astral Plane has its own unique set of elements. They're an extension of the physical plane's elements that are already listed on the periodic table. Astral specific elements each have their own unique properties, behaviors, and characteristics too, but of course, all of them are much lighter in density than the elements found on physical Earth."

I blinked at him.

"If I could bring *any* one of them here, there are hundreds, just for a tick in time, and record it, then I can prove the existence of the Astral Plane."

"Okay, this actually makes sense," I said.

"I believe that I am very close, and I would be much closer, but I've desperately needed a capable team. There are very few people that can, or would, study the Astral Plane in this manner. Out of the people that are willing *and able*, an even smaller percentage have the ability to remember what they've studied once they're back in their physical bodies!"

"Hmm," I said, looking over his notes and drawings, genuinely intrigued.

"I haven't even begun to tell you about the power and potential of the Astral Plane—there is so much more, Natasha!" He started coughing.

"Here you two are...I should've known you were down here. Where do you want your tea?" Moon's soft face crinkled once she realized Mikael was in discomfort, "Are you okay Dr. Stepanov?" she asked.

"Thank you Moon, would you mind showing Natasha, the third building please. I'm going to meditate for a while."

"Yes of course." Moon said, and she set down his tea on the observatory desk.

We left Mikael in the meditation room, and rode the elevator in complete silence. Our walk over to the third building, the one that housed the cafe, was also made without saying a word. She open a door for me, and I walked through, sans gratuity. I stopped by the cafe and ordered my own tea before we continued, also, without a word. This building was similar to the middle one, although it had less of a transparency complex, and at least three times as many floors.

We walked toward the elevator, which was located more or less in the same area as the second building. She pressed the button to the top floor. Each level was color coded on the elevator's directory. The one we were heading towards was a light purple, or lavender: labeled Philosophy. The silence between us was louder than any spoken words would have been. She showed me around the rooftop terrace in mime. It was breathtaking, I could see the Atlanta skyline in the background, as well as stone mountain; from this vantage point the city actually appeared peaceful.

"This is my favorite place to think," she said, finally breaking our Cold War of silence, "I come up here when I need to get a better view."

"How old are you?" I piped, peering through the silver telescopes mounted along the wall.

"I just turned thirty," she said.

"Didn't it ever bother you that Mikael abandoned his daughter, and used you as his substitute?" I kept my face in the apparatus.

"Ms. Price, if anything, having someone around him so close to his daughter's age, was something he had to fight *through*, not something he embraced. Dr. Stepanov is a good man, you'll see."

I swallowed, and stared hard into the skyline, "It's nice up here."

"Is there any area that you have particular interest in visiting today, in this building?" she asked.

"The Lucid Dreaming floor?"

"Sure, Onieronautics—no problem."

I followed her back out to the elevator. The Oneironaut floor, color-coded a baby blue, was on the fifth floor. We passed the sixth floor which was the Meditation floor, and it was assigned a rich indigo. I was curious to visit that floor also. Below the Lucid Dreaming floor sat: Altered States of Consciousness, Neuroscience, and Psychology. They were green, yellow, and orange respectively. The ground level—a deep maroon—was reserved for Memory and Dementia patients.

We stepped off the elevator, into a sleep lab. I immediately recognized a tailored lab coat in the center of the room. He was working with a man laying on his back, who was attached to a myriad of sensors.

"I know that man," I said.

"Who, Dr. Joe?" Moon asked.

"Yes, I've seen him for a Lucid Dreaming workshop."

"I'm not surprised, that sounds like Dr. Joe, would you like to speak with him?"

"Oh no...he looks busy."

Moon cups her small hands around her mouth and yells, "Dr. Joe," in a surprisedly soft voice.

Dr. Joe looked up. His stern smooth face melted into kindness. He waved. He finished saying something to his patient, and walked toward me.

"Hello Natasha, hows the journaling going?"

"Good, good," I said.

"I'm showing her around for the first time today," Moon said, "she's considering joining the team."

"That is a wonderful surprise, I sure hope you do. Let me know if you have any questions for me," he said.

"Thank you, your books have been a big help, really," I said.

"Remember, once you have at least seven lucid dreams in your notebook, give me a call, and I'll help you refine your skills if need be."

"I will." I smiled.

"We don't want to keep you from your patients," Moon said.

"Yes, I do need to get back actually. I have one poor soul who can't stop saying his ex-wife's name in his sleep, and his current wife is not too pleased with his, uhm, adventures."

"Oh wow, and I thought my crocodiles were bad," I said.

"Ah yes, crocodiles, you must remind me when I have the time. I want to share with you my theory on their symbolism. Remember to make sure that they're highlighted in your journal with context. I'll see you two later."

Moon and I left the sleep lab. She half-heartedly offered to show me around some more, but we were both exhausted. We reconvened in Mikael's office, and agreed to meet again on Monday morning. This time he gave me the physical address. Moon drove me home that afternoon, even though Mikael had expressed that he really wanted to. It was visibly obvious that he was too fatigued to make the drive, and I felt a twinge of sympathy for the first time since he told me that he was dying.

THE RESCUE

We reached the familiar streets near my apartment complex. The cold black stone at the entrance welcomed me home. Moon stopped her Tesla in front of the building that housed my personal belongings. I thanked her for the ride and carried my weight up the stairs to my unit. I approached the front door. Once again my heart sank at the anticipated silence on the other side.

Once I pushed through, my heart reached the bottom of my stomach. I melted into the sofa. I was surrounded by all of Yumi's fur. I rested my eyes. An obvious idea surfaced out of the darkness. My heart fluttered right back into place. I'm surprised that I hadn't thought of it before. Yes, of course! I could adopt her myself!

Excited energy reverberated up and down my spine. I sprung up from the couch I'd just collapsed on. I pulled up all of the no-kill shelters in my area, on my phone. Sadly, there was a short list of them, but at least it wouldn't be too difficult to locate Yumi's profile. I called the first one,

"Heller," an old man's voice shouted over several dogs barking and whining in the background.

I cringed and hoped that one of those cries weren't Yumi's, "Hi sir, do you have any dogs by the name of Yumi up for adoption?"

"Uh, no ma'am, we don't get dogs with names on em' much... reckon, they wouldn't be here if we did...you lost yer' dog?"

"Yes sir, she's all white."

"Shhhhhh, Ya'll hush now, I'm tryna' hear," he coughed, "uh, she got any spots on'er?"

"No, she's solid white, with no markings at all."

"Sorry ma'am, we don't have *any* dogs like that. I hope you find'er."

"Ok...thanks." I ended the call, actually relieved that she wasn't there.

The next place I called was a little further away from the animal hospital, but they had a picture on their website of a bunch of lovely staff. They were standing in front of their building, all holding either a dog or cat. Every member wore a big smile, a matching orange shirt, and khakis.

"Hello and thank you for calling The Peach Humane Society, how may we help add joy to *your* day?" A peppy woman with a northern accent answered.

"Hi...yes, I've lost my dog, she's all white and fluffy. I was wondering if you might have found her?"

"Oh I am so sorry to hear that, but it's possible! We have a standard procedure for missing pets though. You have to come in and speak with someone, and fill out some paperwork. If we think we might have a match, then we require proof. You know, vet records, photos, these sort of things."

"Thats fine, I can do all that, but this is an emergency, please, it's been a long two weeks, can you just tell me if you even have a dog that matches that description?"

"Hmmm," I heard the click-clack-click of a keyboard, "you said, female, white—about how much does she weigh?"

"She used to weigh about seventy to eighty pounds, but, it could be less now," I said, with guilt weighing down the last of my words. I hated myself for even adding them at all.

"Oh I am so sorry, no, we definitely don't have any babies that big here. And white and fluffy ta' boot? She would stand out here for sure. You know, anytime we get any of the husky-types they're gone as fast as they come in. They're so popular around here and—

"Okay...thanks, got it," I hung up.

I looked up to let gravity pull the tears back down through my ducts. I said a silent prayer. I called the last no-kill shelter within sixty mile radius. As the phone rang the thought crossed my mind, that Dr. Rue could have been lying.

What if she just wanted my Yumi, all to herself.

"Hello," a male teenage voice answered.

"Hi, I am looking for a solid white, fluffy, female dog. Large breed."

"Weird."

"What? What's weird? You have one?"

"Well, yeah, I'm looking at a profile just like that in our index right now...she's an owner-surrender from Atlanta. Poor girl, says here she was nearly starved to death. I can't imagine what would make someone do that. Ugh people make me sick, ya know?"

"You never know what people are going through," I blurted out.

"uhm...sure, I guess?"

"I just mean, sometimes things aren't what they seem, anyway, so this dog is still available then?"

"Yes, she's currently in temporary foster, says here, 'with the vet technician that found her.'"

Found her. My blood was reaching a boiling point. I tried my best to sound like a normal person and stabilize my tone.

I pushed words through my teeth, "All right, I would like to adopt her."

"Uhm okay," he popped his lips, "I'm going to email you a link to a form to fill out, it's just a few questions. Then we will need you to send a picture of your ID when you send in the questionnaire. Then you pay the adoption fee, and she's all yours."

"My ID?"

"Yeah, any ID is fine, it doesn't have to be a drivers license, we will need to verify your address for the adoption center, and for payment, and in some cases, we might need to follow-up."

"Yeah that makes sense, it's not a problem," I said.

"Bet. I will call you back after I receive those forms, oh and sometimes I leave here early on the weekend...so I would return everything quickly if you really want her—thanks."

I opened my email, tapped the link, filled out the questionnaire in a blazingly fast fashion, signed some type of waiver, and then clicked the link to pay for my Yumi. Two hundred and fifty dollars, it seemed like such a small price in comparison to living without her. I received a call back immediately.

"Hi Tasha, so we already have your ID attached to Yumi's file, and you're not allowed to adopt her—or any of our animals actually, so please don't call here again." He hung up on me.

I stared back at my face in the black screen of my phone.

Given my current mental state, it was probably a good thing that Yumi was *not* physically in that shelter, and it was a very good thing that I didn't know where the veterinary technician lived, or where that smug teen lived. Furthermore, it was an even better thing, that within the last twenty-four hours, I now had something tangible to live for— the new company with the bad name. And finally it was perhaps the best thing, that I knew Bryan would adopt her...for if *all of these things* were not so, then my story would have had an orange jumpsuit kind of ending.

"Hi You've Reached Bryan's Voicemail Please leave a message at the beep."

"Hi Bryan, I need your help, somethings happen with Yumi. It's a lot to explain on a voicemail, but they've taken her away from me. They have her at a shelter and they won't let me adopt her. I need you to answer the phone now please!"

Since time was of the essence, I called Jesmitha to see if she could do it instead. Unfortunately her line went directly to voicemail after the first ring.

What if they were off somewhere together?

Maybe both of them were watching their phones ring: laughing at my name flashing on his phone, and then on hers, having a romantic dinner at some steak house, enjoying our favorite wine. *Wine.* I deserved at least one glass. I'll ask dad—or Mikael, to adopt her tomorrow morning. He was in no position to refuse any requests from me. I poured a glass of wine, and took a big gulp, letting it settle over me like a weighted blanket.

I turned on the television: it was some documentary on microscopes. The show was unusually interesting to me, and held my attention far longer than I expected. *I'm going to be fine without any of them. I'll start a brand new life with Yumi, but first, I want to say goodbye to Nathan. He deserved that much, everyone deserved at least that much.*

22

THE ASTRAL PLANE

Nathan sits on a park bench in an open field. I sneak up on him from behind, hoping to surprise him.

"Congratulations on the new job Natasha, I'm happy I get to see you again, before I leave," he says, still facing forward.

"How did you know," I ask,

"How did I know you were behind me? Or how did I know about the job?"

"Both?"

"Your dreams," Nathan turns his head to look at me, kindness warms his face, "even when *you don't recall them*...but if I hadn't, I could still make a pretty good guess." He follows me with his eyes as I take a seat next to him on his glowing bench. "Your solar plexus chakra has taken up quite the charge since I've seen it last in this realm, and your mental energy field has expanded beautifully."

"Can you imagine if everyone was this discernible on Earth?" I say.

I try not to think about all of the dirty dreams I've had over my lifetime; now knowing that Nathan has had a front row seat to them all —if he so chose to watch—a peeping soul that used to be my husband in a past life. *Whew, now that's, "a lot," Doctor Doom—*

"Natasha," he says.

"Yes?"

Nathan smiled, "Talk to me about the new job."

"I think you'll like it, I'm taking over my fathers work," I hold back the best part for a beat, in order to savor the moment. I want to remember his expressions, and study any of the changes that occur in his energy fields, "with the Astral Plane," I punctuate with enthusiasm.

"What are your intentions in studying the Astral Plane?" He asks with the steadiest of tone.

There is not a single flicker in any of the perceivable energy fields that surround his body. If any of them did alter, I didn't catch it.

I considered my answer. "I want other people to understand the transformative power of this place. It's changed my life in such a short time. It gives me a wider perspective on my life, and something bigger to believe in; Ironically when I thought there was nothing left for me— on Earth. I see everything differently now."

Nathan looks at the ground, "Different how?"

"I view life with a deeper understanding of eternity, but I also appreciate the present moment even more, it's a strange paradox."

"You've a new found appreciation for the infinite concept: it exists in the present moment *and* eternal life. It's the same energy in both." Nathan stands up taking the bench we had been sitting on along with him. He catches me before I fall and pulls me to standing.

"A warning next time would be nice," I say pushing him back.

Nathan's face is sour, "How about a warning of actual consequence? The Astral Plane is not a place for those who are propelled from ego-centric energy."

My hands find my hips. "If you disagree with me taking over the company, why don't you just tell me not to do it? Wouldn't that be better than threatening me, and pulling chairs out from under me like a child?"

Nathan laughs."You misread me…I welcome this path for you. I'm happy that you chose this one; but, it means that I have much more to teach you, and I am out of time," he grabs my hands, "but as long as you are using the power of this place to learn, teach, and evolve with humility and altruism, then you will be fine. But, if you use this place for your own benefit, then you'll be corrupted beyond recognition. Someone with gifts like yours is susceptible to falling into a trap of ego-driven power at worst, or escapism at best."

"I don't understand how I could become powerful just by accessing the Subtle Realm?"

"You will understand, with time," he says, "and when that day comes, I know you will do the right thing."

"I'm actually going to take a break from this place for a while, until I learn how to balance it with my physical world, that's why I'm here."

Nathan smiles. "You're reaching frequencies of enlightenment right now, I'm proud of you," He admires the areas around my body.

"I'll never get used to someone reading me color-by-number. Thankfully you're the only one I know who can—" I realize that this might be the last time I ever speak with Nathan. "Will I ever see you again?"

"I'm not sure, but I will be with you until I ascend into the Celestial Realms. Until then, I can meet you in your dreams of course."

"But if you're not here to help me through the veil then how will I ever reach this place again? What if I can't find the Subtle Realm without you?"

"Natasha, I may have guided you here, but you have always accessed the Subtle Realm through your own will—just like driving a car, the vehicle moves when you will it too. You take the action to drive," he says.

"Well, technically you drove," I say.

"I was the passenger, the entire time, but you felt more comfortable with me in the drivers seat, so I let you, *let me,* lead."

"I was the driver?" I ask.

"You are the driver," he says, "remember how powerful thought is. If you intend to go to the Astral Plane—you believe it and you can see it happening in your mind—then you've only have to allow it to happen. You do not have to be dreaming to travel to the Astral Plane, that is only one path. Just let your body relax into a deep state of comfort through meditation. Bring your mind right to that thin line of sleep, and as your body drifts down to its ultimate state of rest, you'll keep steady with awareness: too focused and you can't relax, too relaxed, and you might drift off to sleep."

I nod.

"Then comes the tricky part, it's similar to peeling a sticker off in one whole piece. Slowly and gently you will detach your awareness from your sleeping body. Your subtle awareness might feel like a dance, an ebb and flow of consciousness. In and out it goes, as you delicately balance your concentration in order to reach the veil—or the selective membrane—that allows your consciousness to pass through, via the facilitated diffusion of intention. The energy you cultivated from your heart chakra just before the meditation began, will be the energy that propels you through to the other side. Darkness might blink for a tick right before your third eye opens, allowing you to fully perceive the Astral Plane. You can do this."

"For some reason, I feel like I already know most of this but I don't know how I could have." I take in his face, and try to commit it to memory as best I can. "I love you."

"I know," he encompasses me with his energy, "I love you too, Natasha."

If warmth has an emotion, this would be it. We stand, a rainbow of energies marrying in centrical motion. I close my eyes and take in this moment of purity, joy, and completion. I feel lighter. The sensation moves me to open my eyes, but it's not me, it's Nathan.

He is ascending before me.

23

A GOOD BYE

Before I was aware of the new day's light around me, I heard a familiar voice in my head—the voice of an old friend, *It's our own responsibility to educate ourselves. Knowledge is power. It's mined out of both Realms. Wisdom is given to anyone who asks for it, graciously delivered from the Source.*

Both are paramount to our evolution."

There was a heaviness on me, a peaceful presence, at least for a short while, until my head began to throb—no, no, no, not again. I could tell by the way my body ached that I was away for far too long. I grabbed my phone off the charger from my nightstand: five days!

I rummaged through the makeshift emergency kit on my bedside table: waters, vitamins, meal bars, and my latest edition, a fresh pair of panties to replace the Depends—I was getting too good at this.

After I reached an equilibrium, I checked my phone; I had almost eighteen missed calls from Mikael. They all ended abruptly about twenty-four hours ago. I feared the worst, and called him immediately. No answer. I called his assistant Moon. She picked up on the first ring, and explained that Mikael's condition had worsened. He was admitted into the hospital yesterday afternoon.

I called the number that she gave me. "Hello, I believe you might have my," I hesitated, "father, his name is Dr. Mikael Stepanov? He came in yesterday. I'm his only living relative."

"Hello, one moment please," I waited, "yes, he's here in the ICU, but if you want to see him you should hurry—

I hung up before she finished her sentence. I rushed to the hospital. I

174

didn't stop to catch my breath until I reached his floor. If Mikael was already dead, then I would lose everything! I hadn't signed a single document, and I never accepted his proposal. I never got the chance to...say goodbye. The sentimental grief confused me.

I stopped at the nurses station on his floor and asked, "Which room is my father in? Dr. Stepanov?"

One of the nurses looked up, "Hi, yes, we just spoke, he is currently in room number eight two nine, but..."

I took off towards the rooms, as soon as she gave me the number. She also said something about visiting hours, but I couldn't hear her over the sound of my own panting. I searched the numbers that jutted out above the endless rows of doors.

#808, #813, #814, #826, #827, #828, #829!

I approached the steel handle shyly—afraid of what might be on the other side. I held my breath before entering. The room was dark and quiet, save for the humming and beeping of the machines. It took a few minutes for my eyes to adjust in order to see his face clearly. All of my familiar features laying there. I sat in a chair about a foot away from his bed and stared at him. I almost thought I saw the first layer of his energy field, that etheric bluish grey light, but I blinked my eyes and it was gone. I moved in closer to try and get a better look. He opened his eyes, startling me, and relieving me at the same time.

"Mikael," I whispered, "I thought you were gone," I said with my voice quivering, I felt a deep sense of guilt throb in my chest with every word.

The time consumed, yet again, was priceless. Although he wasn't dead, it was apparent from his thin yellow skin and his animatronic movements, that he would be leaving this world soon.

Why am I so emotional, I couldn't fully rationalize.

In a slow, breathy whisper he said,"Don't cry girl." He raised one arm, and with it a web of wires. He motioned me closer, "We missed out on a beautiful relationship," he drew in a deep wheezy breath, "and what are all of these things to me now...at least they will not die with my body because my true legacy sits right before me."

He started coughing. He sat up, grimacing all the way, from the pain the adjustment brought with it.

In a slightly stronger voice he continued, "I hope that my death can give you a new life...provide for you a solid foundation. I've laid down deep roots for you...my work will become our work. We are of the same mind—you have always been like me."

The resemblance was undeniable, looking into his eyes were like looking into my own. In those mirrors, for the first time in twenty-eight years, I finally had a clear vision for my life; a decisive direction, a tangible trajectory, and an open road. It was a feeling of pure lucidity, a feeling somewhat foreign to me but strong, persuasive, and alive. The moment in that hospital room wasn't perfect in itself, but there was an opportunity to make it so. I still had my disagreements with what he did, *and* his rationalizations, but half of me understood why he chose to dedicate his life to this field. Hell, I had only had a few interactions with the Subtle Realm, and it nearly ruined my life.

It would have ruined my life, if it weren't for him.

The irony slapped me in the face. I took his hand, his facial expression softened. I stared at the image of our hands together. I couldn't remember the last time I held his hand, and I didn't want to forget this time.

"I continue your work—it will be our work, Dad. I'll run the company to the best of my ability. You can rest now. I'll stay here with you tonight, so you're not alone."

He hung his head in relief, and laid back down. He closed his eyes. He seemed to be at peace. I made myself comfortable in the visitor chair, extended the recliner, and clicked on the television. I flipped through the channels and eventually settled on an old Seinfeld episode. Although I was comfortable in the recliner, it was unlikely I'd get any sleep tonight.

A BETTER MORNING

I watched my dad's ribcage rise and fall all night, and the television when my mind and heart would allow. Sleep never came just as I suspected. I glanced out the window to witness one of nature's most alluring episodes, it was just beginning.

The sky was a wide canvas of robin's egg blue, fading evenly into an easter green. There were lazy broad strokes of electric orange painted across it all. Small clouds popped out in opposition to the pastel background, presenting themselves as deep navy shadows—it was like they had been cut out from a different painting entirely. Slowly, the oranges converted into hot pinks, and the pinks darkened into purples, while the navy clouds shifted into grey's and silvers. I watched until all of the colors softened together, their edges compromising with one another like watercolors, in order to welcome us gently into an iridescent morning. Every color seemed to be making way for the sun. The ball of fire rising slowly over the horizon—the star of the show— radiating into the world with his blazing red aura.

I felt a peace wash over me. There were also elements of renewal and hope, things that I hadn't felt in a long time. Things that sunrises are uniquely capable of reminding me of.

A doctor with short curly brown hair came in while Mikael was sleeping, and introduced himself to me, "Hello, you must be Natasha," he said, "I'm Dr. Rain."

I nodded from the under the blanket in the chair.

"Mikael speaks of you often—he's a proud dad. I've been his doctor for the last fifteen years, so we've gotten to know each other quite well."

My heart stopped. *Fifteen years?*

That would mean that he has been sick the entire time that he's been gone. Is It possible that my dad left, in part, because he didn't want us to watch him die, or because he didn't want to be a burden?

Dr. Rain said, "I'll come back later when he's awake but it's nice to finally meet you though."

"Wait!"

"Yes?" he asked, pausing on his way out.

"How much time do we have?" I asked.

"It's hard to tell, it could be a couple weeks, or he could live a few more months; he's already outlived five years pass his prognosis, so you really never know with these things."

"But not today?"

"No, not today. He should be find to go home this afternoon, after we get his levels stable again."

"Okay thank you Dr. Rain."

"Sure thing Natasha," the Doctor turned to leave again, "and for what it's worth, I hope that he proves us all wrong." He nodded, and walked out the door.

A few hours later Moon showed up at the door and I waved her in.

Mikael and I were playing *War*, the card game, on his bedside table.

She whispered in her kind voice, "Hello...are we ready?"

"Ready for what?" I asked.

"Ready for you to get a job," Mikael frowned, as he placed a King beside my Joker on the tray between us.

Moon pulled out a matte black folder from her Kate Spade Satchel, "We just need your signature, we already have everyone else's."

"Everyone else's?" I asked, and swept both cards into my already-impressive pile.

"Yes, the rest of the board, you'll meet them later," she looks at Mikael, "we didn't want to...overwhelm you." She handed me the papers.

I accepted the documents and signed my name on every page.

HOME

When I finally left the hospital, I had been up for twenty four hours straight, and I was quite delirious. I parked in front of my apartment and looked at the foreign sight—total darkness inside my home. All the lights were off, something that still looked odd, since I always left the them on for Yumi. I sat in my car stalling, the worst part of coming home was opening the door, and having to remind my brain as it prepared to release it's trained dopamine response, that no, there was no one there. No one would greet me with unconditional love, no wagging bodies, or flappy tongues under happy eyes to see me. It didn't matter that it had been weeks, because every time I walked through that door my hopes rose and sunk again, like a phantom limb syndrome. I knew she wasn't there, I knew she wasn't going to be there, but the pain of her not being there remained. Begrudgingly, I exited my car and kicked an abandoned eyeglass lens along the path to my staircase, abandoning it again once more.

I walked inside my apartment and as expected, the pain hit me like a backdraft. I let it burn through me. I flopped down on my couch. She was everywhere. Her memories permeated every inch of this place. I could even hear the sound of her collar jingling. It was so vivid in my mind, so rich in acoustic, that I thought I was finally losing my last grip on reality.

I heard a knock at the door.

I jumped up from my couch, and I was at the door in two long leaps of a step. My heart was racing when I swung it open.

"Yumi!" I cried, wrapping my body around her.

Her body bounced awkwardly off of mine as she spun in circles and licked my face. She placed both paws on my shoulders, and knocked me to my back. She continued to shower me with her affections as she stood over me. Every so often she would whimper loudly, as if she was telling me about her perilous journey home. Tears of joy splattered the floor between Yumi and I. I gave her one more big hug after she had calmed down enough for me to do so. Eventually she settled into my lap, her body and fur ridiculously overlapping mine. She smelled of sweet lavender.

A strong hand reached down for mine to help me to my feet and I accepted.

"I thought you might want this back, I heard you lost it," Bryan said.

"I love you." I hugged him and buried my soaked face into his shirt, "Yes, thank you, how did you find her?" I asked.

"I called every shelter in the city, right after I got your message, I asked them for a female dog, over sixty pounds, spotless white, fluffy, with copper eyes, and it turns out there are not many like her. I only had one dud, and I honestly thought about taking her home too," Bryan pulled out a card behind from his back jean pockets and handed it to me, "Oh, and Happy Birthday."

"It *is* my birthday…" I said.

"You forgot?" Bryan eyed me curiously.

"No…yes," I said. "Thank you," I opened the card.

"Happy Birthday Tasha!

Celebrating your birthday always feels like a gift for me too, because it means you're still in my life. I used to get sad when I thought of family, but now I only think of you. You, Yumi and I, are meant to be together, I think that's obvious. We're bigger than our problems. I've loved you both for years, and I want to help make our dreams come true, whatever that looks like.

Love Bryan."

"You look confused," Bryan said.

"It's perfect, but it seems like something you would write to a lover —not a friend, Bryan."

"Is that what you really want Tasha, a friend?"

"What I want is a fresh start, and I think I finally have that chance, but I'm not—

"Not what—

"But I don't know if that means us." I said.

Yumi walked over to her couch, and flopped down. She seemingly looked like she was begging us to do the same.

"What about you and Jes?" I said, walking over to join Yumi.

Bryan looked like he was evoking some type of deep self control, "We've been over this?" Bryan followed us to the couch.

"Sure...but then you guys take a trip, and *all of the* texting between you two, and the romantic steak dinners."

"We didn't go on that trip *together*, yes it was a work trip, but I took our new hires and Jes stayed back and practically ran Club Daze for us. She did an incredible job Tasha, you would have been so proud of her. We've been texting so much because of you! *All of our texts* are about you, planning things *for you*, worried *about you*, fixing things...for you, and I have no idea about these steak dinners you speak of?" Bryan handed me his phone, which embarrassed me immediately. I was grateful that he couldn't read my aura like Nathan, although I hadn't ruled that out.

"I don't need to see your phone Bryan."

"I'm just trying to make a point, there's nothing there—and Jes is dating some fireman or something, I think they're serious? I thought you knew all of that, but maybe she's been too busy to talk. She's always exhausted when I see her, we both are. And the only thing that Jes and I have in common is that we want you healthy and back in our lives...and back at Club Daze," he pulls me closer, "it's what I've aways wanted. I've had a lot of time to think."

"I can't, Bryan. I'm sorry."

He released me, "I get it, you need to focus on yourself...I know, I assumed a lot."

"No, I mean, I can't come work for you...but...I would like to try us again."

"Oh," he said, surprised, and then more confidently, "well thats good, because technically...Yumi is mine now, and this was about to get real awkward." Bryan pulled me all the way to him, hugging me in his arms.

"You're hilarious." I said.

He kissed my forehead, then my nose.

"I have a new job."

"You do?" he asked.

"Yeah, it's kinda a long story though," I said, "do you want me to make us dinner?"

"Who are you? You have a new job, you're going to cook, and then, actually eat, dinner? This I gotta see."

I pushed him off, and Yumi barked in her usual role of honoree referee. It felt so good to have her home, to have everyone home. I wanted to freeze this moment to keep it safe.

Snuggled on the couch, I ordered impossible burgers and fries off of a delivery app on my phone. While we waited for our food to arrive, I told Bryan the story about my father, and   explained the situation involving his company. I strategically left the parts about the Subtle Realm, I figured that it would be best to keep somethings close to my chest for now. I told Bryan that my father was ill and that he had no one to inherit his equity…which was true.

After the food arrived, we all ate and Yumi collected her French-fry tax for being such a good girl. We talked about my new therapist, my suspected sleep issues, and how my dad's company might even be able to help with them.

Bryan complained about how his club: was now going to be short staffed, and how Rick was *always* asking for me. We took bets over how long Rick would last at Club Daze after he realized we were dating. I watched Bryan glow as he explained how he wanted to, "elevate the music-experience," for his patrons, and, "make it more about the entire experience," or the vibe, and less about all of the toxins consumed. We laughed a lot that night, especially when we tried to decide if we liked Jesmitha's new boyfriend, *solely* from his Instagram page. We dissected everything from his hashtags, down to his selfie-to-food post ratio.

After we finished eating, all three of us watched a movie about a video game system that became a real world; Bryan loved the movie but I thought the book was better. This is what family looked like to me, the soft glow of the television bouncing off of Bryan's profile, and the outline of Yumi's curled up body— incrementally expanding with life. As the credits rolled, I took his hand and led him into my bedroom, confident that my late husband, from my past life, was moving on to bigger and better ventures.

24

ASTRAL ACADEMY

"Good morning boys and girls!" I said, to the three semi-conscious, masses in my bed.

Bryan yawned. "We really need to get a bigger bed."

"I'm not the one who brought home a whole new dog." I said.

Curled up tightly beside Yumi, lay a slightly smaller, but even fluffier, all white pup, now named Yuki. Which is a much more appropriate name than what the shelter's employees were calling her, which was *Rooster*. Apparently she used to howl, early every morning. She hasn't done that here yet. Her eyes were the darkest brown. They appeared black, and you would have to look into them very closely to see where her pupil began and her iris ended. She looked like a miniature polar bear. Bryan returned to the shelter about a week after they'd mistaken her for Yumi, to swoop her up. He surprised me with her as a *late birthday present*, but it would be more accurate to say, that it was an early birthday present to *himself*.

"Look at that face," he said, "who could leave that face?" squishing her face and his words into baby talk, which he did for no-one, ever.

I got up and went to the kitchen to get breakfast started, and Yumi followed closely behind. She had been favoring me ever since Bryan brought Yuki home, I think she was jealous, or annoyed. Regardless, I was thrilled that she loved me more now, even if it was only out of spite.

I was still getting used to wearing professional business attire, but I have fully embraced it. I felt powerful in my new wardrobe. That morning, I wore billowy champagne slacks, and a pristine white blouse, with a thin Hermés belt, and a pair of brown Valentinos. I took the liberty to do a little shopping this past weekend with my new salary. Bryan came out of the bedroom, just as breakfast was ready. He was sporting his typical Monday attire; grey sweatpants and a navy, henley t-shirt.

He leaned on the doorframe, "Do you have time to eat before work this morning?"

"As matter of fact I do," I said.

We sat down at the kitchen bar and enjoyed a veggie omelet and our coffee, while we watched the morning news.

I looked around at my apartment, "You know I think we need a bigger place. You could sell your condo, and we could buy a house together. We could finally get a yard for Yumi."

"And Yuki," he said, with his mouth full.

"Yes, and our new little snowball," I said.

"Hows your dad?" he asked.

"He's doing as good as can be expected. He's not coming into the office any more, but he's still working from home. I spend Monday, Wednesday, and Friday at the company buildings, and Tuesday and Thursday at his home office now. I imagine I'll do that until..." I finished my eggs, "he said he likes you," I took the last sip of my coffee, "and that you're patient with me."

"That I am," Bryan collected our plates, and walked over to the sink. "Maybe we can have dinner again, if he's feeling up to it."

Yumi and Yuki were playing tug-o-war with a bedroom slipper; which Yumi knew was a definite violation of our terms and agreements, but she also seem to be aware that Yuki didn't know all of the house rules, and that made it okay. Bryan ruined all of their fun and stole their prize item, switching it out with a rope—that was actually purchased for that very game they liked to play.

"Do you want another cup of coffee before you go?" Bryan asked.

"I would love one, but I better get going," I stood up and leaned over to kiss Bryan goodbye for the day. "Have fun on your walk with the girls."

I pulled up to my new company, my new baby. It still hadn't fully set in that this was really mine—well mostly mine. I still shared it with the members of the board. The board of which I was going to meet with for the first time today. Standing outside to greet me was my right hand woman Dr. Moon. She waved stiffly as my car approached, and it made me giggle. She seemed to be genuinely as excited as I was to start our new chapter.

"Good Morning, Ms. Price, we have a stacked day today so we should get right to it, just to recap, there are seven board members as of now: you and your father, Mr. Tony Scavo, PhD Min Lim, Dr. Alexis Bard, Dr. Joe, and Miguel." Moon looked at me for signs of comprehension so she could proceed. We walked through he entrance of building number two.

Moon began again, "Tony is over pharmaceuticals, PhD Lim is—"

"Is she your mom?" I asked.

"Yes she is," Moon lit up, "she's a philosopher and an author." I admired how spoke of her, the pride in her voice. "Dr. Stepanov and my mom worked very closely on the Astral Plane project, ever since I can remember," she said.

I stared at, or into and through, the translucent floors and walls. I'd been coming here for almost a month and it still was such an unusual and marvelous sight. It made me long for the Subtle Realm, but also happy to be released from its grasp, at the same time.

"Ms. Price?" Moon piped.

"Can you call me Natasha?"

"Yes, Natasha," she smiled.

"Great, continue," I said.

"Dr. Alexis Bard is over the Neuroscience departments. She specializes in the Pineal gland research, but she also oversees the department head in Memory and Dementia. You already know Dr. Joe, and then there is just Miguel, whose is over Psychology—easy right?"

"Right?" I asked,

"Miguel is a bit of a flirt," Moon said.

We walked towards the board room. From where we stood, I saw that four of the members were already in the room. Only one man was missing, so it was either Miguel or Tony.

"Don't worry, I'll always be with you, and everyone is really nice— well except Tony. But it will be fine, it always is...eventually."

The doors slid open and we walked inside. In the room sat a large ornate crystal table, oblong in shape with eight chairs. The door swished shut behind me. The room was completely sound proof.

"Hello Ms. Price," a toned, but petite woman, was the first to greet me.

I assumed this to be PhD Min Lim—Moon's mom. She stood up to shake my hand. It was evident who Moon inherited her baby-soft hands from. The other members followed suit with their hands outstretched to meet my acquaintance. I walked around the table and greeted each one. I noticed that Dr. Alexis didn't appear to be much older than me—perhaps thirty-five; but she could have just looked younger—the melanin in her skin sparing her from premature aging from the sun.

Dr. Joe surprised me with a hug. I was pleasantly caught off guard. He probably still has my mascara stains on his sofa, and he's held my weepy tissues; surely he is allotted a hug, even if I was his boss.

Am I his boss?

"Miguel," a Spanish accent sang out, accompanied by a honey-colored hand.

"Natasha." I lingered a bit in his presence.

"I'm over the Psych. Department, but we are all here for the same reason, more or less," he winked. He smiled with his eyes like we shared a secret together. A smile crept up on my face too.

An abrasive voice from behind me huffed, "Okay let's get this thing started. I have a very busy schedule today."

I smelled his cologne, before I heard his voice. I swung around, happy to be released out from under Miguel's spell.

This must be mean Tony. They must meet early without him.

"Right," Moon stood up from the seat next to me. "So here's the agenda for today's meeting per Dr. Stepanov, we want to introduce and welcome the newest member of our board, Ms. Price."

Most of the board clapped, and I quickly took a seat.

"We also need to continue *the* discussion." Moon added as the applause died down.

"The discussion?" I asked. I looked at that the head of the table, and realized it was left empty. I had probably been expected to take that seat. But my father was still alive, and even if I would have thought to take it, it didn't feel right just yet. On the opposing end, the other head of the table, if you will, sat Mr. Tony and his hair gel. I couldn't help but wonder if he sat there all the time, or if he only sat there now because my dad was absent.

Alexis, whom was sitting across from Moon said, "Yes, the discussion on which direction to take the company in; we need to pivot bit, for uhm, financial and efficacy reasons," she whispered the last

185

part, and adjusted her delicate eyeglasses. "I suggest that we apply for grants, specifically to research Pineal glands tumors so we can see if we can replicate what your father was able to do."

"Is able to do," I said.

"Of course. I'm sorry, *is* able to do." Alexis said. She looked at Moon with wide eyes.

Miguel leaned back in his chair, he was the only person in the room that was dressed casually. "I agree with Alexis, I think we need funding for legitimate—

"And I think that we should begin an entirely different approach," Tony set his attention on me. He scanned me, reaching my eyes last. "Ms. Price, with all due respect, we have been trying to achieve materialization of astral elements for over a decade without sufficient success. We need to drop this child's play and focus on what brings in actual money: drugs." Tony said. "Hopefully your presence will bring a long-needed common sense to this place." He looked around the table at the board like they were all children playing too loudly.

The rest of the board seemed to have a silent conversation, while Tony was speaking to me, without his knowledge.

When PhD Lim spoke up, everyone paid attention, even Mr. Tony. "Ms. Price, I believe that it is worth noting that our lack of success is largely due to the fact that we have been attempting to study the entire ocean with only handful of marine biologists, or the entire universe, with a couple astronauts."

"Or dreamlands with only one oneironaut," Dr. Joe beamed.

Moon smiled at Dr. Joe.

"What are you saying?" I asked.

Min continued, "What if we began teaching a school, or an academy, for astral projection? We could train multitudes of people at one time, from a very young age, to be conscious in the Astral Realm. In this way, all of our disciplines would be able to work together, we could build an entire lab in the Astral Plane if need be, verses only having one or two people with a talent or a true ability to conduct experiments there."

"Or remember them when they come back." Alexis interjected.

"What a silly idea," Tony barked, "But, I guess it's easy to sit *in here* and play make-believe when I'm *out there* generating all the revenue."

"Tony you're not the only one that brings in money." Miguel said.

Tony stood up from his chair.

"Okay." I said, standing up also. I looked directly at Tony.

"Everything is a silly idea until it works—then it's considered genius." I walked to the head of the table. "I like it, and I think dad would like it too." I said.

Something deep inside of me stirred, like this is what I was meant to do all along. I was finally on the right path.

THE NEXT BOOK: *Astral Academy and The Subtle Realm* is set to be released on August, 8th 2022.

AUTHOR'S SOCIAL: @NJSimat or join the team at **www.clubdaze.net** for news, events, and promotions.

AUTHOR'S NOTE: If you enjoyed this novel, **please leave a review** on Amazon or wherever you found it! The success of this novel is in your hands—literally— especially as an indie author. I am eternally grateful for your support. I read every single review.

Thank you
-N. J. Simat
(Melodysta Swirls)

Books of reference:
Hands of Light by Barbara Ann Brennan,
The Astral Plane by C. W. Leadbeater,
Astral Projection & Lucid Dreaming by Mari Silva
Lucid Dreaming by Robert Waggoner.
Websites of Interest/Contributors/Supporters
www.performive.com

CPSIA information can be obtained
at www.ICGtesting.com
Printed in the USA
LVHW091521301021
701980LV00012B/34/J

9 781737 903055